COINCIDENCES
& Consequences

A Novel

BANU TÜLÜMEN

 FriesenPress

One Printers Way
Altona, MB R0G 0B0
Canada

www.friesenpress.com

ISBN
978-1-03-917461-0 (Hardcover)
978-1-03-917460-3 (Paperback)
978-1-03-917462-7 (eBook)

1. FICTION, CONTEMPORARY WOMEN

Distributed to the trade by The Ingram Book Company

DEDICATION

For Turkiwi

FOREWORD

I am not a writer.
To call myself one would be doing an injustice to all the great writers,
past, present, and future.
I am a storyteller who wanted to tell a story.
A story that can take place anywhere.
A story about coincidences that led to consequences.

B. T.

THE WILLOW TREE

The fact that the willow tree can bend in various outrageous poses without snapping makes it a great example of adaptability to a situation.

It is a very powerful symbol of survival because the tree has the ability to survive in even the most challenging of situations such as heavy storms with the strongest winds.

The branches will never easily break no matter how bent by the strong winds they are. In the event that they do break, the branches grow back, and this gives the tree this crooked, scarred look which actually contributes to its overall magnificence.

The willow tree as a symbol of adaptability also encourages expression whether of love, loss, sadness and so on.

It is a tree that symbolizes that even through great loss, there is always an opportunity for something new to emerge, something even better.

www.treesymbolism.com

PROLOGUE

$\mathcal{J}$ane was frustrated. The opening of her first solo exhibition of photographs at the Windfell Gallery was in just one week, and she still didn't have a centrepiece photo that would dominate her show, *TREOW*. She had liked photographing trees ever since she received her first camera from her father at the age of ten. Throughout the years she had travelled the world, accumulating quite a portfolio of some of the most amazing trees. She had won several awards and made a name for herself as a rising star, so she was very excited to do her first solo show.

Anne, the curator of the gallery, had gone over the portfolio, making choices, including those that Jane particularly wanted shown. Anne was the one who had told her to pick a main photo that she could build the exhibition around, and that had proved to be more difficult than she expected. They had settled on a panorama of trees taken at dawn with the landscape covered in a lavender-coloured mist that seemed to flow upward to the sky. It was one of her favourite shots; however, she still felt that something was missing, a feeling she had difficulty expressing. Anne had shown tolerance while Jane hesitated, but as they say, the show must go on, so for now, they had agreed on this centrepiece.

Jane got up from her bed and quickly dressed. She glanced at her watch to see if she had time to stop by her favourite coffee place before meeting with Anne at the gallery to go over the display arrangement and details of opening night. *I have another two hours, so enough time,* she thought, picking up her large bag and portfolio case.

Her loft/studio was close to downtown where the gallery was, so she started walking. It was a fine autumn day with a crispness to the air. Even though autumn was not her personal favourite season, it was good for photographing trees, and as she walked, she glanced around, admiring the changing colours of the foliage.

The coffee shop was busy as usual at this time of the day, and she saw that there was a lineup before the counter. She waved at Tracy, one of the baristas that was working today, who waved back. Jane looked around inside her bag, trying to find her wallet, when she was suddenly accosted by a person behind her, forcing her to stumble forward against the person in front of her.

"I'm so sorry," said the young woman behind her, "clumsy of me, tripping over the doormat."

Jane turned around to look. "Don't worry, I do that too," she replied. When she turned back, she saw that the person she had stumbled into had turned to look directly at her. The first thing Jane noticed was his startling blue eyes. *Clear as the sky,* she thought; the man was looking at her, but not with anger.

"I'm sorry," Jane said, "it's just that…"

"Good morning," the young man replied, smiling and looking behind her at what had caused the commotion. "Are you all right?" he asked.

She had been startled at the question and started to apologize again.

"Good thing we didn't have our coffee yet," he remarked, looking down at her.

There was an awkward silence while he kept looking with a smile before Jane said, "I believe it's your turn," nodding toward the cashier.

He turned around and gave his order ("double espresso please") and moved aside.

What were the odds? Jane thought as she walked up.

"Good morning, Tracy. I'll have the usual, please," Jane said.

"Of course, Jane. Double espresso!" Tracy shouted at the other baristas. The young man glanced at her with a smile.

"It seems we have similar tastes," he said. "Would you care to join me at a table?"

Jane hesitated. The least she could do was have coffee with him since she had stumbled into him awkwardly. He looked innocent enough on top of being charming and very handsome. She glanced at her watch.

"Thank you, I'll join you," Jane said. She waited for her coffee while the young man picked up his and went outside to sit at one of the small tables on the sidewalk.

He got up once Jane came outside and waited for her to sit before sitting down himself. *Courteous as well,* Jane thought.

"Hi, my name is Simon."

"Jane," she answered. She placed her portfolio beside her chair and noticed that he was looking at it. "I'm a photographer," she continued, sipping her coffee, "and I'm on my way to the gallery."

"Which gallery?" Simon asked.

"Windfell," Jane replied.

"It's a good gallery. I know Anne, the curator," Simon said, smiling. "She's a friend. Also, among other things, I must confess: I know who you are."

Jane pushed away her coffee, surprised. "How?"

"You have an exhibition coming up. It's all over the art magazines. What a coincidence, bumping into me today," Simon replied, "and a pleasant one."

Jane was at a loss for words. "I'm off to see her after this," she finally answered, having calmed down.

"*TREOW*, right?" Simon asked. "Interesting choice of name, deriving from Old English."

"You are well-informed."

"What kind of an editor would I be if I wasn't?" he said, leaning back against his chair.

"Oh, what are you the editor of?" Jane asked.

"*Empyreus*," He replied.

"I've heard of it. What does 'empyreus' mean?" Jane asked. "I always wanted to check that up."

"In a few words, it means 'fiery.'"

"Interesting choice for a name," Jane said using his words.

"We're an online medium providing an open platform for communicating. We have a small permanent staff and writers but invite people to share their thoughts and ideas as well," he replied.

Jane looked up at him questioningly. "What does it have to do with me or you knowing me?"

"As an editor, I'm curious and read many other magazines and articles. There was an interview with you recently in *Arts and Culture*. It caught my eye when I saw that you had named your show *TREOW*. I also liked your reasoning behind taking photos of trees." Simon smiled. "You must be excited, your first solo," he continued. "I quite look forward to seeing it now that I've met you."

Jane blushed. "Thank you." Even though they had just met, she felt a sudden warmth inside her when he said that.

"Have you chosen the exhibits?" he asked.

"Yes… I have."

"I notice a hesitation there."

"It's just that I'm finding it difficult to decide on the centrepiece. I mean, I have all these photos, but it just doesn't feel right, you know? It hasn't clicked and come together yet."

Simon looked at her then, and Jane felt the mutual attraction drawing them together. She now saw that he seemed distracted by her crystal earrings that she knew shimmered in the sun.

"What are you looking for, exactly?" Simon finally asked.

"I'll know it when I see it," Jane replied.

"How can you know it if you don't know what you're looking for?" Simon insisted, his blue eyes gazing deeply into her green eyes. For a minute, Jane wondered what she was doing here, talking to this man that she had met minutes ago. Strangely, she was drawn to him, his blue eyes and handsome face and all. He had a quiet demeanour, and she was attracted to his inquisitive mind.

"The word I'm looking for is 'embrace.' I want a photograph that'll embrace the whole exhibition. Something unusual. An experience, a sensation… a phenomenon."

Jane stopped when she noticed Simon looking at her in admiration. She flung her vibrant red hair, flushed with emotions. She did not know exactly how she should proceed.

"Funny you should say phenomenon," Simon finally said. "Did you know there's an NGO called Phenomenon?"

"No, I don't really, what kind of organization is it?" Jane asked.

"It's founded by Sam Ryes and his wife, Jasmine. You might have heard of them?"

"Isn't Sam Ryes a futuristic movie director and an activist?"

"Yes, so is Jasmine, different fields."

"Why the name Phenomenon?"

"The foundation is based out of their home, and they have a special phenomenon in their garden. Do you know what a gemel tree is?"

"I can't say I do." She frowned. "What is it?"

"It's two conjoined trees. It's a natural phenomenon where two trees grow together, first separately, then they touch and intertwine and merge into a connectedness, as if holding each other up." He stopped when he saw her, noticing how excited she looked.

"That's it, that's what I'm looking for! My goodness, can I see it? Will they allow me to see it? Do they have a photo of it on their website or anything?" Jane was so excited that she blabbered out all her questions. Simon looked on, amused.

"I thought you might like it. And yes, they do have a photo on their website." He pulled out his phone, quickly scrolled through the website, enlarged the image, and showed it to her.

Jane looked on, amazed at the image of two trees with their trunk intertwined as if one, holding on with their branches growing up high. She could just imagine the shot she would take. She had to see it in person. She looked up from the phone at Simon's face.

"Are you for real?" she asked him softly.

"Yes, I am," Simon replied, pulling back his phone. "Would you like me to make you an appointment?"

"Do you know them?" Jane asked, surprised.

"I do," Simon replied, "but first, you'll have to allow me to buy you another coffee." He smiled, waiting for her reply.

Jane glanced at her watch, then thought, *Why not?* "I would like that," she replied. Simon got up and went inside.

Jane wondered if she would be able to go and see the tree and take a photo in time for the opening. *I need to talk with Anne first before doing anything,* she thought. She took out her phone and dialled Anne's number.

"Windfell Gallery, how may I help you?"

"Anne, it's Jane. I need to ask you something."

"What is it? You sound excited."

Jane looked up as Simon returned with two cups of coffee. She pointed to her phone and mouthed the word "Anne."

"Anne, I've just met Simon from *Empryeus,* and he showed me a tree I think that would be a fantastic centrepiece for my show. Do you think we have time to put it in?" she asked hastily.

"When can you take the shot?" Anne asked. "We only have a week."

"I know. He's going to make an appointment for me, and if they agree, I can go off immediately."

"You sound very excited, that's good. Well, go for it, and thank Simon for me, we'll just see if we can fit it in. Keep me posted. You're still dropping by today, right?" Anne asked.

"Thanks Anne, I am. See you later." Jane looked up at Simon, who had been listening to the conversation.

"Looks like you're good to go. I'll call them, then let you know. That is, if you'll give me your email and phone number," Simon asked, smiling.

"Of course." Jane searched for her business card in her wallet and handed it over.

"I should be able to give you an answer by this evening, if not earlier." Simon said, finishing off his coffee.

Glancing at her watch, Jane said, "I really have to go now, Anne is expecting me." She got up from her seat. "Thank you for the coffee and giving me inspiration."

"It was my pleasure. May I walk with you to the gallery?" Simon asked, gazing deeply into her eyes as he got up too. At that moment, Jane realized that she didn't want to leave him. Not just yet.

"I'd like that," Jane replied as she picked up her portfolio case. "This has been an extraordinary morning."

"For me too," Simon replied, and they started walking toward the gallery.

oeo

That evening, as Jane sat in front of her laptop enjoying a glass of wine, she received an email from Simon. She quickly opened it.

Hi Jane,

I've got you an appointment at the Phenomenon Foundation for tomorrow afternoon at four p.m. Let me know if you can make it. The details are below.

Simon

She quickly wrote back.

Hi Simon,

That was fast. I'll be there.

Thank you so much for this. I owe you one.

He replied,

I'll take you up on that. Let me know how it goes.

Simon

Jane quickly sent off an email to Anne letting her know and then bought herself an airline ticket.

The next day, Jane took the noon flight out and, after landing an hour later, rented a car to drive out to where the foundation was. The region was famous for its orchards and vineyards, and she enjoyed the spectacular view as she was driving through. She had been here before during a summer vacation as a child but never had the opportunity to come back. She pulled the car over and glanced at the map on her phone. *Ten minutes. Hmm, I'm a bit early,* she thought. *I guess they won't mind.* Jane continued to drive and arrived at a small town, and from there, she followed the directions until she found 55 Willow Drive. It was a dead-end gravel road lined with tall trees splendid in their autumn colours. She drove slowly, curious and enamoured by the surrounding beauty. She passed through open wrought-iron gates and arrived at a court in front of a beautiful house. It was an

English-style cottage, covered with ivy, and she could see wisteria and climbing roses. On the side was an immense willow tree, and through there she caught a glimpse of a beautiful garden. She parked the car and got out, admiring the willow.

"It's beautiful, isn't it?" Jane turned around to see a middle-aged woman at the entrance of the house. "You must be Jane Bartley," the woman said. "Welcome to Phenomenon. Come in."

Jane walked toward her and shook her hand.

As they walked in, Jane noticed a plaque on the wall outside with the word Avalon written in beautiful lettering. Once inside, Jane glanced around, noticing the antique furniture, the paintings on the wall, and the beautiful accessories that were carefully placed. One painting caught her eye. It was of the ocean and waves, a kaleidoscope of blue and green. Jane gave it a second glance before they arrived at a reception area; she sat down as the woman went behind her desk and sat down as well.

"My name is Lilian," the woman said, smiling. "We received the request from Simon that you wanted to see and possibly take a photograph of our trees for your exhibition."

"Yes, if the lighting is good, with your permission I would like to, very much," Jane replied.

Lilian wrote something in a logbook and handed it over to Jane. "Could you please write your full name and sign? We like to keep a record of our visitors. You may go out to the garden; the trees will be down by the pond. If you need anything, just let me know. I'll be here until seven," Lilian said as Jane signed the book and stood up.

After thanking her, Jane slowly walked through the French doors onto a patio. For a minute, she stood still. It was a magical garden, with different types of flowers, bushes, decorative arbours, climbing roses, and steps leading down to a beautiful pond with a waterfall. The cascade of colours was mesmerizing. She walked down the steps and turned around to look at the house. It dominated the landscape, but in a way that it captured the nature around it, becoming part of the landscape. From where she was standing, she could see that there was a conservatory and a greenhouse right behind with what looked like a vegetable garden. She turned back and walked slowly by the pond toward the edge of the garden, when suddenly, she saw it.

Jane stood transfixed, looking at the trees with the trunks intertwined to become one. The left side of the tree had shimmering yellow leaves, while the right side had bright red leaves. At this time of the day, the autumn sun was low behind it and the filtering rays of light through the branches created a misty illusion of sprinkling gold and amber, as if the whole tree had become alive and glowing. *I wonder if this is why Simon made the appointment for four p.m.,* she wondered. *Did he know it would look like this at this time of the day?* It was an image that she couldn't resist capturing. She placed her bag on the ground and walked toward the tree. It was then that Jane noticed that there was a bench on the side with an old woman sitting on it.

"I'm sorry, I didn't mean to disturb you," Jane said. The old woman looked up at her. Jane could see that she must have been a beautiful woman in her youth. Her long white hair was loose on her shoulders. She literally looked angelic in the light.

"You must be Simon's Jane," the old woman said in a soft voice. Jane was startled at the remark.

"I'm not Simon's, we just met yesterday," she replied. "He kindly arranged for me to photograph this amazing tree."

"I didn't mean to offend you. Go ahead," the old woman said, smiling, "and then come sit by me."

Jane never did like an audience while photographing, but she somehow knew that it would be impolite to ask the old woman to leave. So, she took out her camera and took several shots, ignoring her presence. More than an hour passed by when Jane decided that she had enough images. The old woman had been silent throughout, watching her work. Jane packed away her things and came to sit next to her.

"Thank you for this," Jane said, looking at the woman. "I wonder how this happened."

The old woman sighed and reached out to touch Jane's hand. "Do you have time for a story?" she asked, looking at Jane with sadness in her eyes.

"If you have the time, then by all means," Jane replied, leaning back against the bench.

"That's all I have these days," the woman replied.

CHAPTER ONE

The Story

"Jasmine, remember that rosé wine I mentioned to you the other day? The one with the ruby colour? The one I fell in love with?" Willow asked.

"Yes, I do, what was the name of the winery it came from again?" Jasmine replied.

"Laid-Back Estate Winery."

"What about it?" Jasmine asked.

"Well, I looked at their website, and they have these beautiful small suites that they rent out. You can stay there while touring around the area and get wine tastings, and they also have a restaurant too, apparently with a very good chef, and—"

"Mom," Jasmine said, cutting her off, "why don't you go? It sounds fantastic, and you haven't been anywhere for, I don't know, ages."

"I thought I might go there for my birthday since you won't be coming this year."

"I told you, I have to go to this event for the company, otherwise of course I would be there. You know Sam is coming with me too."

"I know, I know, let me look into it and I'll let you know. How are you? How is Sam?" Willow asked.

"We're both working hard, busy running around like crazy."

"Happy?"

"I'm happy. Stop being a mom, will you?" Jasmine laughed.

"I'm a mom, and since you decided not to become one, then I have the liberty of playing the Mom card."

"Go ahead, then. I'll play the annoying daughter."

"Never," Willow said, laughing. "Go on, I won't keep you busy. We'll talk later."

"Love you. Let me know what you decide."

"Love you back."

Willow put down her cell phone. Talking to Jasmine in the mornings had become a weekly habit between them. Willow knew how busy Jasmine was, but Jasmine always managed to find time to talk to her, and she was grateful for it. Willow returned to her computer and again found the website for the winery she had mentioned. The place looked beautiful, and it was just an hour's drive away. She clicked on the link for the suites, which led her to a calendar for availability. She browsed through the dates in search for the month of May and saw that the whole month was fully booked. "So much for fantasies and plans," she mumbled to herself.

She grabbed her phone and texted to Jasmine, *no availability for the month of May.*

A few minutes later, Jasmine replied. *What about now?*

What do you mean? Willow texted back.

Go when its available, like now!

Willow stared at her phone. *Why not, indeed? What did it matter if it wasn't on my birthday?* She looked back at the computer and scrolled around the calendar again. There it was: availability from Monday to Thursday next week. She got up from her desk and went into the kitchen to make herself another cup of coffee. As she waited for the machine to heat up, she pondered the thought of going. She literally hadn't gone anywhere since, well, since James died. She had become a hermit living in her house and garden with just the dogs to keep her company. The more she stayed at home, the more she got melancholic and depressed. It seemed like she didn't enjoy anything anymore and instead lived the same monotonous day, over and over.

Willow picked up her now steaming cup of coffee and went back to her desk. She sat up straight in her chair and looked again at the dates. *I could tour other wineries in the region that I haven't been to and have a couple of nights in luxury by myself. I could leave the dogs at the dog hotel; they're used to going there anyway. And the house and garden can survive without me for a couple of days,* she thought. Here she was, trying to persuade herself to do something for herself and herself only. She was so used to taking care of others that she never did anything she enjoyed or would enjoy. Her fingers hovered above the keyboard, and she took a sip from her coffee and looked outside. *What am I afraid of? Being alone? Something bad happening? I'll be disappointed?* "what?!" she shouted to the room.

All three dogs looked up from where they were lying and tilted their heads. "I know, girls, Mommy is having a tough time making a decision for herself," she said aloud.

Another sip of coffee, and she punched "yes" to the available dates. Another window opened with questions for her to answer. She went through those quickly and finally ticked off the box 'single.' "Down payment required for one night. All right," she said. She found her credit card details and punched those in. *A bit expensive, but breakfast is included with internet and other amenities. Come on,* she told herself, *you spend all that money on plants and flowers. You can afford this.*

I know that, she answered herself.

Send button, and off it went. A few minutes later, she received a confirmation and that they were looking forward to seeing her.

Willow texted Jasmine, *done am going next week Monday to Thursday.*

Jasmine replied, *YAY!*

Willow smiled. She knew Jasmine worried about her.

⌒℮◯

Willow drove to the winery in the coming week after dropping off her dogs at the dog hotel, where they seemed to be happy, trotting off inside without looking back at her. It was a scenic drive along a lake with vineyards, orchards, and farms scattered over the landscape. She had made plans to visit three other wineries on the way before reaching her destination.

Laid-Back Estate Winery itself was in a beautiful location high on a hill overlooking the lake with acres of vineyards surrounding the main building with a beautiful patio. There were several small villas with rustic charm scattered over the vast landscape higher up right behind the main building, which she assumed were for guests, rightly placed to view the beautiful sunset that was just a couple of hours away. She was pleasantly tired and a little tipsy from all the wine tasting she had done on an empty stomach.

Willow parked her car in front of the reception and entered inside. A young woman was behind the desk. "Good evening, how may I help you?" she asked, smiling.

"I have a reservation." Willow handed her the printout she had brought of her confirmation.

"Thank you, ma'am, your suite is ready," the receptionist said while punching the keys on her keyboard. She then turned to get an old-fashioned key from the wall behind her. "You'll be staying at the Merlot suite." Willow looked up. "Yes, all the suites are named after grapes."

My favourite wine, is this a sign? Willow thought to herself. "You don't see these anymore," she said, continuing to look at the key, "it's all key cards now."

"Yes, I know, but we like traditions here, and it goes with the concept of the suites."

"Oh, make no mistake, I love these," Willow said, holding onto it.

"Please take the narrow road between the vineyards, and that will lead you up to the hill where the suites are. I hope you enjoy your stay with us."

"Thank you." Willow looked at her name tag. "Yvonne, is there any way I can order something to my suite? I'll try out the restaurant tomorrow evening."

"But of course. We have a special antipasto tray that can accompany your complimentary bottle of wine in your suite."

"That sounds great, please send it up in two hours."

As Willow walked out, she saw the narrow road between the vineyards on her right. *Hmm, what happens if a car comes?* she thought, but then saw the sign saying Please Alternate. She drove among the vineyards, enjoying the view, and she opened her window to smell the air. At the top of the hill, she saw the five villas with double suites spread out in a semicircle, all enjoying the view down below. Merlot was the third suite, so she parked in front of it and got out of the car. She noticed there were several other cars parked as she opened the door to her suite.

Well, now, this is a surprise, she thought as she looked over the place. The suite was quite large, with double French doors opening outside on to a private patio. On the right side, there was another room with a king-size bed and an ensuite with an old-fashioned bathtub with claw legs and a walk-in shower. On the other side of the room was a small kitchenette and a fridge. Willow walked straight through to the doors and went outside. There were two lounge chairs and beautiful terra-cotta planters with bright red geraniums. The choice of furniture, decorations and the whole construction was very tasteful. *Too tasteful to be done by just anyone*, she thought to herself as she walked back inside. She opened her small carry-on and started to hang up some of her clothes. She placed her toiletries in the bathroom, very tempted to take a bath.

She texted Jasmine, *have arrived its gorgeous.*

Enjoy, Momma! keep me posted with photos, Jasmine replied.

Willow texted back, *Love you.*

She went into the bathroom and filled up the bathtub, pouring a generous amount of the bubble bath from the bottle placed by the side. She had to admit, someone with great taste had decorated this place. She would ask Yvonne tomorrow for more information about the architect and decorator.

After nearly falling asleep in an hour-long bath, Willow finally bundled herself up in the soft bathrobe and walked out on to her private patio. The evening was silent as she gazed upon the scenic landscape. The sky was turning into all colours of pink and orange. *It was a good idea to come here,* she thought. *I should thank Jasmine for pushing me to do so.* She walked back in and looked for the complimentary bottle of wine Yvonne had mentioned. She opened the small fridge, and there was a bottle of her favourite rosé. *How did they know?* She smiled to herself. Just at that moment, there was a knock on the door. Willow opened to find a waiter with a big tray in his hands.

"Please place it on the table inside," she said while grabbing her purse to tip him.

"Thank you, ma'am, enjoy your dinner."

Willow gave him the tip and closed and locked the door. She lifted the cover off the tray to find an amazing board filled with cold meats, cheese, olives, some spreads, and artisan crackers. She took the tray outside onto the patio table and then went to get her wine. She poured a glass and walked outside and sat on one of the patio chairs.

Twilight was one of her favourite times of the day; it was when every-one settled down wherever they were, and all was quiet. She could hear some voices in the distance. *It must be coming from the restaurant below,* she thought.

Willow took a sip from her glass. The wine was cool and smooth on her tongue. She took a bite from one of the hard cheese squares and leaned back. *I can get used to this,* she thought. She sat out there eating and drinking, and by the time she had finished, it had gotten dark, and the lights on the pathways had lit up. It was getting a little chilly as well, so she took everything inside and closed the doors and curtains. She still had a glass of wine left from the bottle, and she finished that up as well before putting on her nightgown and getting into the huge king-size bed. The pillows were soft, and before she could decide whether to watch TV, she fell asleep.

Willow woke up the next morning early as usual. The sun was rising, and she could feel the heat behind the curtains. She got up to pull them open and walked outside. The cool fresh air hit her face, and she realized that even though she had gone through a bottle of wine by herself, she had no headache. She stretched her arms out lazily like a cat. *What I need is a good cup of coffee,* she thought, and she went inside and made herself some from the fancy coffee machine on the kitchenette counter. She noticed the brand. *Hmm, no ordinary coffee here. They sure are treating their customers well,* she thought. Breakfast arrived by the time Willow had finished her second cup of coffee: French toast with fruit compote and cream, along with three slices of bacon and a bowl of fresh fruit, all presented with style again. *This should keep me well until dinner time,* she thought as she dug in.

It was late afternoon when Willow came back from her day of wine tasting. She felt the sun on her face and noticed that her cheeks were rosy, and she had a glow that she hadn't seen for a long time now. She felt good and looked forward to tasting the food at the restaurant. She had made a reservation for seven o'clock, so she rushed into the bathroom to take a quick shower.

Later, she dressed up in some casual pants and a long chiffon shirt over her tank top. She had brought some sensible flat shoes to go with the outfit. Now for her hair. She looked at herself in the bathroom window. She had stopped dyeing and cutting her hair five years ago, and now it was totally white and long. She piled it all up in a haphazard way and pushed two sparkling combs to hold it up. *Not bad,* she told herself. Along with the hair, she had stopped putting on any makeup except the occasional moisturizer, but this time, she had brought along her compact powder and mascara. *Barely making a difference,* she thought. To top all off, she put on some crystal sparkling earrings, her favourite. *There. Much better for a woman of sixty-five. Yes, it was definitely a good decision to come here,* she thought.

Outside, she hesitated between walking or taking the car to go down. She had noticed a pathway down to the restaurant. She glanced down. She should be able to make it back up, but she didn't trust herself, so she backtracked to her car and drove down. She saw that there were already many cars parked by the entrance of the restaurant. The region was a popular destination for wine lovers, and apparently, the restaurant here was one of the best.

"Good evening," greeted the young man at the door.

"I have a reservation for seven under the name Willow."

"Of course." He glanced down at his list. "Will someone be joining you?" he asked politely.

"No, a table for one, please."

"Of course. Please follow me."

He showed Willow to a small table at one corner of the patio that had a beautiful view. *Must be the white hair,* Willow thought. The young man handed the menu he had in his hand.

"Can I get you some water?"

"Yes, please, thank you."

He walked back inside, and Willow glanced around. There were several couples, a large group of young people, and what she assumed a family of four. She glanced down at the menu. Everything looked very inviting, and she was famished, having not eaten anything since breakfast. A waitress came back with her glass of water.

"Would you like a drink?"

"I'll have some wine with my dinner, so I'll let you know once I decide what to eat," Willow replied, smiling.

As the waitress left, Willow looked down again at the menu when she heard a group of people arriving. She glanced up to see the group walking toward the entrance. Behind them, a couple was conversing while following the group. The woman was talking excitedly, while the man was listening with his head bowed. They walked by her. Something about the man seemed familiar, and then Willow heard his voice as he replied to what the woman had said.

Her head shot up. As the man casually turned to look at the patio, she quickly hid behind her menu, trembling before he could see her. But she didn't know that more was in store for her.

Indeed, the man had noticed Willow. His attention was drawn by her earrings, which sparkled as they caught the light. Something was very familiar, but then, he did not at once recognize her. She had been sitting alone at one of the tables, with beautiful white hair that was piled up, held by sparkling combs that matched her earrings. That sparkle resonated with him, and as much as he tried at first, he could not remember why and where. She had been holding the menu high in her hands and seemed not to have noticed him looking at her, or so he thought.

"Alan, are you listening to me?"

He turned around to his sister as they entered the restaurant. "Yes, I am. It's just that…" Suddenly, he stopped.

"What's the matter, Alan? You look like you've seen a ghost."

"I think I just have." Alan shook his head. "Give me a minute, OK? You take care of the seating arrangements." He excused himself, turned, and walked out—but the woman had somewhat disappeared. Frustrated, he looked around, but she was nowhere to be seen. *What, again?* he thought.

By then, Willow had already left her table in a rush. *The waitress, along with all the other customers, must think I've gone mad,* she thought. *Of all the places I could be.* She hurriedly walked out toward her car when she saw some hidden steps on the side leading down to the vineyards. She quickly walked down a few steps and sat down. *What were the odds, really? What were the odds that I would choose to come here? Had he seen me? Had he even recognized me? What was he doing here, anyway? I knew something was going to happen. I should literally kick myself for coming here.*

All these thoughts rushed through Willow's head, which by now was throbbing. She could feel the fast pace of her heartbeat. Seeing him again after all those years had triggered emotions she thought had gone away. She could hear sounds of conversation streaming down from the patio. *What do I do? Go back up to my suite and sulk? Get drunk?* And she hadn't eaten anything. *That would go down so nicely,* she thought. As she was deliberating all this, she noticed how peaceful it was out here. Maybe she could sit down and cool off.

That was when she noticed the dog watching her from a distance. "Hello," Willow said in a calm voice. "Who might you be?" The dog sat and looked at her, tilting its head. "Come and sit with me," she said, patting the stairs. Slowly, the dog walked up and stared at her. Willow didn't move.

"Do you want to sit with me?" she whispered. The dog stood still and then walked up the steps to reach her side. Willow could now see that the dog was a female and looked like a cross between a border collie and a retriever.

"What's your name?" Willow asked. Then, she noticed the dog tags and slowly reached out with her hand. The dog sat down and placed her paw on Willow's knee.

"Aww, sweetie, you're beautiful." Willow petted the dog on her back and slowly reached out to read the tag. "Roxy?" She laughed, leaning toward the dog. "That's a beautiful name." The dog slowly lay down by her side and looked up at her.

"You're friendly, aren't you," Willow whispered in the dog's ear. "I have three dogs you know." She scratched behind the dog's ear.

"She likes you."

Willow recognized the voice. She turned around to look up.

"May I?" the man said, pointing to the steps.

"By all means," Willow replied, moving aside a little. Roxy got up and started wagging her tail.

"Good girl." He petted her head as she settled down next to him. There was an awkward silence. "How are you?" he finally said.

She turned in surprise. "I didn't think you remembered. I saw you looking at me, and you seemed to not recognize. But of course, it's been many years now, and I've changed. Gotten older." Willow laughed, trying to disguise the trembling of her voice.

"No, you haven't. Yes, the hair threw me off at first—but the sparkles, that's so you."

"Sparkles?" Willow asked, confused.

"Yes, the first time I saw you, it was your sparkling earrings that had attracted my attention again."

"Like twelve years ago," she replied.

"Has it been that long?"

"Yes, it has."

"What are you doing here?" Alan asked.

"Wine tasting. Funny, of all places I could be, I brought myself here, not knowing. What are you doing here?"

"I own the place," Alan replied casually.

"I never connected this winery to you," Willow replied in surprise.

"Would you not have come if you knew?"

"I don't know." Willow looked at him. "I never saw your name on the website when I looked over the winery."

"We just recently bought this company. We needed an establishment to make our own wine our vineyards produce. The owners of this company were ready to retire, so it was a mutual agreement and advantage to both parties. We haven't gotten around to changing the website yet," Alan replied.

"Funny, I recently discovered the remarkable rosé this company produces at the liquor store and was curious to see the place."

"That rosé you like is produced from the grapes from our vineyards, hence the reason to expand. Remember? I mentioned it to you once."

Willow smiled. "What are the odds? Really, a wine brought me here." She shook her head.

"I didn't even know you lived around here. Daisy, my daughter, is in charge of marketing, and tonight's dinner is a business meeting to discuss strategies to start off the season with the new name and brand. That's why I'm here."

"You haven't changed much," Willow said.

"Oh, yes, I have. My hair may not be as white as yours, but it's getting there. Wrinkles and bruises and scars are there to remind me of the passing years." He brushed his hair with his hand.

"So, you live here now?" Willow asked.

"Yes, I moved here about ten years ago. Took over the management of the vineyards when my father died, but it's my sister Robyn who's the winemaker. I just oversee things. And everyone, I guess." He smiled.

"In a way, you're the CEO?"

"If you want to call it that."

"Quite the family business. What happened to architecture, then?" Willow asked.

Alan was pleasantly surprised by the question. "Put aside as a hobby. My youngest daughter, Grace, became an architect, though. The renovations for the buildings are my design when we took over. What about you? When did you move here?" he asked.

Aha! The architecture and decorations. Now I know. Why hasn't he mentioned his wife? Willow thought. "I moved here about eight years ago. I live an hour away. However, I'm staying at one of your suites for three nights as a treat for myself," Willow replied.

"Dad?"

They both turned around.

"They're waiting for you," said the young woman, glancing at Willow.

"I'm coming." Alan stood up. "Come, let me introduce you to an old acquaintance. Willow, this is Daisy, my eldest daughter."

For a minute, Willow thought that there was recognition in Daisy's eyes when she heard her name. "Hello, Daisy," she said.

"Pleased to meet you. Dad, are you coming in?"

"I'll be there in a few minutes."

"All right," Daisy said as she turned to go back.

"Go ahead, please. Don't mind me. You shouldn't keep your wife and guests waiting."

Alan stood still. "Wife?"

"I saw you together as you walked by," Willow said.

"Willow, I'm a widower. My wife passed away eleven years ago. That was my sister Robyn that you saw."

It was Willow's turn to be silent. "I… I'm sorry to hear that, Alan. I didn't know."

"What about you?" Alan changed the subject. "Are you married?"

"I'm a widow too. Three years now."

"So, you remarried in the end?" He looked deeply into her eyes.

Willow didn't answer him because suddenly, old memories came rushing back, making her head pound. She struggled to control her voice.

Before she could say anything, he said, "Look I have to go, but how long are you here?"

"I leave Thursday morning," Willow replied.

"What are you doing tomorrow?"

"Visiting different wineries, trying to know the region."

Alan looked at her. "Let me show you around. We can visit my vineyards, have lunch, and talk. We need to talk."

Willow didn't reply immediately. On one hand, she wanted to accept the offer, but on the other hand, she knew this would be asking for trouble. After all she had been through, to do it again would be punishing herself.

"I don't think that would be a good idea," Willow answered finally. "Besides, you're busy, and I'm sure you have better things to do."

He looked down at her from the top of the stairs. "You know, you haven't changed. You're doing it again."

"Doing what?"

"Making excuses. This time, I'm not backing down. We'll meet at nine here, and don't you dare stand me up. We have much to talk about, don't you think? Twelve years. And anyway, you're staying here, so I'll just show up at your door if you aren't here at nine. How's that?"

"All right, all right, I'll be here at nine. Go now before Daisy comes out again."

Alan looked at her questioningly. "Did you finish your dinner?"

"No, I didn't even start. I sort of ran away."

"Then come on. We'll go back together." He offered her his hand as Willow stood up.

"Thank you, I'll manage," she said, not knowing what she would feel if she touched him.

They walked back, and Willow saw that her table hadn't been cleared. Her glass of water was still there, along with the menu.

He stopped before going in. "It's good to see you again, Willow."

"It's good to see you too, Alan."

He went in. Willow turned and walked back to sit at her table. *What have I done?* she thought. *Why did I accept? Was it because I wanted to see him again after all these years? Do I still have feelings for him?*

"Is everything all right?"

Willow looked up at the waitress who had shown up silently. "Yes, yes, thank you, I'm fine. I'll have the risotto and a bottle of your rosé wine, please."

After the waitress left with her order, Willow leaned back and remembered. Remembered back twelve years, when she first met Alan.

CHAPTER TWO

·◦· ⊶❧⊶ ·◦·
Coincidences

*A*lan was tired. It was the first day of an early spring, and the sun was shining brightly outside the international terminal of the airport. He was walking slowly among the rush of people since he didn't need to get anywhere soon. He had a lot of time to kill before his next flight and he was trying to get to the business lounge and find a quiet spot to sit down so his tiredness could ease off.

It was another crowded day at one of the busiest airports in the world, and he was amazed at the variety of people he was seeing and the many different languages he was hearing. This was one of the reasons why it took him a while before he noticed his cell phone ringing inside his jacket. He stopped to answer and saw the name Robyn flashing. He smiled.

"Hello, Sis."

"Where are you?"

"At another airport," Alan replied.

"So, how are you?"

"You know, it seems like I've spent the last three months on the move. The hotels arranged by my—or should I say, Patrick's clients were very comfortable, but I can't seem to fall asleep. A habit that I picked up these days along with the travelling."

"And Caroline isn't helping, I'm sure," Robyn said.

Alan stared at the phone in his hand. "Are you being psychic again?"

"Please. Give me credit. You think no one knows how you feel about Caroline? How we all feel? Don't worry, everything is under control here—but seriously, it's time to make some changes. You can't keep living like this."

Alan was suddenly at a loss for words. He pulled his hand through his hair, further mussing up the already untidy image he was presenting to the world. "And now, another ten hours of flight. Thanks for business class. But you know, we should just buy a corporate plane. I know we can afford it."

"You keep saying that. Well, it's good you're coming home. Besides, you might catch up on some sleep. By the way, Dad says hi."

"Hi, Dad."

"Why don't you go and get a good, relaxing book? Something light. I bet it's been a long time since you read anything just for the pleasure of it. Maybe you'll even fall asleep," Robyn suggested.

"You wish. Yes, I guess I can do that," Alan replied.

Robyn sighed and said, "Take care now. I worry about you."

"Don't worry. What's the worst thing that can happen?" he whispered into the phone as he looked around the crowd. "I already have a miserable love life, a hectic and chaotic business, and a family that adores me. How's everyone else holding up? I talked to Daisy the other day, and she seemed troubled."

"You know teenagers. I'll talk to her today. OK, I'll let you go now."

"Thanks for the call. Love you."

Alan stood and closed his eyes for a while. *Robyn is right. I should take care. I'm sleepless and tired. So very tired. Maybe I should just go ahead with her suggestion and look for a book. Something to distract me from business and love,* he thought.

As he walked toward the business lounge, he decided to stop by the bookstore. Alan gazed at all the bestsellers strewn on the big tables in the centre of the shop. He picked up a novel and started to read the back cover when he noticed her. In fact, it was her earrings that he noticed first. She was wearing delicate earrings of small crystals that shone brightly, casting tiny lights over the books as the sunshine caught them. It was a mesmerizing sight, and for a minute, he stood still, just looking at the cascade of lights. Then, he looked up at her.

She was glancing over the book covers while walking slowly, so he couldn't see her face as she traced the covers with her fingers. She looked as if she was dreaming and took no notice of the way her earrings were creating a festival of light. She stopped walking and picked up a book. All the while, Alan stood still, holding his breath. What was it about her that caught his attention? Why was he so intrigued by her?

Suddenly, she looked up at him. He was astonished to see that there were tears in her eyes.

Taking a deep breath, he looked away, fumbling around with the book in his hand. Her look had shattered him, and he became overwhelmed with emotion at the sight of her tears. At that precise moment when their glances met, the world had stopped for him. His surroundings had become a blur, and the only thing that was clear to him was her expression. She had brown eyes, shimmering with tears, looking at him. It was a look that seemed to pierce his soul. He shuffled his bag and dared to look again, but she was gone. He froze. *What the hell?* he thought. Alan looked around, but she was nowhere to be seen. He couldn't understand why he suddenly felt awkward, but he wondered why she had been crying. It had been such a personal moment that he was surprised how he felt about it and how much it had disturbed him. Why had it tugged at his heart so?

Alan dropped the book on the table and walked out. He walked around aimlessly, looking for a woman he had just once seen, and finally gave up and sat down at one of the bars and ordered a beer with the hope that he might catch a glimpse of her. He took a sip and looked at his watch. He sat there until he finished his beer, but there was no sight of her. He shrugged. He paid the barmen and, picking up his bag, walked toward the business lounge.

Alan fell into the habit of glancing around among the rushing crowd, and he felt helplessly silly. It was as he was passing the duty-free shops that he noticed the earrings again. Funny how they seemed to attract only his eye and no one else's. He looked around, wondering if anyone else was watching, but everyone was in a rush to get from one place to the other and had no time for sparkling lights. He stopped and stood still.

Suddenly, his cell phone rang again. Cursing silently, he struggled to find it. The name Patrick flashed on the screen.

"Hey!"

"Hey yourself. Where are you?" Patrick asked.

"Waiting for my flight," Alan replied, still looking at the woman who hadn't seen him yet.

"So, everything went well?" Patrick asked.

"Yes."

"Did you get the offer?"

"Yes."

Patrick, somewhat puzzled, said, "You sure are short on answers."

"Can't talk now," Alan whispered.

Patrick whispered back, "Why not?"

Alan looked at the woman with sudden relief. Not knowing why, he felt that he had to be next to her. Protect her. From what? He kept staring.

"Hello? Alan?" Patrick shouted on the phone. "Man, you're creeping me out. What's the matter?"

Alan hesitated. "I just saw this woman in the bookstore, and now I'm sort of stalking her around the airport. Look, I'll call you back, OK?" he said and put his phone back in his pocket.

Logic says that I should move on and get myself to the business lounge and sit down. But I want to stay and observe. What do I do? Alan thought as he glanced up—and then noticed that she was gone. *What, again?* He frantically looked around, but she was nowhere to be seen.

Alan silently cursed his luck. *This is like playing hide-and-seek,* he thought. *Maybe it's for the best.* What was he going to do if he did indeed find her? He finally reached the business lounge and, after showing his boarding pass, walked in.

The lounge had a cosy atmosphere with subtle lighting, nothing like some lounges he had been in before. The armchairs looked comfortable and inviting, large enough for his long legs.

Alan walked up to the bar and ordered a dram of single malt. Anything that would take his mind off the woman and how tired he felt. He took his glass and glanced around for a seat. He noticed a corner seat and walked in that direction when he saw her again. *This can't be,* he thought. *Of all the places, I find her here, in the business lounge. What were the odds?* Taking in a breath, he peeked at her. Amazingly, she was sleeping, regardless of her environment. There was a seat right next to her, so without another thought to it, he sat down. He settled back, placing his bags next to him, and folded his arms. Under half-closed lids, he looked at her.

He stared at her hands. She was wearing a ring on her right hand, which looked like an antique. *Is that an heirloom?* he thought. She wasn't young, looked to be in her forties, but she had a regal, poised demeanour about her.

She stirred. Alan closed his eyes and pretended to sleep. He heard her fidgeting and moving about, but he was too afraid to open his eyes to look. He heard a sigh, and then all was quiet again. He dared to lift his eyelids. Yes, she was sleeping again but was huddled up as if she was cold. He frowned. He saw from the corner of his eye that she had turned more toward him and had placed her hand on the armrest of the chair.

Why am I attracted to her? She's not even my type. What's the pull? I don't know. Is it because I saw her crying, or is it the crystal earrings that sparkle? Maybe it was her silent poise, tall and regal. I don't know. I don't know, but I can't stop thinking about her, he thought.

Alan noticed that she slept with a wrinkle in her brow, as if she was dreaming. She was hugging herself, and he again wondered if she was cold. She was wearing a soft grey cardigan zipped up in front on top of black pants. Her feet were covered in sensible black shoes with perfectly tied shoelaces. *Funny how you notice these things at the weirdest moment,* he thought. She had a scarlet pashmina around her throat that gave a soft rose pallor to her face. And of course, the crystal earrings shone on their own, sparkling on and off.

Should I? Should I place my jacket on top of her to keep her warm? Or will she wake up and shout hysterically? She definitely doesn't look the type that would shout, but... I don't want to be seen as coming on to her, which I'm definitely not. But I can't stay away from her, so what does that make me? Thoughts ran through his mind.

The ring sparkled. *What is with her and the sparkles? I know that if I reach out, I can touch her hand. It's so close. I hate myself for thinking about it. But she looks so cold,* he said to himself silently. He drowned his drink in a gulp.

Alan took off his jacket and looked around to see if anyone was watching him, but everyone was minding their own business. He bent forward and slowly, carefully draped his jacket over her body. Holding his breath, he waited. No sign of her waking up. He breathed out and leaned back again. He closed his eyes, but sleep refused to come. He opened his eyes and glanced back at her. She looked peaceful while sleeping. Her hand was still resting on the arm of the chair. He smiled to himself and closed his eyes again.

After some time of closing his eyes, he felt the woman place his jacket back on his body. He opened his eyes suddenly, and they stared at each other without saying a word. She was the first one to look away and stand up.

"I guess this is your jacket," she mumbled.

"Yes, you looked cold," Alan replied with a deep, husky voice, as if having awoken from a deep sleep. In fact, he had just closed his eyes to rest.

"Thank you. I was. Please take it—you must be cold now, and I have to leave. My flight leaves in an hour."

Alan looked at his wristwatch. "I should be going too. My flight also leaves in an hour."

He quickly struggled to get up and in doing so accidentally bumped into her. Her right foot got caught up in his chair, causing her to lose her balance, and she fought not to fall back.

"I'm sorry, are you all right?" he asked anxiously. He grabbed her arm to steady her and consequently pulled her up against his chest. She stood still for a minute, mesmerized as if she were a cat.

"I'm all right, thank you. Now, I really must be going. It was very kind of you to give me your jacket," she said, somewhat out of breath. She put out her hand to say goodbye. Alan looked down at it, then at her face.

"Where are you flying to?" he suddenly asked, putting on his jacket, not noticing the discomfort that he had caused her just a while ago.

The woman frowned. He still hadn't shaken her hand. It was still up there in the air between them. Alan suddenly stood still. She pulled her hand away. He slowly turned around and stared at her.

"What is it?" she asked.

"You still didn't tell me to where you're flying."

Silence. She struggled to find something to say, but no words came to her mind.

"I have to use the washroom," she finally said, turning her head while fumbling with her bag. "Thank you again for the jacket, and have a safe flight."

Alan gathered his things, and when he stood up, he was a head taller than her. "It's been a pleasure. You have a safe flight too," he replied.

Alan walked away, realizing that he wasn't registering any details surrounding him. *What just happened back there?* The moment when he had her in his arms, he had been... aroused. He had never felt like this before. He was a grown man, and yet here he was, stalking this strange woman. Really, when he came to think of it, what chance was there that he could be travelling to the same destination? How many passengers passed through this airport, and what was the chance that they would end up on the same flight? He was trying to cope with the sudden rush of feelings and thoughts that he failed to understand. Besides, he was feeling very uncomfortable, wondering if she had felt the same thing just a minute ago. *And why didn't she say where she was flying? Strange,* he thought.

⤮

The woman Alan was thinking of had rushed into the washroom and was staring at the mirror, trying to focus.

When the man had steadied Willow earlier after she had nearly fallen, she had found herself looking closely at his white shirt and smelling a faint cologne that had awakened her. No, she hadn't been all right. The feel of their bodies at close proximity was just another reminder of how long it had been since... She suddenly felt dizzy. The hand that had grabbed her had felt like a vice around her arm. *Where did the strength come from?* She wondered. He also had the most beautiful smile, which illuminated his whole face and reached his eyes.

"Are you all right?" A woman turned to look at Willow, who was staring at her reflection. "You look very pale."

"I'm all right, thank you. It must be the jet lag," Willow replied.

She continued staring at her flushed face. She turned on the water and splashed some water. *Time to brace the world again,* she thought as she walked out. She checked the lounge and noticed with relief that the man she had been thinking of had left.

She reached her gate and saw that there was already a long queue for a security check. As she stood in line, she saw that the same man was inside the boarding lounge, sitting down and working on his laptop.

What the... she thought, trying not to look at him. He had a puzzled and concerned look on his face, and he looked so handsome that she felt an ache in her stomach. It had been such a long time. Such a long time since... She refused to think. *I'm going to see my daughter, and nothing can upset me,* she thought.

"Lady, this way." She looked up to see the security guard motioning for her to move forward. She dumped her bags and passed through the checkpoint.

This is such a weird day, she thought. *Now what?* She walked toward the windows and looked outside with her back turned toward the man, hoping he wouldn't see her. The odds were playing against her today, first at the bookstore, then at the lounge, now on the same flight and same business class. *Murphy's Law,* she thought. *Please go away.*

Alan closed his laptop and put it away in his briefcase. He leaned back, watching as people came into the lounge area. From the corner of his eye, he noticed the woman standing by the windows looking out. *What do I do? Tempt fate? Or just play safe? Give me a sign. A sign that I should pursue this. Anything? Is that Bach I'm hearing?* he thought.

He realized, as the woman fumbled around in her purse, that it was her cell phone ringing with Bach.

"How are you?" Alan heard her say, somewhat out of breath.

He stared at her. She had undergone such a striking transformation that he couldn't believe it. Her eyes had widened, and her smile lit up her whole face. It was as if her whole body came alive. She glanced at him. He pretended not to listen.

"I'm waiting to board, yes. I'll let you know once we land. Can't wait to see you. Bye." She turned off the phone and placed it in her bag. He still feigned ignorance.

Alan realized he wanted to see her animated face once again. She had looked so different. Would this be the sign he was looking for? Suddenly, there was a crackle, and then the announcement for the passengers to board began. Soon, the ground crew invited the business class passengers to board, and he saw her slowly walking forward.

"Fancy seeing you here again," he said when he came to stand behind her. "I think we got off on the wrong foot," he continued. "My name is Alan."

"Willow," she answered.

"What a beautiful name," Alan replied, continuing to look at her as they walked. "What do you think the odds are that we're seated together, now that we've come so far?"

"Too bad I don't believe in coincidences," Willow replied.

Alan didn't answer. *You think you have me outwitted,* he thought.

"Hmm. Well, I do," Alan said. "But it was nice talking to you again. Have a good flight."

"Thank you."

Willow smiled politely, thinking, *Well, so much for that. What did I expect? Oh well. This is going to be one long flight, and I just hope that my neighbour won't be a chatterbox. I don't need to talk at this moment, especially after all this. I just want to close my eyes and relax. Have some champagne.* Willow smiled at the flight attendant who glanced at her boarding card and invited her in. It was a double seat, and Willow had the window.

Willow sat down in her seat. She rummaged around in her bag, trying to find her phone to check whether she had turned it off, when she noticed a pair of brown suede shoes standing next to the seats. The shoes reminded her of something. As if she had seen them somewhere before. The flight attendant joined in.

Willow heard a familiar voice say, "Thank you for changing my seat, much appreciated." A deep voice. A voice that she now remembered. She looked up, staring.

Alan continued, regardless of her stare. "You see, the lady and I are long-lost friends, and we would love to travel together."

The flight attendant smiled. "Of course. Would you like me to hang your jacket, sir?"

"Yes, please," Alan replied and handed it over to her but kept his briefcase with him. He sat down and smiled. "By the way, you turned off your cell phone in the waiting lounge."

Willow kept looking at him, at a loss for words. Her nerves were tingling all over as she felt the large man sitting next to her, felt his warmth and strength. Mixed thoughts rambled in her mind as she sat. *Now what? I ask for deliverance, and this is what I get? And why has he done this? He said he wanted to, but why? Why with me? Now I'm in real need of that damn drink. Maybe I can make the best of all this and just enjoy. How long has it been since I enjoyed the company of a man? And especially a man like him? And after all, it is a long flight, and I should enjoy the company.*

So, he thinks he can outwit me. Well, two can play at that.

"Champagne, madam?" the flight attendant asked, holding out the tray in her hand.

"Thank you." Willow took one of the flutes.

"You, sir?"

"Thank you, I will," he said, smiling at her.

Willow watched as the plane took off. Alan was pretending to read the in-flight magazine, but she could see that he was just glancing at the pages.

Maybe he's as nervous as I am. Maybe he's already regretting what he's done, she thought. Willow knew he was throwing her anxious glances, trying to understand what she was thinking. *What should I say?* Willow thought. *He was totally mistaken about me, and he couldn't have any interest in me, could he? Not when he could have any woman swooning over him at any given time.*

Swoon? Where do I come up with these words... Too many romantic novels, I guess. She saw him glancing at her sideways from the corner of her eye.

"Business or pleasure?" Alan finally asked, looking at her.

"Pleasure," Willow replied. "And you?"

"I was on a business trip but am now returning home."

"What kind of business are you in?" Willow asked, thinking she might as well have a conversation.

"I'm an architect."

Willow shook her head, and her earrings sparkled. "I studied interior decoration. We're colleagues, in a way."

This time, Alan stared at her. "Really?"

"Really. Well, it was a long, long, long time ago," Willow replied.

"Why?"

"Why what?" Willow was puzzled.

"Why has it been such a long, long, long time ago?" Alan repeated.

Willow smiled and said, "I'm not that young, you know." *Better that he knows my age,* she thought.

Alan smiled back. "Yes, I know. But that's not answering my question."

"What answer do you want me to give you?"

"Well, you can tell me why you stopped doing it a long, long—three times, was it?—long time ago." Alan leaned back.

Willow looked down at her feet. "Ahh… you're making fun of me."

"I am not," Alan said softly.

Willow insisted, "Yes you are."

"No, I'm not." Alan glanced sideways at her.

Willow did turn around to look back. "Anyway, it's a long story."

Alan still looked on. "It's a long flight."

At that moment the flight attendant came to their seat with wet towels. Willow rubbed her hands and noticed that Alan had beautiful hands with long fingers and clean-cut nails. It was always the first thing that she noticed in a man.

"Why was it a long time ago?" Alan asked after placing the wet towel on the tray that he opened.

"Originally, I wanted to be a child psychologist. However, interior decoration was my second choice."

"That's interesting. Why didn't you become a child psychologist?"

"I'm an only child, and my mother and grandmother didn't want me going away to a college in a different country," Willow said, remembering the arguments she'd had with her mother. "So, I stayed and instead attended the Academy of Fine Arts and studied interior decoration. I always had an interest in the arts. I also painted."

"Really? You're a very talented woman," Alan said admiringly.

"You haven't seen anything. How can you tell?" Willow replied jokingly.

"I can tell, believe me." Alan looked at her.

This time, the flight attendant came to get their requests for drinks. "What would you like to drink, madam?" she asked, offering a napkin and a bowl of nuts.

"Gin and tonic, please," Willow said.

"And for you, sir?"

"I'll have the same, please."

"I'll be right back."

Once they had their drinks Willow said, "Cheers," and saluted his glass.

Alan saluted back. "Cheers." He took a sip. "So, what happened later?" he continued while munching on a peanut.

"After a couple of years, I became dissatisfied with it all and established my own company, offering hospitality services and event planning," Willow replied calmly.

"Like a wedding planner?" Alan asked.

"No. My company specialized in organizing medical conferences and exhibitions, along with publishing seven medical journals."

His hand stopped midway with his glass. "Anything else? You're like a jack-of-all-trades."

Willow tried hard not to laugh. "I believe so. Nothing was planned, though. It just turned out that way."

"Are you still in business?" Alan asked.

"No, I retired two years ago after twenty-something years in the business," Willow replied reluctantly.

"Why did you retire?" Alan asked.

"I didn't want any ties in my life," Willow said sadly as she slowly turned her head to look outside. Alan threw her a glance, and she was grateful he decided not to ask any more questions for a while. They both read the menus the flight attendant handed out and gave their individual orders, along with wine choices. Shortly, their food was served, and they ate in silence.

"I'm sorry I snapped then," Willow offered after a while in an apologetic tone.

"Don't be." Willow turned to look at him. He wiped his mouth on the napkin. "Don't apologize. I should not have asked. Not yet anyway."

The flight attendant came along. "Can I get you anything else?" she asked politely.

"I'd like some more white wine, please," Willow replied. Alan raised his eyebrows questioningly.

The flight attendant turned to him. "And for you, sir?"

"I'll have more of the red," Alan said, and then leaned toward Willow's ear as soon as the flight attendant had left. "How bad is the wine? The truth, now," Alan asked.

"It's quite good, surprisingly," Willow replied, looking at the label.

"Not bad as far as flight wines go. Do you like wine? If that's not too personal to ask." Alan said.

"I love wine. I'm very partial to Merlot for red, I love fruity white wine, and rosé, well, that's a different story. I still have to find the perfect one."

"Hmm. You should taste some of mine, then," Alan said. She turned to him in surprise. "My family owns vineyards."

"A winemaker on top of being an architect. That's a lot of things to juggle, isn't it?" Willow said jokingly.

"I don't personally oversee the winemaking, I just enjoy drinking it. My sister is the winemaker. We're a large family, so lots of uncles and aunts, brothers and sisters to take care of it all."

"I wouldn't know. I come from a very small family," Willow said, hesitating. Thankfully, Alan didn't dare ask more. He instead continued the conversation.

"What's so special about finding the perfect rosé?"

"To be frank, I don't really know. It's just that for me, it's fresh spring water with a scent of summer. Spring has always been my favourite time of the year."

"I've never heard wine described like that. Now you really have to try our wine," Alan replied.

"Well, give me the name so I can look for it at the liquor store," Willow said, finishing her food.

"You won't find it there. You have to come for a visit."

"Maybe I will," Willow replied, looking directly into his eyes. Alan looked back. There was an awkward silence, yet neither of them could look away from each other. The sun shone into his green eyes, and Willow could see that there was a ring of blue around his iris which slowly turned into a darker shade of green. In fact, she could swear that his eyes were now blue as he continued to look at her without blinking. Willow wished she had such interesting eyes, but unfortunately, they were just plain brown. So why was he staring at her as if they were the most beautiful eyes that he had seen? she thought.

Suddenly, she couldn't keep looking at him anymore. She turned away. From the corner of her eye, she saw him down his glass of wine. Willow said, "It's warm in here, isn't it?" and she pulled off her pashmina and leaned forward and placed it inside her bag. Her earrings sparkled in the sunshine.

"You have quite spectacular earrings. They were the first thing that I noticed about you."

"Oh, how's that?" Willow turned to look at him.

"Well, remember at the bookstore, you were looking at the books? The sunshine had caught your earrings, just like a minute ago, and all these sparkling lights shimmered on the book covers. That was what I noticed first." He paused. "Then you looked up."

"I know. You saw me crying," Willow said softly.

"Yes," Alan reluctantly replied.

"I was just sad."

"I noticed. They're quite beautiful you know, your earrings."

"Why, thank you."

Alan hesitated before continuing, "Why were you sad?" he asked.

"I believe it's because of the changes in my life. Some by choice, but some I was forced to do." Willow looked up into his eyes. "I've just gone through a messy divorce."

"How long had you been married?" Alan asked.

"Thirty years," Willow replied.

"Thirty years? That's such a long time. How old were you when you got married?" Alan asked, surprised.

"I know, I can't believe it myself," Willow said, ignoring his question.

"Why after thirty years?"

"Because he cheated on me with my best friend," Willow responded calmly. Alan nearly choked on his drink. He looked at her questioningly. "I know it sounds corny, but it's the truth. They say the wife always knows, but I didn't. Or maybe I did but just didn't want to admit it."

"Excuse me for asking, and you don't have to answer if you don't want to, but how did you find out?" Alan asked.

"I saw them on the street, hand in hand." There was an awkward silence then. It seemed like Alan hesitated in asking further questions because she had become troubled, but Willow continued anyway. "I think that during a marriage, it's the woman that grows up while the man stays the same as the day he got married," she finally said after calming her senses. She paused, then continued, "I just can't understand why men in general feel the need to be with a younger woman. Don't they know that their wives were once that young woman? That during their marriage, she supported him through the ups and downs, health and sickness, money problems, children, and bam! They reach their midlife crisis, and they have to go prove to themselves that they're still a man. Have you heard of any man leaving their wives for an older woman?

"And what about the wife? Do they know how the wife feels upon seeing the new couple? How humiliating it feels? And what about the children? How do they perceive what's happening with their father? Do they… know how…" Willow stopped. *What am I doing, anyway?* she thought. *Talking about this to a stranger.*

Alan laughed nervously. "You're very angry."

"Oh, does it show?" Willow said sarcastically.

"You can't assume that's true with all men. Anyway, you should stop talking about it if you feel uncomfortable."

"Not if you are."

"It's all very… intriguing," Alan finally replied.

"This isn't funny."

"I didn't say it was. You have me captivated."

"This is serious, you know."

"Well, I am serious. I know this is serious."

Willow glared at him. "You don't sound serious."

Alan glared back. "You don't know me enough to judge whether I'm serious or not. Come on, you need to lighten up a little."

"I should've known," Willow said.

"Known what?"

"That you would be like the rest of them," Willow continued.

"Rest of whom?" Alan persisted.

"Please don't pretend that you don't understand. Men, of course."

Alan laughed. "OK, now you have me lined up with all the bastards out there. I can live with that. You do know that there are women who cheat also, and sometimes with younger men?" He took a sip from his wine.

Willow fiddled with the entertainment system in front of her.

Alan leaned to look at her. "So, are we not talking anymore?"

She looked at him, then continued toying with the controls.

"I sure would like to hear the rest of the story." Alan mumbled to himself. No answer. He bowed his head to look at her.

"I normally don't talk to strangers about my personal life, I apologize," Willow said finally.

"You know, you tend to apologize a lot. This is the second time you've apologized to me since we met. Why do you play the underdog all the time?" Alan asked.

"I don't," Willow said stubbornly.

"Oh, yes, you do. You don't have to apologize for everything that you do, you know. It's not always your fault, so stop taking the blame for everything."

Willow didn't reply.

"I acted like a total ass just a minute ago, so if someone should apologize, that's me. It sure isn't you," Alan added.

Willow smiled. "Apology accepted."

Alan swirled the last of the wine in his glass and drank it.

"You sound lonely," she said when Alan turned to look at her.

"Sometimes. But it's my choice." He paused to reflect.

"It looks like you've been too harsh on yourself." Alan looked up in surprise. Willow noticed that he had suddenly become thoughtful at her words. Was it because they had been discussing details of their love lives? she thought, knowing they were two strangers who had just met.

Willow shrugged her shoulders. "As for me, I guess I just grew up. I'll never marry again."

"You're lonely now, though."

Smiling, Willow remarked, "Yes, but it's my choice."

Alan waited patiently as Willow stared into her glass of wine, staring as if she was going to see the answer there in the white wine. She hoped Alan didn't notice the vein throbbing on her neck and realize that she was actually trying very hard not to cry. *Thank you, thank you for not asking anymore questions,* Willow thought.

Finally, after a lengthy silence, all Alan could say was, "I'm sorry. It's all for the best, you know."

"Yes, but it will be difficult to adapt and arrange a new life. Being a woman and at a certain age... I..."

"What is it with you and age? You keep mentioning it, and frankly, I couldn't be bothered with it, you know. You can't frighten me with your age. What are you, eighty?" Alan asked.

Willow gave him a disgusted look.

"Come on, tell me. I can see you're very keen on me learning how old you are."

Willow was now very angry. "You're impossible."

"Well, you're the one who keeps bringing it into the conversation, so I'm assuming you want me to know. Let's have it."

At first, Willow didn't answer. She didn't like the way Alan had turned the conversation around to her.

"It's just that I never imagined myself in this position, especially at this age. Once my daughter had left home, I'd assumed that my husband and I would travel and build a new life around our retirement, but apparently, I'd assumed wrong," Willow said.

"How old is your daughter?" Alan asked.

"She's twenty-six. She'll be meeting me at the airport."

Alan looked at her questioningly. "How many children do you have?"

"Just the one. She's the love of my life."

"Was that who called you at the airport?" Alan asked.

Willow looked surprised. "Yes, it was. How did you know?"

"Your face became so animated when you were talking. I was fascinated with the change," Alan remarked.

"Yes, she was my support throughout the whole... well, you know."

"So now you've cut all your ties and embarked on a new journey?" Alan asked.

"Yes, at the age of fifty-three," Willow finally admitted. *Better he knows*, she thought.

Alan looked surprised. "You have to be kidding, you can't be. You look much younger."

"You flatter me," Willow replied, "but there you go, now you know."

"You're just three years older than me." Alan said.

Now it was Willow's turn to be surprised. "Now then, I can return the compliment, you don't look at all your age."

"It's just the genes," Alan laughed. "We just like to look young and fool people. Anyway, age is just a number."

Willow was tempted to ask about his personal life but decided to wait for him to come forward with it. By this time, the flight attendant had cleared their trays, and the lights were dimmed for passengers who wanted to sleep.

"If you're going to sleep, please do so, I'll watch a movie," Willow offered.

"Will you be sleeping?" Alan asked.

"No, I rarely can sleep on planes, but like I said, if you…"

"I would rather talk with you, if that's all right," Alan said, looking at her.

Willow looked back. "I would love that."

"How about a nightcap?" Alan asked.

"Why not?" Willow smiled, and Alan got up to find the flight attendant. She leaned back and wondered why it was so easy talking to this man she had just met. How they had somehow connected, two strangers who met at an airport. Alan came back with two glasses filled with a honey-coloured liquid.

"Brandy," Alan whispered as he handed her the glasses and sat down in his seat. He took back a glass and sipped.

"This is nice," Willow said, after she too had taken a sip. "So, tell me, what kind of architecture do you design?"

"My idol and inspiration is Frank Lloyd Wright, not that I claim to be like him. I don't know if you…"

"Of course, I know of him," Willow replied. "My favourite has always been Fallingwater, I love that house."

"My partner, Patrick, and I, we've designed different structures like offices, high-rise buildings, hotels, houses, always trying to stay in harmony with the environment, what Wright called organic architecture."

"That's so interesting, can you show me any designs that you've done?" Willow asked.

"Here, I have my laptop, let me show you."

Alan excitedly bent down, grabbed his briefcase, and removed a laptop from it. Willow watched as he turned it on, the screen casting a light on his animated face. He scrolled through several folders and then opened one and turned the laptop toward her.

Willow looked at the images, fascinated at the concepts, admiring the designs. "They look amazing, Alan," Willow said softly. "You're a very talented architect."

"Thank you," Alan replied while he opened another folder. These were the sketches he had done on a special software, and as he scrolled through, Willow saw something.

She leaned toward him. "What was that just a minute ago? You passed by it so fast." Alan scrolled back onto said sketch. It was a design of a house, high on top of a cliff, jutting out toward the ocean, laid into the landscape much like Wright's design, yet so different. "What is this place?" she whispered. "Where is it? It's beautiful."

Alan looked down at her head as she peered into the screen, the glow illuminating her face. "It's a design I'm working on for myself. I haven't built it yet. It may never be built. I just bought the land recently imagining this," he admitted.

"You have to build it, Alan," Willow said. "It's so beautiful, it's so… so serene. You should call it Serenity." She turned to look at him. For a minute, their eyes stayed connected, and at that moment Willow realized that this man she had met just today understood her in ways nobody had. *How could this be* she thought *this is so surreal.* All she wanted was to reach out and kiss him right there and then and she saw that he somehow wanted the same thing. Willow leaned back suddenly against her chair.

"Thank you for sharing," she finally said as Alan closed his laptop and put it away. There was an awkward silence. Most of the passengers were sleeping, so the plane was quiet except for the hum of the engines. They both sat and stared, waiting for the other one to speak first.

"This is what happens when you drink too much. I need to go the lavatory," Willow said, unbuckling her seat belt, "sorry to trouble you."

Alan got up. "No worries."

By the time Willow came back, Alan had fallen asleep. With some difficulty, she crossed over to her seat, trying hard not to wake him up. She buckled her seat belt and, with a sigh, turned to look at him. Alan was fast asleep. Willow smiled and lifted the control command to turn on the entertainment set in front of her. From the movie selection she picked out an old favourite, *Pride and Prejudice*, and settled down.

"Miss Bennett."

"Mr. Darcy."

Suddenly, Willow felt Alan's head turn and finally rest on her right shoulder. She hit the pause button and took a sideways peek at his face. He really was sleeping deeply, and Willow once again relived the first time she saw him in the bookstore at the airport, remembering when they were sleeping in the chairs next to each other. How he had placed his jacket over her. She shook her head and returned to her movie.

"Ladies and gentlemen, we are now descending…" As the announcement continued, Willow glanced down from the window at the mountains still covered with snow and the scattered glaciers. She was excited at being so close to seeing Jasmine again. She turned around at the sound of Alan yawning.

"Well, well, good afternoon to you sir."

Alan continued to yawn. "I'm sorry, I just closed my eyes while waiting for your return. Why didn't you wake me?"

"And spoil your dreams? Never."

"So, you want to watch a movie?" Alan asked.

Willow laughed. "You've been sleeping for five hours. We're already descending."

"What?" Alan exclaimed.

"And here you were telling me you had problems sleeping. Didn't look like that to me."

"Five hours? That can't be. No way." Alan continued, amazed.

"Are you calling me a liar?" Willow teased.

Alan looked around. "No, I didn't mean… I was very tired and really, I haven't slept this soundly for a long time."

"I'm glad I made you sleep," Willow replied.

"I didn't mean that you made me."

"I know, I'm just teasing you. Come on, you slept, so what? I watched some movies."

Alan shook his head. "I can't believe I fell asleep. I've been travelling in so many time zones, I guess it finally caught up with me."

They were both quiet as the plane landed with a soft thud and the brakes came on. They were still quiet as the plane taxied to its stop, Willow lost in her thoughts and Alan likely the same. Alan got up once the seat belt sign turned off. The flight attendant brought his jacket.

"Can I help you with anything?" Alan asked Willow as he picked up his briefcase.

"No, I have everything here." Willow replied as she too got up. They were among the first to get off. They walked together, first passing through security, then to the baggage area. Alan helped her with her two suitcases and loaded them on a cart while he picked up his and pulled the handle to roll it.

"That was quick and easy," Willow remarked. Alan nodded in response. Suddenly, they ran out of words to say, each knowing that the voyage was about to end and realizing that they didn't want it to.

As they came out of the terminal, Willow saw Jasmine waiting by the side. She rushed forward, pushing the luggage cart in front of her, and at once, they were embracing each other. Willow could no longer hold back the tears.

Jasmine was a tall girl with streaky blonde air piled up on her head, wearing a black military-style jacket over grey-blue pants. After hugging Willow, she looked up at Alan. "Mom?" Jasmine questioned. Willow turned around.

"Jasmine, this is Alan. We flew in together. That is, we were seated—"

Alan put out his hand and cut in. "You must be Jasmine. She hasn't stopped talking about you."

Jasmine stared at her. "Really?"

Slowly, a security guard approached them. "Ma'am? If you'll just walk ahead, you're blocking the passengers coming out."

"Oh, sorry. Come on, Jasmine," Willow said, taking her arm and pushing the cart. Alan followed. They reached the exit doors in no time.

"Do you ladies need a drive? I have a car picking me up," Alan offered, gallantly smiling at both.

"Oh, thank you, but I brought my own car," Jasmine answered.

Alan smiled weakly. He seemed disappointed. "Well then, I shall say goodbye."

Willow turned around. There was an awkward silence while she looked at him. Jasmine just smiled and waited.

"I would like to see you again," Alan said finally.

"I would like that," Willow answered.

"Can I have your phone number, then?" Alan made for his inner pocket to retrieve his cell phone.

"I'm sorry, but I'm going to get a new carrier and number here—let me give you my email address. You can always reach me through that."

"Or I can give mine, Mom," Jasmine offered.

"It would be great if I can have both," Alan said.

"Sure, let me give you my business card," Jasmine said, opening her bag. She rummaged around, finding the card case, and pulled out a card. Meanwhile, Willow took out a pen and wrote her email address on the back of the card.

"This should have you covered," Willow said as she gave the card back to Alan.

"Thanks. I'll look forward to seeing you again. Both, of course." Alan smiled and put out his hand. Jasmine shook it after Willow. Alan waved goodbye and walked out. Both Jasmine and Willow stared after him.

"Mom? What was that? What's going on?" Jasmine asked, smiling mischievously as they walked toward the parking area.

"What?" Willow answered innocently, pushing the cart while Jasmine took out her car keys.

"Mom? Who was that, hmm? Handsome guy, isn't he?"

"Really?" Willow walked on, feigning ignorance as they reached the car.

"Mom, he's gorgeous, if you haven't noticed. Where did you meet him?"

"I'll tell you over a bottle of wine. Come on, I'm here finally. Isn't it great? I've missed you." Willow picked up her luggage and placed it in the car. Jasmine went to pick up the second piece.

"I thought we would never get to this day. It's great to have you, Mom. I really missed you. And I'm sorry I wasn't there for the difficult days."

"You were always there with me, my darling, don't worry. It's all over now. Come on, let's go home." Willow opened the front seat door and climbed in. Jasmine started the car, and they drove off.

CHAPTER THREE

Prelude

*A*lan glanced out of the window of the car that had picked him up at the airport. It was rush hour, and everyone was speeding on the highway toward downtown. *I wonder what she's doing,* he thought. What a flight it had been. And sleeping for five hours—what was he thinking? Here he was, complaining of sleep deprivation, and yet he had fallen asleep in a plane beside a stranger, an intriguing woman.

"To the office, or shall I drive you home?"

Alan glanced at the driver who was looking at him from the rear-view mirror. "Home, I think, Trevor. Long flight."

"All right, sir." Alan looked out of the window again.

After Trevor dropped him off at his condo in one of the upscale high rises, Alan poured himself a drink, and while pacing around his living room with the glass in his hand, he called his younger sister, Robyn. He could sense the surprise when she picked up, and he understood why. This wasn't the way he usually acted; he never called her unless something important was going on. Even to himself, he sounded troubled, yet excited.

"I met this woman Willow on the plane—no, I met her first at the bookstore. You told me to go to the bookstore for a book, remember?" Alan said.

"I did, but what does that have to do with—" Before Robyn could finish her sentence, he cut in.

"I first blinked at the books wondering if I was seeing lights in front of my eyes. You know, I was so tired, I could have easily been imagining things, but then I looked up and saw her. This woman. Willow. She wasn't looking at me. A few minutes passed, and I didn't move, and I began to wonder if I was really reading or just standing there, not knowing what to do."

"So, what happened next?"

"She noticed me. It was too late for me to look away."

Robyn was mystified. "What is this with this woman and you? I mean, was she just too gorgeous to miss out?"

"You're totally wrong this time. She's not even my type. She's tall with light brown hair that was tied up in a ponytail. She has a face that's... She looks young for her age. She kept making remarks about it at first, then finally confessed. She had these deep brown eyes that sparkled." Alan paused to remember. "That I thought sparkled."

"But then I noticed that they were tears when a teardrop suddenly fell from the corner of her eye, and I felt something shatter inside me. She looked so sad," Alan remarked, pacing the room. Robyn waited patiently for him to continue.

"I don't know. At first, I thought she looked to be in her forties. There were small lines here and there on her face, but of course, it's always the hands that shows a woman's true age."

"And where did you hear about that?" Robyn laughed.

"I can't remember. Some magazine or other."

"Divorced? Widow? Single?"

"Divorced. Can you imagine, after thirty years? She looked sad enough. And angry. It somehow felt good to have my jacket lying over her. As if I was protecting her. From what, I don't know." The memory made him smile.

"You got all this from a ten-hour flight? No woman talks to a stranger about her personal life," Robyn observed.

Alan didn't explain that he'd talked as well. "I could kick myself for delving too quick into her life," he said after a while.

"Did you tell her about Caroline?" Robyn asked. Alan remained silent. "Alan, did you?"

"No, I didn't."

"How could you? How can you not tell her?"

"I don't know. I didn't want her to get the wrong impression."

"Wrong impression of what? You've sure messed this up, haven't you? You can't just have a fling like this. I hope you're not going to call her or anything."

"This isn't a fling. Something about her just connected with me. I can't describe it, and I think she felt it too."

"You're my big brother, but you can't do this, not at this time. You haven't even come home to see Caroline and father yet, for that matter," Robyn said angrily.

"I know, I know, you don't have to tell me what kind of mess I'm in. I'll come once I get this new contract designed and approved, which means I have to travel again. I know this is hard for you. You've sacrificed more than I could ever have asked for."

"Just promise me you'll end this before something happens that you'll regret. It's not fair to this woman or to you and your family."

"I don't know, Sis, I'll think about it. I promise I won't do anything rash," Alan said, not believing a word.

"Get some rest and we'll talk again. Love you, Alan."

"Love you back." Alan put down his phone and sat down on the couch. He put up his feet on the coffee table in front of him. *What to do,* he thought.

ᘡᘓᗢ

Willow and Jasmine had finally made it back to Jasmine's apartment where she lived with her husband, Sam. After a joyful greeting by both parties, Willow sat down, pulling up her legs underneath her. Jasmine opened a bottle of red wine while Sam was busy preparing dinner to give mom and daughter some privacy.

"I thought I was dreaming. A dream that smelled wonderful. But then I thought, how can a dream smell? It reminded me of the ocean. I imagined waves and sunshine. I imagined walking barefoot in the sand. I felt the sunshine on my face. And it smelled so fresh and… so like a men's cologne." Willow hugged her knees and looked at Jasmine. "I mean, how could the sea smell of cologne? And how come the sun felt warm but heavy on my body? It made no sense, but of course, it was a dream, and dreams never make sense, do they?"

"Mom, you really are a dreamer," Jasmine said, smiling tenderly. Sam glanced up from where he was working.

"I know. I knew at that moment that I should wake up because this dream didn't feel like a dream at all. I opened my eyes. And held my breath. The man I had seen at the bookstore was sleeping on the chair next to mine. Alan. His head had fallen sideways, so I got a close look at his face. I had noticed him before at the bookstore and had wondered why he was looking at me. He had glanced down immediately when I looked, but not before witnessing my tears."

Jasmine looked at her with a worried look in her eyes. "You were crying? Not again."

"I was upset, OK? Anyway, I remembered him because he was so handsome to look at. Tall, with that light brown hair streaked with sunshine, or maybe they were greys. It was tumbling down on his forehead and curled up behind his neck. He was elegantly dressed, carried himself with strength, but he looked tired. His eyes were closed so at first, I didn't see what colour they were, but I remembered that they were light-coloured." Willow paused.

"He looked quite fit, really, as if he exercised regularly. He had this mature look that made it hard to determine his age, probably a lot younger than me, I thought then. It turned out that in fact, he was just three years younger than me, which caught me off guard. He had the most beautiful smile. No wedding ring on his finger," Willow continued.

"Well, most men don't wear them. I read that somewhere. Some magazine or other. As if it matters, really. By the way, he did have a beautiful smile," Jasmine said casually.

Willow was shocked. "Jasmine! You're impossible." She glanced at Sam, who was laughing silently.

Jasmine just shrugged her shoulders. "What? It doesn't kill to look."

"Well, I thought it was just sheer coincidence that we met, but then I remembered Francis saying once that there was no such thing as a coincidence."

"So, you told yourself not to be stupid enough to think that this man had searched and found you and then sat next to you just because you had made eye contact some time ago and you'd been crying." Jasmine got up her from her seat to pour some more wine. "You should write a book about this."

Willow gave her a hurt look. "Exactly. It was then that I noticed the jacket. I looked down and realized that the faint cologne was drifting up from the jacket, and that plus the warmth emanating from it was what had woken me up. I looked at him, then at the jacket, and then at him again, trying to figure out whether it was his." Willow stopped speaking and took a sip from her glass.

"Well, come on, don't stop now. Was it?"

"I looked around and he was the only one sitting in his shirt, so logically, I assumed it was his. When did he put it on top of me?

And why? I couldn't remember, but I could still feel the heat from his body trapped inside the jacket, warming me." Sam looked up from the kitchen counter.

"I was a little sharp in answering his questions. He was just trying to get to know me better, that I understood, but I didn't know how to handle that. It's been a long time since I've been socially active, and I knew that I had no right to snap at him like that. I felt like he really did want to get to know me better, but something about that bothered me."

"Why, for heaven's sake? You're an incredible woman, when will you ever believe in yourself?"

"I never had a man like that take a personal interest in me, and I felt awkward like a young girl," Willow added.

Later that night, Willow found it difficult to fall asleep. Sam and Jasmine had retired to their own bedroom and had opened the hide-a-bed in the living room for her. Willow was going to stay at their place for a couple of days until she got some furniture for the townhouse she had rented. Jasmine would be taking her shopping tomorrow with her car. Willow wanted to get out as soon as possible and settle into her new life. There were a lot of things she needed to set up, and the faster she returned to a normal life—if you can call it that—the better she would feel.

As she got up to get a glass of water, she noticed it was past midnight. It was at that moment that she heard her laptop signalling that she had received an email. She walked back to look. It was a message from Alan.

I know it's late, but I just couldn't fall asleep. I thought about you and was wondering if you're all right. Of course you are, you're with your daughter. Anyway, just wanted to check in. Alan

Willow took in a breath. Why was she getting excited? She sat down to write a reply.

I'm awake as well. Everyone's gone to bed, and I was just thinking of the things I need to do tomorrow, or should I say today. How are you? Willow

She sent it off. There was no reply for some time.

What are you doing up? Alan wrote back.

What are you doing? Willow replied.

I was hungry, so I made myself a sandwich.

What kind of sandwich?

Rye bread, mayo, lettuce, ham, and cheese.

Yummy!

Alan smiled to himself. *Want some?*

Willow wondered what to say. She got up and walked around the room, then came back to sit down again.

Yes.

It was Alan now who took his time to reply.

All right, what time and where? he wrote back.

Willow regretted saying yes, but it had been an impulsive move, as she realized that she did indeed want to see Alan again.

I'm going shopping for furniture today, and they should be delivered sometime next week, hopefully. I don't know when my other stuff that I shipped will arrive, so I'll be waiting for that too, which means I'll be too busy to shop for food. Why don't I let you know which day, and you can bring the sandwiches? Willow wrote back hesitantly and waited.

And wine? Alan asked.

I'll make sure I buy wineglasses, then, Willow wrote, now enjoying the casual banter.

I'll bring the corkscrew, Alan wrote back.

Willow leaned back, smiling to herself. *He does make me feel like a young girl,* she thought fondly. *Could this be happening, and so soon? Was Murphy asleep this time around?*

Go to sleep, Willow wrote.

To which Alan replied, *Only if you will*

See you soon Alan, good night
Good night, Willow

Willow closed her laptop and lay back down on the bed. She fell asleep shortly.

⁓

The following week passed by in a rush. Jasmine took Willow shopping for furniture and the other things she needed. Willow didn't mention the conversation she had had with Alan that one night.

It had been a heartbreaking moment for Willow to leave the home she had created over the thirty years she had been married and venture on a new life. Her mother had said that there had never been a divorce in the family. Her grandmother had said, *Why don't you forgive him? Men do things like this.* It was only her father who had encouraged her to leave everything behind and start anew. *You don't have to stay and look after us,* he'd said. *You deserve better. Go and start a new life. Move next to your daughter, who will help you forget this unfortunate turn of events.*

His words still echoed in her ears as she unpacked the boxes and furniture that were delivered Saturday morning with Jasmine and Sam. Sam was busy putting together her bedroom units with Jasmine's help. Willow had taken what she wanted mostly after the divorce, things that she had an emotional attachment to, but she had left the majority behind, unable to bring it with her. This would be the first time that she would be living by herself, and truth be told, she was a little wary about it all. A new city, a new home, a new life. Willow also had not forgotten her promise of telling Alan that she had moved into her new place. *Maybe he forgot about it,* she thought. The internet was connected yesterday, and she had a new phone number. She had been quite busy these past days. *Am I making excuses?* Willow thought.

"Mom, you want to come and take a look?" Jasmine shouted from the bedroom.

"Coming," Willow replied, dropping the paper wrapping in her hand. She walked upstairs to the bedroom and saw that they had put up everything as she wanted.

"It's beautiful, wow, look at this!" Willow exclaimed as she walked around the queen-size bed frame and nightstands. She walked into the ensuite where her suitcases were. "I'll deal with all this later, thank you so much."

"We'll just bring up the mattress, and you'll be good to go," Sam said, walking down the stairs. Once done, they all came back down, and Jasmine opened the fridge and pulled out a bottle of champagne. "Here, I'll rinse some glasses," Willow offered as Jasmine popped the cork.

"Here's to a new life," Jasmine said raising her glass. "Be happy and do the things you like. No one to judge you." Willow smiled at her comment.

"Ditto that," Sam said as they all sipped from their glasses.

"You guys should go," Willow said, "I know you have a dinner engagement. You've spent enough time with me, and I appreciate it so much."

"You sure you'll be all right?" Jasmine asked with a worried look.

"Hey, I'm a big girl now, I can manage. Go and enjoy your evening. We'll talk tomorrow."

Jasmine and Sam both hugged her, and Willow saw them off from the front door. Once they disappeared from her sight, she closed the door and locked it. Turning around, she looked at her new home.

Willow had resisted the idea of renting a condo in a high rise because she didn't want to live in a glass tube. It was good for young people, but she needed some sort of outdoor space. Those condos had only a tiny balcony, not enough for someone who was retired and often at home. This townhouse was small, with one bedroom and bathroom and a den, but it had a spacious kitchen and living room area. What had attracted her to the place was the small patio in the back that overlooked a park with tall trees. The house she had left behind had a large garden, and she had planted every rose, every tree, every flower with her own hands. All left behind for her ex and her best friend to enjoy. Willow shuddered at the idea and felt negative vibes coming through. *I will not let that happen,* she thought, *not this time. Look at me, I did this, I survived, I broke through, I did what I set out to do, I did it,* she thought, then shouted out loud, "I did it!"

Willow finished off her glass and looked around. It was then that she remembered Alan and looked around for her laptop. It took her a while to find it since she had put it upstairs in the ensuite when she had brought over her belongings from Jasmine's place. She took it down to the kitchen counter and turned it on. She saw that there were fifteen emails in her inbox. She again searched for her eyeglasses, which again turned out to be upstairs. *I don't need to go to the gym,* Willow thought, *just put everything upstairs and go up and down the stairs.*

Willow scrolled through the emails. There was an email from her mom and dad separately, some from her friends who had stayed friends with her after the divorce, emails from the internet provider and TV cable, and finally, an email from Alan. She clicked it open.

Still waiting for the call. I haven't forgotten.

Alan

He had written it two days ago. Willow glanced around at the mess. *Maybe I should wait until I have everything organized,* she thought. But then she would have to wait another week when her other belongings would arrive by truck. Willow looked at herself. She was dressed in jeans and some old sweatshirt. She had swept up her hair to get it out of her eyes, but they were threatening to come down anytime. She saw that there was a little bit of champagne left in the bottle, so she poured it into her glass and pulled over a high stool next to the kitchen counter and sat down. She stared at the screen of her laptop. *Here goes,* she thought.

⤳ ⤲

Back at his home, Alan was busy sketching at his drafting table when he heard the ping from his phone. He pulled it toward him and looked. His heart skipped a beat. *Could it be?* He opened his inbox and stared at the words.

Got any sandwiches? I'm famished.

Alan smiled foolishly.

Where and when would you like it delivered? he wrote back.

How about now? Are you free?

Alan looked around. The plans would have to wait. He could always come back and work through the night.

Give me an hour and your address, Alan wrote.

Take all the time you need. It's 15 Brownman Street

Alan put down his phone and got up from his chair. He had kept all the necessary ingredients for the sandwiches in case Willow called, so he walked into his kitchen and delicately prepared four sandwiches. He looked inside his wine fridge and noticed that he had run out of the special rosé from the family vineyard. *Damn,* he thought. He then looked at the wine rack and picked a Merlot, remembering that was her favourite red. He put everything into a bag and went to his bedroom to check up on himself. He hadn't shaved so he had stubble, but he thought that it looked good on him, so he decided to leave it as-is. He was wearing jeans and an old T-shirt, so he changed into a polo shirt and grabbed his blazer jacket. *Not bad, Alan,* he said to himself as he checked himself in the mirror. He grabbed the bag, his keys, and his phone, and walked out. He lived on the top floor of a high-rise building, so it was a long ride down.

Once outside, Alan looked around for a taxi, then noticed the gourmet shop across the street. *Maybe I should get a dessert,* he thought, so he crossed over and walked into the shop. It was a busy evening with people doing their last-minute shopping for a Saturday night, and he briskly walked toward the dessert counter and peered into the display. *What to buy,* Alan thought.

"May I help you?" asked the young woman behind the counter.

Alan knew he had to be careful with his choice but was having difficulty deciding between a cheesecake and a strawberry tart with whipped cream. The young woman was still waiting.

"I'll have the strawberry tart, please," Alan finally said, and he waited while the young woman prepared the box.

"Here you are, sir, have a good evening," she said, handing it over.

"Thank you," Alan replied, thinking, *I hope so.* As he was walking toward the cashiers, he passed by a stand with flowers. He stopped and returned. *Flowers would be nice, I'm sure she doesn't have any,* Alan thought and looked at the display. Roses were too... well, not for tonight, and the wildflowers were too simple. Then Alan noticed the bouquet of fragrant lilies and picked it up.

Willow was still opening boxes and unwrapping items. She placed two plates, two glasses, and matching cutlery on the counter while putting away the rest. She glanced at her watch. *Alan should be here any moment now,* she thought, when the doorbell rang. Willow smiled to herself, thinking, *My sixth sense is still working.* She pushed the intercom button on the kitchen wall.

"Yes, who is it?"

"Delivery, ma'am," Alan replied. Willow giggled and walked to the front door and opened it. She stood there with her dishevelled hair, jeans, and old sweatshirt. She looked up and down at how well-dressed Alan was.

"I might have overdressed for the occasion," Alan said, laughing, noticing her look.

"You look just right, come in," Willow answered, closing the door after them. Alan looked around at the empty living room. There was a TV on the floor and two high stools in front of the kitchen counter.

"I see you've been trying your hand at minimalism?" Alan asked, placing the bag down. "Flowers for the lady." He handed over the bouquet.

"My favourite, they're beautiful. Thank you, Alan," she said, opening the bouquet. He looked on as she took a carafe out from the cupboard behind her and filled it with water. Alan took off his jacket and looked around for a place to put it.

"Here, give it to me," Willow said and opened the closet door next to the entrance. She placed the jacket on a hanger and hung it up. She returned to place the flowers in the carafe.

"Just what the place needed," she said to Alan, brushing aside her hair. Alan kept looking at her.

"You look happy. Very different from the woman I met at the airport."

"I'm happy because I did it. I survived the turmoil, and here I am in a new city, new home, new life." Willow sat down on one of the stools and peered down at the bag beside Alan.

"I'm sorry, yes, the sandwiches." Alan leaned down and picked up the bag. "Here's wine, sandwiches as promised, and a dessert, which I thought would be appropriate."

Willow looked at Alan, smiling. "You sure know how to treat a woman," she said softly, and for a minute, their gazes locked. Alan was the first one to look away.

"No corkscrew though, it's a screw top. I also found out that I had run out of the family rosé, so I brought you Merlot."

"Another favourite," Willow remarked.

Alan looked at her then, "I know." Once again, there was an awkward silence.

Willow pulled over the box and opened it. "Strawberry tart! That's one more favourite, how did you know?"

"That I didn't," Alan said as he opened the bottle of wine and poured two glasses. They sat on opposite sides of the counter with the carafe of lilies on the side. *All we're missing are candles,* Willow thought, *and this would be a first date.*

"To your new home and new life," Alan said as he raised his glass.

"Gotta love this Merlot," Willow replied as she opened the wrapping on her sandwich and took a bite. Willow glanced up to see him looking at her, seemingly mesmerized by something. Was it her appetite, or was it her dishevelled looks? "I was hungry," she said apologetically, noticing he hadn't unwrapped his sandwich yet.

"Don't be, I'm glad you like my sandwich." Alan started to eat. "So, tell me, I thought you were going shopping for furniture. What happened?"

"I did go shopping. I bought a new bedroom, some items for the kitchen, furniture for the den and for the patio. A new TV as you can see, but the rest will be coming in next week. From my previous home," Willow added.

"That must have been tough for you," Alan remarked. Willow looked up at him.

"You have no idea. Choosing what to bring, what to leave behind. In a home of thirty years, you tend to accumulate." Willow took a sip from her glass, remembering the days when she cried and packed at the same time.

"Couldn't you have stayed?" Alan asked.

"No, never. Knowing what went on, I couldn't stay. My ex bought my share of the house. That's how I'm here now." Willow stopped speaking and finished off her sandwich. "I never go back when I decide to leave," she added.

Alan looked on quietly. "Another one?" he asked, handing her a sandwich.

"Why not? They're very delicious." Willow shrugged off the gloomy thoughts. "And more wine, please."

"How did you find this place?" Alan asked, looking around. "I remember these buildings going through renovations a couple of years ago."

"Jasmine found it for me. I signed on immediately when I saw the patio in the back."

"Can I see?" Alan asked.

"Of course." Willow got off the stool and walked toward the tall doors at the end of the living room, and Alan followed. She pulled them open to walk onto a small patio facing a park with tall trees. Not all townhouses had patios, so there was enough privacy for comfort. He noticed the large terra-cotta planters lined up against the iron rail. There was also a table and some chairs folded against the wall.

"I can see what the attraction is. It's rare to find such a place near downtown."

"I know. I loved my house, but I have to adapt to my new life now, rental and all," Willow said as they walked back in. They both sat down again on the stools to continue eating.

"Where do you live?" Willow asked. For a moment, she saw Alan hesitate.

"I live in a high rise, top floor so I have privacy."

"Oh, the penthouse?" Willow smiled.

"Not really. I just have a nice view. And it's conveniently located close to my office. I do have a similar set up at home as well so I can sketch and work, even though everything is computerized nowadays. I just like the touch of paper and pencil," Alan replied.

"I agree on that, I still like to write down notes and make lists. Jasmine keeps telling me to use my phone, but I'm old-class. What are you working on?" Willow asked.

"It's a museum for Indigenous art, with a main building, workshops, and an art gallery. It's privately owned by this family, and I've never designed a museum before, so it's quite a challenge for me. They were interested in our style of organic architecture, and the whole construction will be environmentally friendly and solar-powered. That's where I was coming back from when we met. We'd just signed the contract."

"Sounds exciting. How many at your office?"

"It's me and my partner, Patrick. We also have a staff of ten, a mix of technicians and architects. We do hire temporary staff when needed, like for this project, since it's a big one. I was sketching some ideas I wanted to add when I saw your email. Soon, I'll have to travel again," Alan remarked, looking up at her.

"Shall we have dessert?" Willow asked, changing the subject. She brought the box toward her and opened it. She deftly cut a slice and put it on a plate and handed it to Alan. She served herself a slice as well. Alan poured more wine into their glasses, emptying the bottle.

Willow started eating the tart. "Goodness, this is delicious," she said, licking her lips. Alan looked on.

"I see you enjoy food as much as I do."

"I know, it's a curse really enjoying food this much." Willow drank her wine and leaned back against the stool. "Thank you for all of this. You know, when my other stuff arrives, I'll invite you to a proper dinner and you can see the place decorated. It won't be minimalist, that's for sure." Willow laughed.

"I would love that," Alan said, looking at her. They had an awkward moment of silence again as they both finished their dessert. Alan glanced at his watch, and Willow looked at hers as well and noticed that it was getting close to midnight.

"I should be going," he said, getting up from the stool. Willow joined him, and they walked toward the front door.

"Thank you again," Willow said, touching his arm as she handed him his jacket.

Alan looked down at her hand, then at her face. He hesitated for a moment, then said, "You're most welcome. I'll see you soon. Good night."

"Good night." She opened the door for him, and watched as he walked down the short flight of steps to the pavement. He turned around and waved, then started walking away. Willow closed the door and leaned against it. She was sure that for a moment, he'd hesitated in kissing her but had backed away. *Maybe for the best,* she thought. *No need for romantic entanglements. Not yet, anyway.* Willow slowly walked around turning off the lights and went upstairs to her new bedroom.

CHAPTER FOUR

Soulmates

*I*t was the following week when Jasmine shouted, "Mom, your phone is ringing" from the patio. Willow came out of the kitchen wiping her hands on a dish towel. Jasmine handed her the cell phone.

"Hello?" Willow said, pushing a strand of her hair behind her ear.

"Hi, how are you?" It was Alan. Willow suddenly blushed. Jasmine looked back quizzically, then smiled in recognition.

"Alan, what a pleasant surprise." Willow paused. "So, how have you been?"

"Working. Too much. How about you?" Alan asked.

"Well, I've been spending some time with my daughter. Arranging the new stuff around the house." Willow stopped when she saw Jasmine grimace and mouth the word "Mom."

What? Willow mouthed back silently.

"Listen, the reason I called you was to ask if you're free this Thursday."

"Oh, Thursday... I'm..." Willow hesitated. "Well, I have other plans for that night. I'm sorry, Alan."

"It doesn't matter. We'll make it another night," Alan replied. He tried to keep the disappointment out of his voice, but Willow could still hear it.

"I really am sorry. I was going to call you too about that dinner I promised. Is Friday good for you?" Willow asked.

Alan sounded pleasantly surprised. "I'd love to. What time?"

"How about eight o'clock?"

"All right, I'll be there."

"Good. I look forward to it. And again sorry about Thursday night."

"Goodbye."

Willow stared at her phone. *I wonder if I should have told him about my plans for Thursday,* she thought.

"Why didn't you tell him, Mom?" Jasmine asked, standing up.

"I don't know. I just don't know."

❦

That Thursday, Alan entered the heritage building with Patrick and his wife, Jeanette. It was a black-tie fundraiser event with a live band playing in the centre of elegant dinner tables scattered in the plush gardens surrounding it.

He was gazing down from the balcony when he saw Willow. At first, Alan didn't recognize her. It was his first time seeing her all dressed up, and he was taken aback at how beautiful she looked. Her hair was gathered up with two sparkling combs, accompanied with the dangling earrings that sparkled with the lights. He remembered that image fondly. Willow was in earnest conversation with another elderly woman when a very handsome tall man with a full head of grey-white hair approached her. He leaned forward to kiss her on the cheek and placed his hand on the small of her back. Willow looked fondly at him. Alan was startled with the sudden fit of jealousy that overwhelmed him.

"I see you know Francis." Alan turned around to look at the stunning woman that had approached him.

"Yes, we did some business together several years ago."

"And do you know the lady standing next to him?" the woman continued, leaning on the balcony rail.

Alan turned around to look at her. "As a matter of fact, yes. Do you know her?" he asked.

The woman smiled mysteriously, turning and leaning backward. A waiter approached with champagne. She picked up one while Alan declined.

"Just by name. She's very beautiful."

Alan was bemused. "You're a far more striking woman than she is. And that's not a compliment but a fact," he added.

"Why, thank you. But you're missing the point. She's a beautiful woman because she has a beautiful soul." The woman finished off the rest of her glass.

Alan was astonished. "How can you see that?"

"You men are always the last to see. Not all, of course, but most." She laughed. "How long have you known her?"

"About a month."

"And you think that gives you enough time to judge?" she added.

"What about you? How come you know so much about her? You just said that you know her by name."

"Francis told me." She glanced over her shoulder at the garden below.

Alan suddenly felt a cold shiver. "Count Francis von Tauberg?"

"The one and only."

"But? How... I mean..." Stunned, Alan looked into her grey eyes.

"We haven't been introduced. I am Evelyn von Tauberg"—she smiled—"soon to be ex." Alan was at a loss for words. "They're soulmates, you know. Oh, yes, they've known each other for the past twenty years and write to each other practically every day. I've just been married to him for four years."

"How do you know all this?" Alan finally asked, recovering from the information she had given.

"Francis told me. When we decided to get married—that is, when I offered to get married and he accepted—he told me about her. Said that they were soulmates and that they wrote to each other, they needed the contact, were close confidantes, and that I had to accept this fact."

"And did you?"

"It was innocent enough, I'd thought. We had other issues to deal with. Not that it did much good to our marriage in the end, as you can see." It was then that Alan noticed Patrick and Jeanette waiting for him.

"It was lovely meeting you," Alan said to Evelyn, and he joined his friends. Together, they walked down the stairs.

⌒ℯↃ

"Good evening, Willow."

Willow turned around.

"Alan! What a surprise. I didn't know you would be here." Willow said, somewhat agitated. She was nervous and looked at Alan, then at the man next to her. "Oh, I'm sorry. Let me introduce you to Count Francis von Tauberg. Francis, this is Alan Peters."

"Hello, Alan," Francis said, "it's been a while."

Willow looked between the two men. "You two know each other?" she asked, surprised.

"Yes," said Francis, "we've worked together in the past." There was an awkward silence then and Willow suddenly felt very uncomfortable with the knowledge.

"Well, I just wanted to say hello, I should be getting back to my friends," Alan said and, with a glance at Willow, turned and walked away. For a minute, Willow looked after him, feeling guilty. Before she and Francis could exchange words, however, the host of the event invited everyone to be seated, so they walked in silence to their designated table. Willow was seated across from Francis with people she really didn't know, but she started a polite conversation while glancing about to see where Alan was seated.

The evening went smoothly with a three-course meal, and the wine kept flowing. Willow picked at her food, engaged in her thoughts, answering questions with a smile that inside she knew was fake. The live orchestra kept them company, and she saw that couples had gotten up to dance as dessert was served. She looked down at her plate.

She continued to eat and listen to the animated conversation at the table when suddenly, Alan's voice came from behind her. "Willow, shall we dance?"

The rest of the group at the table stopped talking and turned to look. Francis lifted his eyebrows and looked across at her.

Willow blushed. "Of course," she finally said, slowly placing her napkin on the table. She stood up. Francis also stood up and looked at the pair of them, bowed his head in acceptance, and sat down again. Everyone resumed talking as Alan led her away.

It was a slow jazz number, and he theatrically swung her around and into his arms.

"Ahh, I'm not very experienced with this," Willow said, out of breath.

"Don't tell me you've never danced before?" Alan asked. He looked astonished at the idea.

"Of course not. It's just that... I haven't had much experience lately."

"Nothing to it. Just follow my lead." Alan tightened his hold around her waist, bringing them face-to-face. Willow held her breath and looked into his eyes.

"Take a breath. You'll need it," Alan whispered.

The music suddenly changed into a waltz, and Willow found herself swinging, with Alan commanding the whole show. She felt a little dizzy and very sensitive at the points where her body touched his, which seemed to be everywhere. Willow looked around and saw Francis looking.

"Are you enjoying this now?" Alan asked.

"I'm just afraid I'll trip over my feet and fall flat on my face," Willow responded. "Please, this is enough, let's stop."

"Why? You move so well."

"How come you know so much of dancing?" Willow asked, trying desperately to hold on.

"My grandmother. She was a grand old lady who believed that you could win a woman's heart on the dance floor. So, she insisted that I learn ballroom dancing. Which I did, thank goodness."

"Meaning you won many ladies' hearts?" Willow laughed.

Alan smiled down at her. "And believe me, much more."

The music slowly came to an end, and Willow found herself suddenly swirling around and then bent over Alan's arm. He looked down at her.

"See, you can dance," Alan said, staring into her eyes. Willow slowly rose up. Never in her life had she felt like this before. "Are you all right?" he asked.

"Yes, yes. That was very… very entertaining. I'd like to sit down now," Willow said. Alan led her back to her table, nodded to Francis, and walked back. Willow sat down and quickly drank some wine.

"That was some dancing," Francis remarked. Willow blushed but didn't comment.

"I have to go to the washroom, excuse me," she said to Francis as she got up. He too got up and came by her chair.

"Be careful," Francis whispered in her ear.

Willow turned to look at him with surprise. "Whatever do you mean?" she asked.

"We need to talk when you come back," he replied.

Willow walked away from the table, still thinking of what Francis had said. *Be careful of what?* she thought as she climbed the stairs and entered the main building. "Where are the washrooms?" she asked one of the passing waiters.

"It's on the left as you go toward the entrance."

"Thank you."

Willow looked at her face in the mirror of the washroom. She looked flushed. She tidied some of the hairs back and washed her hands. She didn't really need to be here, but she wanted a moment of reflection after the dance. *What are the odds that Francis and Alan would know each other?* she thought. Another coincidence that shouldn't have happened. She still thought about the words Francis had said. *Be careful.* Of what? She couldn't wait to get back to the table, so she went out and looked around. As she reached the balcony, she noticed that Alan was speaking with a group of people. His back was turned to her, so he couldn't see her coming. Willow slowed down, and as she was just about to pass them, she heard a woman talking to Alan.

"And how is Caroline? It must be difficult with the children, even though they're grown up."

Willow felt as if the world had stopped still. Her head was pounding, and she was trembling. Her heart skipped a beat, and she gulped in air in panic.

The woman who had just asked the question looked behind Alan at Willow. "Are you all right?" she asked.

Alan turned around to look, and Willow saw him freeze, paralyzed with shock.

"Is this true?" Willow asked quietly, trying to control the anger and dismay in her voice. "Who's Caroline? Are you married? With children?" Alan reached out to hold her arm. "Don't you dare touch me," Willow growled and hurriedly walked down the stairs. Alan ran after her.

At some point, Francis had noticed the commotion on the balcony from where he was seated and now ran toward Willow. "Are you all right?" he asked when he saw her face.

"I have to leave. I'm sorry." All Willow wanted was to get out, run away from this place, this moment. She could feel the tears burning behind her eyes. Francis followed her.

"Willow, wait, tell me, what happened?" Francis asked, grabbing her arm. She stopped and turned around.

"I want to go home, Francis, I can't talk to you now." Willow turned around to Alan, who had reached her side by now. "I have to go, now. I don't want to talk to either of you." She walked toward the parking area in the hopes of finding a taxi to take her home.

"Willow," Francis said, "let my driver take you home, please, we'll talk later."

Willow continued to walk at a fast pace, and Francis followed behind, calling his driver on his phone. The car came forward immediately from the parking area. Francis opened the door of his car.

"Marcel will take you home. We'll talk later," he said as Willow got in the car and left. As a result, she never saw Francis turn around to face Alan and say, "You never told her you were married."

⁓

Later that evening, Willow sat on her couch with a box of tissues by her side. She poured herself a dram of single malt and drank it in one gulp, the liquid burning through her throat. She had her cell phone with her, hesitating to call Jasmine. It was past midnight, and she didn't want to worry her. *I'll call early morning,* Willow thought and poured herself another drink. As she was about to pick it up, she received a text message. *May I call you?* It was from Alan. She deleted the message. A few minutes later, her phone rang. Willow stared at it, not wanting to answer, but realizing she needed to know why.

She answered the phone without speaking.

"Willow, let me explain," Alan said.

"Explain what? What is there to explain? God, Alan, how could you do this to me?" Willow asked, her voice close to shouting.

"I never lied to you," Alan said.

"Oh? You call not mentioning that you're married a truth? Oh, please, give me credit. I may be a lot of things, but I'm definitely not stupid."

Alan hesitated on those last words. "I never told you I wasn't married. When I first met you, I thought that—"

"You thought what? That it would be a fling? How can you do that to your wife? How could I do it to her?"

"Willow, my wife and I are separated, but yes, I am still legally married to her."

Willow didn't answer, trying hard not to cry. "I can't believe you did this to me. After all we discussed, you haven't understood one bit of me. And here I was, thinking that I'd found a man that was different, that could... Oh, you're all the same. I can't believe I fell for you."

Alan reacted, "You fell for me?"

"Have you not understood anything? How can you be so stupid? How can you be so blind? How can I have been so blind?"

"I want to continue this relationship."

"It isn't even a relationship."

"Then what is it?"

"You lied to me. Why didn't you say you were married? That you were separated, that... I opened my heart to you."

"Oh, yeah? What about Francis?"

"Francis? What has Francis got to do with this?"

"You never told me about him."

"Because there's nothing to tell."

"Oh? Soulmates and all that stuff? I saw the way he looks at you."

"Where did you hear that? You're making this all up. Francis is a very close old friend."

"Who happens to be also your soulmate."

"Define 'soulmate'."

"You want me to get a dictionary?"

"Don't be absurd. You're distorting the whole issue. Typical male behaviour. Subjecting me to humiliation while you rise above your lie."

"You would know."

"Frankly, I do. I've been there, as you very well know. So don't lecture me. I don't care if you're separated or that you're going to get a divorce, you made a mistake, admit it. This is major."

"I didn't make a mistake. I just thought that it wasn't relevant."

"Relevant? What do you take me for?"

"I just didn't want to ruin it."

"I deserved to know the truth. That's what hurts most."

"What's going to happen now?"

"Nothing. I won't talk to you or see you again. Please stop calling or texting or anything at all. I want nothing to do with you." Willow turned off her phone then, hugging her knees, burst into tears.

After a sleepless night, she turned on her phone to see several text messages and calls from Alan. Francis had also called but left no message. Willow promptly deleted all without reading or listening. She then called Jasmine.

"Mom? Mom, is that you?" Jasmine said. All Willow could do was sob. "Mom, are you all right? What happened?" she asked frantically.

"Can you come over?" Willow managed to say between sobs.

"Sure. I'll be there in twenty minutes," Jasmine said.

Willow was sitting on the couch with paper tissues strewn everywhere, sniffling and sobbing, and she left the door to her townhouse open so Jasmine could quietly enter. Jasmine arrived and closed the door silently behind her.

"Mom?" she ran over and bent down close to Willow. "Are you all right? What happened? I thought Alan was coming over for dinner tonight?"

"Don't you ever mention Alan to me."

"What happened at the gala? Come on, stop crying. No man is worth it, you know."

"I know. I'm not crying for him; I'm crying for myself."

"Here, I'll get you some water. You look like you've had enough to drink," she said, noticing the empty decanter.

Jasmine got up and walked into the kitchen. She picked up a glass from the counter and, after filling it with water, came back to sit beside her mother. "Tell me what happened."

Willow drank the water heartily, not realizing she was thirsty, and leaned back. Jasmine listened as she recalled what had happened. By the time she finished her story, Jasmine looked dismayed.

"What did Francis do?" Jasmine asked.

"He put me in his car and had his driver bring me home. Apparently, he called last night, but I didn't hear it because I'd turned off my phone. I'll call him later. Sorry about all this," Willow said, looking at Jasmine.

"I'm always here for you. What are you going to do now? Come and stay with us this weekend," Jasmine offered.

"I just want to take a shower and get my thoughts together. I'll give you a call, all right? Thank you for coming over this fast, but I just needed to tell someone, I guess." Willow leaned and kissed her daughter on the cheek. "Don't worry, I'll be fine. Go, you have to be at work."

Jasmine got up from the couch. "My offer stands. Don't be alone. Come and stay with us. He can't reach you there, I'll screen your calls."

"You're sweet, but go, I'll give you a call later," Willow said and saw her daughter off. Once she returned to her couch, she called Francis, who picked up on the first ring.

"Willow, are you all right?" Francis asked with a worried voice.

"I will be, it's just been a shock. What a turn of events. Thank you, though. Where are you?"

"Listen to me. I'm at my hotel at Bentley Lake. I'll send Marcel to pick you up this afternoon and bring you here where you can spend the weekend away from everything. Nature and open air will do you good, and we can talk."

"I don't know. I mean, thank you, but..."

"I will not have no for an answer. Marcel will be there at two."

"Please, I don't know, really..."

"Get out of the city. Come here, you've never seen the place anyway. It'll do you good, and like I said, I'm here for you. Please get ready by two," Francis insisted.

Willow gave in. "I'll be ready."

"Good, see you soon. Take care now, nothing and no one is worth your tears." Francis hung up. Willow wondered how he knew she was crying, but then again, Francis knew her well. She dialled Jasmine's number.

"Mom?"

"I talked with Francis just now, and he's sending his car to pick me up and take me to his hotel at Bentley Lake. I'll be spending the weekend there," Willow said.

"That's wonderful, get out of the city and give me a call when you get there. Love you."

"Love you back."

Marcel was punctually at Willow's door at two p.m. Willow handed him her small suitcase. Once out of the city, the drive took two hours as the highway turned into a winding mountain road when finally, they reached the hotel. It was situated at the top of a hill overlooking a golf course and the lake in the background. Willow got out of the car and looked around. The view was spectacular. She followed Marcel into the lobby and the reception desk. The young man quickly signed her in and gave her an envelope. Willow recognized Francis's handwriting. Another young man came forward with her key and, picking up her suitcase, walked her to her suite.

"Thank you," Willow said, tipping him, and closed the door. It was a beautiful suite with a fireplace overlooking the lake. She sat down on the bed and opened the envelope.

Welcome, dear soulmate. When you're ready, come and have drinks with me. I'll be in the lounge. Francis

She texted Jasmine. *Have arrived, beautiful place. I'm fine. Love you.*

Shortly, Jasmine texted back, *enjoy, and don't think about anything. Love you back.*

When Willow met with Francis later in the evening, she asked, "Is it true? Did you know he was married?" Francis didn't answer, but she understood from the look on his face. "Why didn't you tell me?"

"Because you never told me that it was Alan you were seeing. You just mentioned you'd met a man at an airport and things were going steady between you two. You sounded so happy, I had no suspicion," Francis replied sadly.

Willow sat, swirling her wineglass. "Is that why you tried to warn me at the gala? I didn't understand, did I?" she asked.

Francis sighed. "It was quite a shock to see that he was the man you'd been talking about. Yes, I knew he was married. I also knew that he was separated from his wife for a long time. I thought that maybe you would figure it out for yourself. Or that he had explained himself to you. I never imagined you didn't know."

"How was I to know? I was so thrilled to find someone." She looked up at him. "OK, a man was interested in me, so I probably didn't see any signs. Why are they separated, do you know?" she asked.

"All I know is that they live apart, but why, I don't know. I thought he might have told you, but I realized that he hadn't, and you were getting too involved, like you already are."

Willow sat quietly, thinking over what Francis had just said.

"So, what are you going to do now? You can always stay as long as you want at the hotel. I would enjoy the company," Francis said.

"That's very generous of you, but I'll just stay the weekend. I still have plenty to do at home. Anyway, I wouldn't want to get in your way, what, with all the investors you're expecting," Willow replied.

Francis reached out for her hand. "I insist, then."

"What about Evelyn?" Willow asked in a small voice.

Francis frowned. "What about her?"

"I mean what, how… She wouldn't mind me being here?"

"Why should she mind? You're my friend."

"Come on, Francis. She's your wife."

"No, it's you who's making it difficult for yourself. What I do is my business, and what Evelyn does is hers. She knows we have a very different relationship, and she understands that. I'm not hiding it, and neither are you."

Willow didn't answer at first.

"Right?" Francis insisted.

"You're making this very difficult for me, you know."

Francis placed his glass on the table. He looked like he was trying to curb his anger. "Why? Really, you're impossible. What do you want me to say? Anyway, I should have told you before, and you're going to hear about it anyway. We're getting a divorce."

"What, again? I guessed as much," Willow said.

"What?" Francis said at her reply.

"You said you were having troubles these past few months, I remember. That you would try to work out this one. Is it the distance creating a problem with both of you traveling most of the time, and now this hotel investment?" Willow asked.

"I don't know, frankly. Maybe I'm not cut out for marriage. God knows I've tried, especially with her," Francis replied.

"Who wants the divorce?" Willow asked.

"Why, Evelyn, of course."

"No. Oh my God… Now I remember last night Alan mentioned something, but I didn't realize what he meant until now."

"What did he say?"

"He said that even if certain things changed in my life, he would fight for himself." Willow paused. "I never did understand what he meant."

"He must have spoken to Evelyn," Francis said to himself.

"Maybe she spoke to him," Willow offered.

"Why would she do that?" Francis asked, surprised.

"She is a woman, Francis. No woman likes to be measured up with another woman. It's a pity she feels like this. You're a wonderful man, and she's certainly a gorgeous beauty."

"Well, life goes on, and if she wants to leave, she will, and there's nothing I can do about it now, is there?" Francis leaned back and looked at her sadly.

"You're very calm about all this," Willow remarked.

"I've learnt in life that no matter what you do, what is meant to be happens," Francis answered, resigned.

"Fate?" Willow asked.

Francis laughed. "Call it what you like. It's just that three unsuccessful marriages make me look kind of bad. Oh well, I'll get over this one too. So, you see, I need you to stay."

"And feel sorry for ourselves?"

"Never! Why should I feel sorry for myself—or, as a matter of fact, why should you? I've tried, you've tried, we have had some happy years and wonderful kids to be grateful for, so no. No regrets and no self-pity. Or I'll kick you out of the hotel. Come on, let's have dinner," Francis said as he got up and took her hand.

"I know you're changing the subject," Willow said, smiling. He chuckled.

❧

After a good night's sleep, Willow woke up early next morning and went for a walk around the property. The sun was rising over the lake, casting its first rays of sunlight over the still water. As she slowly walked to the main building in search of coffee, she saw the fitness centre situated on the basement level that had windows all around overlooking the landscape. She noticed Francis, who was on the treadmill with his back turned toward her. Willow smiled. *There he is, early riser as usual,* she thought and proceeded to enter the building. The servers were putting the final touches to the breakfast room. One of them noticed her.

"I know I'm early," Willow said, "but I was wondering if I could get a cup of coffee."

"Of course," said one of the servers. "I can also get you something from the bakery, they're just out of the oven."

"Would you have a croissant, by any chance?"

The server smiled. "I'll be back, please have a seat."

Willow sat down at a small table by the windows as she was served her coffee and a large croissant that looked very inviting.

"Thank you," Willow said and took a sip.

"You're up early." She turned around to see Francis with a towel around his neck and a sweaty T-shirt. "They told me a guest was having an early breakfast." He smiled and noticed the croissant. "They got to you?"

"Oh, yes, they did." Willow said, munching on the tip of the croissant as the flakes fell.

"I have to go, but come back later and find me," Francis said and waved goodbye. Willow looked fondly after him.

Later in the morning, after returning to her suite and taking a shower, Willow dressed up for the day and walked back to the main building.

"Have you seen Mr. von Tauberg?" she asked the receptionist.

"I believe he's in the dining room, having breakfast with one of the guests," the young woman answered.

"Thank you." Willow walked into the dining area and looked around. She saw Francis sitting at one of the long tables in front of the windows with the magnificent view of the lake. There was another large man sitting with his back turned. She hesitated and stopped. Francis caught a glimpse of her as he turned to talk to the man, and he got up and waved.

"Willow, come and join us."

She tried to say no with her hands, and then the other man turned to look behind him. "Professor Millan?" she asked, surprised.

The man struggled to recognize her as he got up, holding his napkin.

"Professor Robert Millan?" Willow said as she walked toward them. "What a pleasure to see you again after all this time. I'm Willow from Excorp."

"Willow? Oh my, it is you, really. But you've changed so much."

Willow, with a smile, said, "I hope for the better."

"Certainly, you have. Goodness, what are you doing here? Have a seat." She sat down as Francis looked at her with a puzzled look.

"Professor Millan came to visit about five years ago with a group of surgeons, and I had the pleasure of organizing their stay," Willow explained as Francis sat down.

"And what a great success it was. She was magnificent, as I'm sure you know." Willow smiled as a waitress came up. "I'll have some black coffee, thank you."

"Is that all you're having?" Professor Millan asked as he bit into a pancake.

"I had my breakfast very early in the morning."

"Yes, she gets up around five thirty," Francis offered, giving her a smile.

"So do you." Willow smiled back.

"Tell me, what are you doing here?" Professor Millan finally asked after wiping his mouth on his napkin and leaning back.

"I've come to live here in town now and am in the process of moving. Francis is a very old friend, and he's kindly offered for me to stay for a couple of days at his hotel to rest and relax."

"How's the business going?" Professor Millan continued, looking over his cup of coffee.

"I closed it down two years ago," Willow replied quietly, glancing at Francis, who said nothing.

"That's a shame. You were doing so well."

"I had some problems with my partners, so I had to fold," Willow offered, realizing that it still hurt to say it.

"And your charming husband?" Professor Millan asked.

"Divorced him."

The professor looked up suddenly. "So, the change comes from there. I'm sure you know what you're doing. You always looked like you had courage and stamina. What are your plans for the future?" he asked.

"I haven't really thought about it yet," Willow replied, glad to get over the subject. "But enough of me. What are you doing here?" she asked, looking at Francis questioningly.

94

"I met Professor Millan and his wife when they came to my hotel in St. Vincent. We've been in contact ever since. Robert is a keen golfer," Francis offered.

"Really? Professor, don't tell me you're retiring," Willow said as he laughed heartily.

"My wife has been insisting that I relax and start to enjoy life again. Forty years of cancer research is a long time. She wants to travel and be with her grandchildren. I just want to play golf," the professor replied.

"Is Carol here with you?" Willow asked, remembering the elderly lady with fondness.

"Of course. We came for a medical conference, then Francis here kindly invited us over for a stay. She's at the spa, getting pretty."

Willow laughed. "How long are you staying?"

"We're leaving tomorrow morning."

Francis stood up. "I should go. I have some guests coming in, and I have to go to the airport. Professor, I'll see you tonight at dinner."

"Sure, sure, go ahead. I have Willow to keep me company."

Francis nodded at her and left. Willow looked after him.

"So, how long have you known him?" Professor Millan asked with a soft, understanding smile.

"Who? Francis?" Willow asked, surprised. The professor just continued to smile patiently. Suddenly, Willow felt very embarrassed. "About twenty years now. We met for business."

"Charming fellow, isn't he?" he continued, folding his napkin.

Willow stared at him, puzzled. "Yes, he is."

"So, tell me," he continued, "what he's after. He seems preoccupied and a little agitated. It's not like him." Willow hesitated to say anything. "Come on, you can trust me. I like the damn guy. Is he in trouble?"

Willow gave in. "No, no, of course not. It's just that he wants to renovate this place and turn it into a larger spa and golf resort, and he's looking for investors. He wants to set another golf course on top of the cliff here so that you can enjoy the view of the lake while playing. He wants to improve the restaurant as well, bring in a new chef, and he wants to expand the spa services too. Some of the buildings here need to be renovated and some redecorated, the usual stuff. He's already put in a substantial amount of his personal money into buying the complex in the first place."

"How much?" the professor asked.

"How much what?"

Professor Millan placed his fork and knife on the plate and drank the last of his coffee. "How much is he looking for?"

"Forty million dollars."

"Whew!" exclaimed the professor.

"Unfortunately, yes. But it's going to be spectacular, I know. He has such great taste and knowledge, and he does know how to sell the place. I know it'll be grand. It's just finding the financing that's killing him. Today, he has these prospective investors coming in to take a look."

"Hmm. You trust Francis this much?"

"Yes. He's been through a lot in his life. Family, business, friends, but he always rose above the problems and more than surviving—he succeeded. Look at what he's done. Look at his portfolio of hotels," Willow said.

"And look what an admirer he has. You should be his PR," he said, smiling. Willow waved aside his remark.

"I'm sorry if I got carried away. It's just that I can't do anything to help him, and I see his frustration. But it'll turn out well in the end, I know. We have to stay positive. He would hate me to say otherwise."

"Well, darling, I should be going," Professor Millan said, pushing back his chair. "It's been lovely talking to you. Will I see you tonight?"

"I'm around. I would love to say hi to Carol," Willow replied, also standing.

"What about drinks then, around six?" he asked.

"Would love to, thank you," Willow replied as the professor gave her a hug and waved goodbye. She sat down again and looked out the window, wondering if she had talked too much.

After lunch, Willow took one of the trails down to the lake. It was a beautiful day, and the fresh air was revitalizing. She was trying hard to push thoughts of Alan out of her mind. She walked a little by the lake and back up the trail, which proved to be harder than she thought, and she was out of breath by the time she reached her suite. *I need to exercise more,* Willow thought. She heard the phone ringing and ran to pick it up.

"Hello?" she said.

"What are you doing? You sound out of breath," Francis said.

"I guess I'm out of sorts. I just came back from a walk down to the lake. Where are you?" Willow replied.

"I'm back at the hotel. Picked up the guests, had lunch downtown, and then drove up. They're now settling in their rooms, then I'll be taking them for a tour around the property."

"How's it going so far?" Willow asked as she sat down on the bed.

"We shall see. I called to invite you to join us for drinks at the lounge bar."

"Oh, I'd love to, but I accepted drinks with Robert and Carol at six."

"All right then, I'll see you at dinner," Francis said, sounding slightly disappointed.

"OK, I'll see you then."

"Wish me luck," Francis said suddenly.

Willow was surprised. "Hey, is this the suave, cool businessman I know? Of course, everything will be all right. I know."

"Don't quote me." Francis laughed. Willow was relieved to hear his laughter.

"Go, go, before I say something else. I'll see you later." Willow placed the phone slowly in its cradle. As she glanced at her watch, she saw that there was time for a nice bath before meeting the Millans. She got up and walked into the bathroom.

At six o'clock, Willow slowly walked into the lounge bar and looked around. She noticed Francis sitting in one of the corner tables with a group of men, talking animatedly. One of the men glanced up at her and returned to look again, this time admiringly. Willow was wearing a sleek black top over black pants. The crystal necklace and earrings dangled and sparkled from the spotlights in the ceiling. She had piled up her hair in a French chignon, but already, some wisps of hair had escaped from it, and she hastily tried to push them back in vain. Francis turned to see what had caught the man's attention, and he too did a double turn to look again. Willow smiled and waved.

She finally saw Professor Millan and his wife seated out on the terrace. She walked out, reaching out her arms toward the elderly woman who sat facing her. "Carol, what a delight to see you here again."

"Willow! Fancy seeing you here, Robert told me that you'd changed, but this is a transformation."

Willow kissed her on one cheek. "Stop, you're embarrassing me, Carol. You look great yourself."

"Thanks to the spa. Sit down, sit down, and tell me everything. Robert, order her a drink. Darling, what will you have? I'm having a wonderful martini."

"I'll have a glass of red wine, please."

"Any special kind?" Robert asked.

"Merlot, please," Willow replied.

He went inside to find a waiter while Willow sat down, facing Carol.

"Tell me, when did you get divorced?" Carol asked, sipping her martini.

"Word travels fast."

"Don't blame Robert. I asked how you were. Are you settled down now? It must have been hard. And fancy your daughter living here."

"Yes, in the beginning it was. But I rented a place, and I intend to live here. Difficult to let go of certain things, and I have my parents back home," Willow said.

"The time we spent with you was spectacular, and you were really extraordinary in arranging that program."

"Let's go back, and I'll arrange a different one this time," Willow said as Robert approached with a glass of wine. "Thank you."

"Can't. Have four grandchildren now, and I want to spend as much time as I can with them," Carol said.

"Professor Millan has told me that you want him to retire," Willow added.

"Yes, enough is enough. You don't get any younger, and he needs to see that there's a life outside the clinic."

"Is she complaining about me again?" Robert asked, settling down.

"No, no, we were just talking about retirement." Willow raised her glass and took a sip. Robert was enjoying the peanuts in the bowl on the cocktail table.

"Tell me, Willow, how well do you know Francis?" he asked seriously.

"Why do you ask? I thought you'd met him before," Willow replied, surprised.

"Yes, we did, but it was always a courteous relationship between host and guest," he replied.

"What he wants to know is, how well do you know him, and how much do you trust him?" Carol offered.

"Why do you ask?" Willow asked, looking at them both.

"Just curious," the professor replied, continuing to munch on the peanuts.

"Robert, stop eating and tell her why you want to know," Carol said.

He leaned back in his chair and looked directly at Willow. "I might have a solution for his problem," he offered.

"What problem?" Willow asked.

"You know, finding investors," he continued. Willow suddenly found that she was unable to hold the wineglass in her hand, so she put it down on the table with shaking hands.

"Are you serious?" Willow finally asked.

"Very."

"But how, I mean, who… What do you mean?' Willow asked.

"Darling, Robert and three buddies of his were looking into buying a golf resort for their retirement," Carol said.

"Buy? A golf resort? What?" Willow knew she wasn't making sense.

"Robert, do something, she looks quite white with shock." Carol laughed.

He chuckled. "Willow understands what I'm saying but finds it hard to believe. You know, it's just pure coincidence that we met here."

"No. No, it's not a coincidence. Nothing happens by coincidence. I… I was… I guess I'm here for a reason… You're here for a reason…" Willow stuttered and stopped speaking. She hesitatingly glanced inside but couldn't see Francis and his guests.

"My dear, you're trembling. Why are you so agitated?" Carol leaned forward to hold her arm.

"It's just that… it's so weird meeting you here, me being here… I just can't understand." Willow gulped down her wine and leaned back, brushing back the tendrils of hair.

"Willow, I believe it's a sign that we met you here," Robert offered. "Listen, what Carol is trying to say is that my friends, doctors from the same clinic, we've been looking into investing. We're all keen golfers, so we thought we would put our money on a resort where we could play freely and make money. Now, what you've told me about this place makes more sense. It's a beautiful spot, no doubts about that, and what he wants to do with it has intrigued me. No use trying to build something on our own when we can have someone else take care of it all and we can just enjoy the benefits. Of course, I'll have to discuss this with them, but I'm sure they'll say OK if I am inclined to say yes. As for Francis, I'd like to know more about the man."

"Did you know that he's a count?" was the only thing that came to Willow's mind.

"What? We didn't know that, did we, Robert?" Carol asked, amazed.

"A count?" Robert said, dropping the peanut he had in his hand.

"Yes, he comes from a very old family, connected to the royal family from a long time ago, I'm not sure how exactly. He retains the title only for official business. He separated from his father when he was ten years old, refusing to follow in his footsteps, claiming that he wanted to know the world." Willow stopped talking when she saw Francis, walking toward them.

"Shall we go into dinner?" Francis asked.

"Of course," said Professor Millan, and they all stood up and joined Francis.

◦⟳◦

It was past midnight by the time Willow returned to her room. She quickly changed into her nightgown and walked into the bathroom to take off her makeup. After washing her face, she closed the bathroom door, crossed the large bedroom toward the wide terrace windows, and looked out. It was raining heavily. She turned around and put on the electric fireplace. The fake flames were nothing compared to a real fire, but it still warmed her. She returned to the bed and pulled down the bedcover. After dimming the lights, she had just gotten cosy when the phone on her night table rang. Surprised, she reached to answer it.

"Hello?"

"Are you in bed?"

Willow stared at the phone. "Francis?"

"Are you in bed?" he repeated.

"No—yes, but I—"

"Good," he said, quickly cutting her off.

"Francis? Hello? Hello?"

Suddenly, there was a knock on the door. Willow stared at the phone in her hand, then at the door, then at the clock on the night table. The knock repeated, and Francis's voice followed. "Willow?"

She got up from the bed and slowly walked toward the door. "Francis? It's one thirty in the morning. What happened?"

"Will you please open the door?" he asked quietly. Willow looked around at her room and then walked into the bathroom to grab a bathrobe. She put it on and walked back to the door to unchain it. Francis was standing there with a bottle of champagne and two glasses. She looked at Francis, then at the bottle in his hand.

"Isn't it a bit late for this?" Willow said, smiling.

"Can I come in?" Francis asked, looking inside the room.

"Sure." She opened the door wide. He walked in and placed the bottle and glasses on the coffee table by the fireplace and suddenly grabbed her by both arms and pulled her into the middle of the room. The door closed slowly by itself.

"What have you done?" Francis asked suddenly.

Surprised, she replied, "What do you mean? I haven't done anything."

"Sit," Francis said.

Willow sat down in the armchair. "What is it, Francis? This is so not like you."

"I know, and I'm frightened myself. You don't mind, do you?" Francis said, walking up and down the room.

"What, you coming to my room in the middle of the night? No, of course not. But what will everyone think? Think of the scandal." Willow smiled, trying to understand what was going on.

He suddenly turned around to look at her. "Are you serious? Should I leave?"

"I'm kidding. Tell me what happened."

He stopped in the middle of the room. "What did you do?" he again asked.

"I don't know. You're freaking me out. Tell me."

Francis walked toward her and knelt in front of the armchair. He reached out for her hands, and she was so overwhelmed by the touch and what was happening that she couldn't look into his eyes and instead just stared at his hands.

"You talked to Robert and Carol," he said finally.

"Oh, no! I didn't mean to and no, they promised not to tell you, no, I'm sorry, I just—" Willow tried to explain.

"Will you just shut up for a moment and listen?" Willow looked down at him. "I'm sorry. I didn't mean to shout," Francis apologized. "I know this is very awkward for you, but right now, I really need to talk to my soulmate."

"Sorry," Willow said in a quiet voice.

"Don't be." Francis reached out with his hand and softly caressed her cheek. It was then that she remembered that she had no makeup and had pulled down her hair, which was now lying softly on her shoulders. She had never been this natural in front of Francis before, and she tightened the opening of her bathrobe so that he would not see the top of her nightgown.

"You were in bed," he suddenly said.

Willow smiled and said nothing. "I didn't want to ruin this extraordinary moment."

"As I was saying, I need to talk to you. What did you tell Robert and Carol?"

"They wanted to know a little about you. So, I talked about you, your hotels. Just simply tried to talk about you," Willow replied.

"Looks like you've done so much more."

"What do you mean?" Willow asked, worried.

Francis gazed into the distance. "Something no one has ever done for me before."

"What do you mean?" she asked again.

"You stood up for me. You did something extraordinary for me. No one has ever been so giving like you've been."

She hesitated. "What happened?"

"Robert wants to invest with his three partners. He's going back tomorrow to discuss the details and wants me to come over sometime next week to present the project."

Willow lay back in the armchair. She saw Francis staring at the carpet and reached out to touch his shoulder. "I'm so glad for you. I'm so glad that I was able to do something for you. But what about the investors that came in?"

"Oh, they looked around and said they would get back to me sometime in a couple of weeks, but I think they're looking into a bigger investment than this place. You can't imagine what you have done for me," Francis answered in a shaky voice. He sat down on the carpet and leaned back against her legs, holding her hand but facing away. "I never told you much about myself, did I?" He was talking toward the fireplace.

"No, never."

"My father used to beat me, you know. Said it was discipline." Willow was too shocked to say anything. "He wanted me to be like him, and all I wanted was to be a chef. A famous chef. He threatened to disinherit me."

"And your mother?" Willow asked.

"She died when I was five. I barely remember her. Just this beautiful lady with golden hair and green eyes. I ran away from home when I was thirteen."

"It must have been horrible for you."

"Believe me, it was. You don't want to ask me what I saw or lived throughout those troubled years."

"Where did you go?"

"After roaming the streets and hitchhiking through countries, I went to my great-aunt. She listened to what I had to say, then she took me in and refused to talk to my father. He went crazy with anger. Threatened to kill her and me."

"What?" Willow exclaimed, surprised and dismayed.

"Oh, yes. I left her too. Studied hotel management. The rest you know."

"Did you ever see your father again?"

"Yes, last year. He was dying and wanted to see me. Ask for forgiveness."

"I'm so sorry."

"You know, I forgave him at his deathbed. For stealing my childhood. My youth," Francis said, fondling her hand.

"I don't know what to say."

"Don't say anything," he replied. They sat for some time in silence. "When I divorced my first wife, she took everything I owned. Everything, from the heirloom plates from my great-aunt to everything that I practically owned before we were married."

"Oh, no" was all Willow could say.

"I just learnt recently that she's without a job, so I gave her one through one of my companies. She invited me to dinner to her house along with her new husband."

"Did you go?"

"Yes, I did. And there, hanging on the hall, were all the things that she had taken from me. I guess she wanted to show them to me as a punishment."

"You must have felt awful."

"Yes, I did. But I managed through that night. And I told myself later that they were just possessions and that I had to let go of the past." Francis paused. "I always wondered why she did that."

"Maybe she wanted to keep a piece of you," Willow volunteered.

Francis suddenly looked back, surprised and shocked. "You know, you may be just right. I never thought of it that way. She couldn't let go of the past. For some, it's difficult. That's why my second marriage was a failure from the start. And now the third one..." He stopped. "So you see, what you did with the Millans means so much to me. I would have never imagined it."

Willow leaned forward. "Francis, I'm your soulmate. You would have done the same, no? You've already done so much for me. This was the least I could do. And I really didn't know what would happen, believe me. I'm as surprised as you are."

Francis turned around to look into her eyes. "They speak of you as if you're an angel."

"Which I'm not." Willow laughed.

"I guess I should open this bottle now," Francis replied, uncorking the champagne with a smooth move and pouring it into the glasses. He handed her one and picked up the other. "Here's to new adventures."

They clinked their glasses, and Willow slowly took a sip. They talked about old times and the things they had done together and laughed at some of their stories.

It was then that he noticed the clock on the night table. "It's very late. You should go to bed," Francis said. He slowly got up from the floor and pulled her up with him. They walked slowly toward the door. He stopped before it and turned around to look at her. They were just inches away, and suddenly, the whole atmosphere changed. Never before had they been this close, and Willow didn't know whether to move or just stand still. Francis was looking at her closely, and for a minute, she imagined him kissing her.

He leaned forward, and their faces were so close that she could feel his breath on her face. Willow closed her eyes. Francis ever so slowly touched her lips with his own. Willow was trembling, and she realized that Francis too was trembling. He pulled away before fully kissing her, then opened the door and left. Willow stood still for a moment, not able to withhold the tears. Then, she opened her eyes to look at the closed door. There was no way that she could sleep now, so she went and poured herself another glass. *What just happened?* she thought.

The next morning, Willow woke up late, having finally fallen asleep just before dawn. She tried not to think about last night but ended up wondering if Francis felt the same. After getting dressed, she walked downstairs to the lobby.

"Good morning," Willow said to the young man behind the reception desk, "where can I find Mr. von Tauberg?"

"Good morning, ma'am. He left early this morning."

"Oh? Did he say when he would be back?" Willow asked.

"No, but he did leave you a note." He reached down and handed Willow an envelope.

"Thank you. Have the Millans checked out?" Willow asked.

"Yes, they left at the same time as Mr. von Tauberg."

Willow walked back to her suite and sat down on the bed. She slowly opened the envelope, afraid to see what Francis might have written.

My dear soulmate,

I didn't plan to leave without saying goodbye but thought it best to not say anything after last night. We have an understanding, you and I, and I hope last night didn't change that. I would hate to lose your friendship.

Stay as long as you want. When you want to go back, just let reception know, and they'll provide you with a ride.

As for me, I won't return immediately. Stay in touch, and know that I'm always here for you.

Francis

Willow dropped the note and lay back on the bed. So, he preferred to run away from last night. She had expected as much, was even surprised that it had gone that far. He had pulled back—whether by caution or by will, she would never know. Willow looked up at the ceiling. He had managed to distract her from Alan, that was for sure.

♾

Back in town, Alan stood up as Francis walked toward the table.

"Thank you for coming," he said, pointing toward the seat opposite him. They both sat down. The waiter came up with the menus.

"Would you like a drink?" he asked.

"No, thank you," Francis responded, placing the menu beside his plate.

"Give us ten minutes," Alan told the waiter.

"Certainly, sir." The waiter bowed and left.

Alan turned around to look at Francis again. "I know you're wondering why I invited you."

Francis looked straight at him. "I'm assuming it's about Willow." Alan smiled. Francis continued, "But what I don't understand is why."

"I'm guessing you know that Willow isn't speaking to me. She's not answering her phone or my emails. Her daughter Jasmine tells me that she doesn't want to see me or talk to me."

"I can understand why," Francis answered. "You should've told her you were married. She didn't deserve to get hurt again, not after her divorce and what her husband had done."

"She talks to you, doesn't she?" Alan asked.

"Did she ever tell you how we met?"

"No."

"Well, it was about twenty years ago. I had partnered up with an old friend, and we were looking around for an office that we could use while we were going through details. My friend said he had heard from another friend of his about this company that provided office rentals and secretarial services to businessmen."

"Willow's company," Alan added.

"That's right. We made an appointment and went to her office. Strange to say, but something clicked between us. Willow looked and sounded like a smart lady, and we sat down to talk details. That evening, we invited her to dinner to continue discussions. We hit it off immediately. She was easygoing, very shy and reserved, and I loved pulling her leg. She eased up a bit later on in the evening."

"So, what happened next?" Alan asked.

"We decided that she would act as our liaison office until our business came through. I returned home. About three months later, I received an email from her congratulating my birthday. You can imagine my total surprise. She never told me how she came to know that."

Alan, with a smile, said, "Something Willow would do."

"Yes, it is. Caught me off guard. So, I replied."

"And?"

"We've been writing to each other nearly every other day ever since."

"What?" Alan asked, surprised.

Francis nodded. "Yes, and she'll have my head if I don't."

"That must be difficult for a busy man like yourself," Alan said.

"It isn't, would you believe it? I quite look forward to her emails."

"Whatever do you find to write about?" Alan asked.

Francis laughed. "You of all people shouldn't ask me that. You know how she is. Willow is an incredible writer. She writes about everything. Absolutely everything."

Alan, now curious, asked, "So what happened next?"

"We continued to write back and forth. She slowly revealed her feelings, her problems about her marriage, and I tried to help her struggle through it all. I was divorced by that time from my first wife. I found it amusing and at the same time thrilling to communicate with this interesting woman from the other side of the world."

"You must have known that she was falling for you," Alan said.

"I wouldn't exactly call it falling. I was just filling a void in her life. True, there was something between us, but I didn't know what to call it. There was an attraction, sure, but I was too busy trying to set up a new life for myself."

"So, you liked her writing to you boosting up your ego."

"Don't be cruel. I tried to be there for her. I gave her no reason to fall in love with me."

"But she was attracted to you. You must have known how striking a figure you must have presented during her tremulous life," Alan said.

Francis smiled. "The problem was how striking a figure she presented in mine. She was like a rock throughout my second divorce. It was very strange to find this extraordinary woman literally by my side, helping me and advising me as to how I should conduct my life. Do you know she flew all the way out to be with me?"

"What?"

"Oh, yes, I was organizing a benefit concert for orphan children. I kept writing about the whole organization and the attending artists, and out of the blue she asked if she could come."

"Did she? Did she come?" Alan asked, knowing the answer.

"Of course. It was funny, though, because the day she was arriving, the star of the show came down with an illness and had to be hospitalized. I was at the hospital when she arrived, so we met the next morning for breakfast."

"I just can't believe she did this," Alan said.

"Willow is an incredible woman with a determination that I've never seen in anyone else. We met the next morning, and I took her around. Then, we paid a visit to the hospital."

"Did you cancel the concert?" Alan asked.

"She told me not to. The tickets were sold, the invitations were out. We promptly got drunk for the next three days until the day of the concert."

"Drunk? Willow?"

"Oh, yes, she can drink you under the table. We drank five-year old rum and got terribly drunk. That was when she started talking about her private life and the problems with her marriage."

"And you discussed all this while drunk?" Alan asked.

"Is there a better way? Anyway, she was beside me throughout the whole week. And the day of the concert, she came and stood beside me and held my hand. She was like a solid rock beside me, encouraging me that all would be well. That was the first time that we believed ourselves to be soulmates."

"And the concert?"

"Was a great success. Even without the leading star." Francis paused to think, then picked up the menu and started looking it over. Alan waited for him to continue. However, he saw that Francis would not say anything else. The waiter promptly showed up, noticing that they were ready to order. After he had gone, Francis leaned back in his chair and looked at Alan.

"Are you strong enough to carry her?" Francis asked him. He gave Francis a puzzled look, trying to determine what he meant. "Not physically, of course."

"Are you?" Alan replied.

Francis smiled into his glass. "I never said that I could or would. It's just that even though Willow might look like a very strong-minded, determined woman who can rule the world, deep inside, she's very fragile, vulnerable, and lonely." Francis took a long sip from his glass. "Needs to be loved and cherished," he continued.

Alan, with a surprised tone, remarked, "You're in love with her."

Francis gave a wry smile. "As you say."

"Does she know?" Alan asked.

"Of course not. I would never tell her."

"But why not?"

"Because I can never give her what she wants. I can't provide her with the life she dreams of. Don't believe the makeup life she's painted for you. She doesn't know what she wants out of life. I would make her miserable."

"But she thinks so highly of you. You've told me that you're soulmates," Alan said.

"I don't deny it. She's my soulmate. She sees through me as I see through her. That's why we get along so well. She fills that empty space in my heart."

Alan didn't know how to reply. He was confused and a little lost with words. "I still think that you should tell her how you feel. I mean, how can she... How can I... What a mess."

"Funny thing is, I believe deep down, she knows. She feels it and knows that I can't or will never declare my love for her. It would ruin the relationship we have."

"And you expect me to go on as if your relationship doesn't exist? How can I?" Alan asked.

"Of course it exists. It's just not as you think it is. Maybe a long time ago, when we first met, something could have come out of the relationship, but she was inexperienced and naive at that time. I watched her grow and flourish. Made her believe in the true woman inside her. Helped her break through."

"You mean to tell me there was no physical…"

Francis laughed. "Never. Not even a kiss. You must promise me never to tell her. Never tell her about all we've been talking about. She must never know I told you." Francis grabbed Alan's arm. "Promise me."

"I promise," Alan solemnly said.

"Good."

Alan bowed his head. "I should have told her right off when we met, but I was struggling with my marriage." He paused. "Still am. The moment I first saw her at the airport, she had this strange pull on me. It was magical. It was as if she was there waiting for me. So, I never did disclose the fact that I was married, and she never asked, so the ruse continued. Quite successfully until… well, until you know." Alan paused, then continued, "I don't want to go knocking on her door. Jasmine said Willow was in a bad state, and it would be better if I didn't insist on trying to see her."

"She's hurting pretty bad," Francis said. He saw the anguish Alan was feeling. "May I suggest something?"

"Please."

"Leave her alone. Pursuing her will lead to emotional distress for both of you. She's just started a new life. She's still vulnerable and self-conscious. If you really care for her, give her the space she needs. The sharper the cut, the sooner it'll heal."

Alan looked at Francis. "You're asking the impossible, but I understand what you're trying to say. I'll think about it," he replied.

"Do it quickly, Alan. Do it before it's too late."

Willow had decided to stay another day at the hotel, relaxing at the spa and enjoying the luxury of the suite. When it was time to leave, the hotel reception arranged a car for her, as Francis had promised, and she returned home, once again flooded with the memories of what had happened with Alan. As she opened her door, she noticed an envelope had been pushed inside. She bent to pick it up. There was no name, but she had the premonition that it was from Alan. She placed her keys and bag on the kitchen counter and left the suitcase by the stairs. She walked and sat down on her couch and opened the envelope. Inside was a letter.

Willow,

It was never my intention to hurt you. I realize now that I made a mistake of not disclosing my personal life, but I had my reasons, selfish they may be. I would have liked to explain them, but I understand that you don't want to see or hear from me again. I will respect your decision. I wish you the best in your new life.

Forgive me.

Alan

CHAPTER FIVE

Reconciliation

*T*welve years from that note, it was needless to say Willow did not sleep well the night of her encounter with Alan at the Laid-Back Estate Winery. She kept tossing and turning, trying not to think, but all sorts of memories kept coming back, some she didn't even want to remember, but nevertheless, she kept thinking of them— especially Alan's last note to her.

Willow got up sometime after dawn and made herself a cup of coffee. She sat outside on the patio. Even though it was chilly in the morning, the fresh air revived her. *It's just going to be a normal day,* Willow thought to herself, *nothing to it. I will not fantasize. Life has taught me that, if nothing else.* She had been through so much and had managed to survive, and she wouldn't jeopardize herself. Not this time. She had been down this road before, even with Alan, even though that had been cut short by herself to protect herself.

And look what that's brought you, she sarcastically told herself.

Willow sat for a while until the day got warmer, and she went inside to prepare. What would she wear? Not that she had much choice, as she had brought the bare minimum on this three-day trip.

She finally decided to pull on her cargo pants and top it off with a long white tunic shirt. She rolled up the sleeves, pulled up her hair into a ponytail, and looked in the mirror. *Woman, you need colour,* she thought and tied a colourful scarf around her ponytail. *There, much better.* She skipped on putting the sparkling earrings and instead went for a pair of small silver hoops. A little makeup, and she was ready to go. She picked up her bag and went outside.

It was a beautiful day, so Willow slowly walked down toward the restaurant. Alan was already there, speaking with someone at the entrance, when he glanced at her and waved. She waved back, noticing that he too had decided to wear cargo pants and a white shirt with the sleeves rolled up, so that now they looked as if they had coordinated their outfits. She laughed silently.

"Good morning," Alan shouted as he turned toward her.

"Good morning."

"What, no sparkling earrings?" he asked jokingly, looking at her face.

"No, not this morning," Willow replied. "How are you?"

"Good, good. Ready to go?"

"Yes, I am." They walked toward the parking area. Willow saw him moving toward a bright red jeep.

"You don't mind?" Alan asked, opening the door for her.

"No, not at all." She climbed in.

"I use this to go around the vineyards." Alan started the jeep, and as he backed out and turned around, she saw Roxy in the middle of the road.

"What is she doing?" Willow asked as Roxy sat down and stared at them.

Alan laughed. "She always accompanies me when I go out in the vineyards. This is her way of saying, 'Aren't you forgetting something?'"

"Oh, let her come, I don't mind."

"Are you sure? I know she won't be a problem, but it's your call."

"Roxy," Willow called as she stood up, "come on, girl."

"She's waiting for me to call her," Alan said. "Let's go, Roxy." The dog suddenly got up, ran toward the jeep, and landed in the back with one jump.

"Good girl," Willow said, petting her. "She's wonderful."

"She's been with me since she was a puppy. I found her abandoned at a construction site six years ago."

They drove about half an hour when Alan pulled the jeep over to the side. "You see there in the distance, the farmhouse with a barn next to it and several other buildings, among the vineyards and gardens?"

"Yes, I do, is that the family farm?"

"Yes, the main building and barn are originals dating back to my grandfather. He was a gentleman farmer. I'll take you there," Alan said driving again. A little further down the road, he turned left in front of a ranch-style gate and passed through, driving down a paved road all the way to the front of the farmhouse. He stopped the jeep, and Roxy jumped out and ran toward the front porch and inside.

"Where is she going?" Willow asked, worried.

"My sister, Robyn, lives here now with her family. There's always someone inside, and Roxy knows she'll get treats. The other building down the river is where my brother, William, lives with his family. He manages the organic produce gardens. There used to be a lot of animals back in my grandfather's time, but now we just keep horses."

Willow gazed at the vast land. She noticed another smaller barn in the distance among tall trees. "What about there?"

"I live there," Alan said. When he saw the look of surprise on her face, he laughed. "I converted it of course; do you want to see?"

"I would love to. I was always curious to see how a barn can be converted, I see a lot of them these days in magazines."

"Yes, it became popular a couple of years ago. After I took on the family business, it seemed convenient to live here. Besides, I'd had enough of the city life."

They started walking among the vineyards, and by the time they reached the building, Roxy had come back running after them.

"She sometimes stays with me when I'm here, but she's usually with Robyn." Alan opened the door. "After you."

Willow entered and stood still. She gazed up at the exposed trusses and beams among the soaring ceiling. The barn had a split level, and Willow could see a sitting area and a bedroom on the second floor. On the ground floor was an amazing open kitchen area and a long dining table with benches on both sides. She saw that Alan had set up office in one corner with a drawing table as well. The ambience was rustic, but she loved the smell and colour of the wood.

"This is amazing."

"I'm glad you like it. It took some delicate planning to make the foundation and frame strong enough to withhold the building, but I'm happy with the result. It's the last architectural work I did."

"The space is just…" Willow couldn't find the words to express her feelings.

As they walked back down between the vines, Willow listened to Alan and realized how comfortable they still felt in each other's presence, as if the past years had been erased and they were once again together. She had been amazed back then at how he seemed to see through her, and she missed that. James had never been like that, and Philip was a long story that had diminished with time past.

"Are you hungry?" Suddenly, Alan stopped and turned to look at her. Before she could answer, he said, "I am, and lunch should be ready by now. Come on, let's go back up."

They returned to the main farmhouse, and Willow saw that a small wooden table and two wooden chairs had been set up under the wisteria-covered gazebo. Alan pulled out a chair for her. She sat down while Alan went inside the building. The view was spectacular, and Willow took off her glasses and leaned back, closing her eyes. It was so quiet except for the occasional birds and labourers working in the vineyard. It was warm for this time of the year, but she wasn't complaining. She opened her eyes when she heard Alan come back with two glasses and a bottle of wine in a bucket.

"Marie will be out with the food," he said as he placed everything on the table and proceeded to open the wine. "Your favourite." He poured the chilled wine into the glasses. He sat down opposite her and lifted his glass. "Here's to coincidences."

Willow smiled and said cheers, remembering that once she had said to him that there was no such thing as coincidences. There was a reason for things that happen. Willow wished she could believe that.

"This place is so peaceful," she said. "I'm glad you brought me."

"I thought you might like it." Alan smiled and looked into her eyes, and for a minute, they stared at each other without saying anything. At that moment, the silence was broken by a little girl, who brought a bowl of salad to the table.

"Hello, Josie," Alan said, "thank you for this. Did you prepare it?"

The little girl blushed. "No, Mommy did, but I helped pick them from the garden." She ran off as a woman came out with a pizza on a wooden board.

"Marie, this is Willow," Alan said as the woman placed it on the table.

"This looks delicious. Pizza, my favourite," Willow said to Marie.

"I know," Alan said, and yet again, Willow had to look at him trying to understand what he was trying to do here.

"Enjoy," Marie said and returned to the building.

"She's the housekeeper here, and she and her family take care of everything and everyone."

"Shall I?" Willow asked, pointing to the salad.

"By all means."

She served the salad onto both of their plates while Alan sliced up the pizza. Willow took a slice and placed it on her plate.

"Excuse the fingers," Willow said as she munched on the pizza. The crust was thin and crispy, melting in her mouth. "Unbelievable."

"I know, Marie makes the best pizza around here. It's the wood-fired oven that makes the whole difference."

After they had finished the pizza and salad and drank more than half the bottle, Willow wiped her mouth and fingers and said, "I'm full. What a meal."

Alan laughed. "You always enjoyed a good meal, as do I." He leaned back in his chair and looked out at the view.

They sat there for a while, Willow lost in her own thoughts, when Alan turned around and looked at her. "What happened to you, Willow?"

She was taken aback by the question. "What do you mean?"

"When I first met you twelve years ago, you were sad but also angry. Now you still look sad, but you look haunted, deeply hurt, as if you're wounded. What happened to you? It can't be just me."

Willow didn't know what to say. She knew that he had an uncanny ability to see through her, but this was unnerving, the way he seemed to know that something had happened to her.

"I don't know what you mean."

"I think you do. What happened? You just disappeared. You just ran off. It was never my intention to hurt you."

"But you did. You broke my heart. You hurt me at a time when I was most vulnerable."

"I know. It was just that—"

"Why? Just tell me why. What if I hadn't gone to that frightful evening? Would you have continued the lie? You knew how I felt about betrayal, you knew how my husband had lied to me, you knew how difficult it was for me to end a marriage of thirty years. The time we were together—no, let me correct that, because we weren't really together. But the conversations we had, you talked about yourself as if you were single, nothing about your family, your children… Alan, you had children and you never let on. Why?"

Willow suddenly stood up in anger. All the memories of that time came rushing back, and she trembled with the emotions of betrayal, fresh as if time had rolled back. She felt the hot tears, but she shook them off, not wanting to show how she still felt, how it still hurt.

"You could have told me you were married when we first met. We could have become friends. I could... I could—"

"I didn't want you as a friend," Alan replied.

Willow turned around and looked down at him. "I wish I had never come here. I wish I hadn't met you again, not after all these years. It's just too painful. I shouldn't have come."

"Sit down." Suddenly, she saw that he was angry.

"Why are you angry?" Willow asked sarcastically as she sat down. "You don't agree with what I said? How you led me on? How you played on my vulnerability? How you—"

"Because I was falling in love with you!" Alan said suddenly, banging his hand on the table and rattling the glasses and plates. The sudden movement reminded Willow of James, and for a minute, she was frightened by the display of anger. However, when she looked up at him, she saw that it wasn't anger, but frustration that had made him do it.

"I'm sorry, I didn't mean to frighten you just there," Alan said. For a minute, Willow looked on, caught off guard with what he had said a minute ago.

"Did I hear you correctly just now?"

"Yes, I said I was falling in love with you," Alan repeated, looking her straight in the eye. Their gazes locked in silence, Willow trying to understand what he was thinking. Alan shook his head and got up, turning his back against her. Willow stared at him then, moments and words said twelve years ago flashing in front of her eyes. She took in a deep breath, suddenly sad with a feeling of loss, as if something had broken inside her. Not knowing what else to do, she took a sip of her wine. Alan was still standing, looking out over the vineyards.

The silence became unbearable. "Please, sit down," Willow finally said, her voice trembling. "Please." Alan turned around and came to sit back in his seat.

He looked at the bottle of wine that was nearly empty and poured the remaining wine into his glass. "We'll need another bottle before we continue to talk."

Willow watched him walk back inside. She still couldn't believe what he had just said. Alan came back out with a new bottle, which he uncorked, and he poured some of the chilled wine into her glass. He finally settled back and glanced at Willow. There was a tremendous sadness in his eyes, and it unsettled her.

"Willow, when I first met you—or should I say, saw you, I found you fascinating. Something just clicked, and I felt this warmth and tenderness inside me. Here was this woman, looking young for her age. You were poised, elegant, smart, with great taste, knew your way around, living by yourself, but sad. So sad. There were tears in your eyes. That was the first thing I'd noticed about you. On the outside, you seemed happy, but there was sadness in your eyes. You'd been hurt. I still don't know the full story, and now you look even more hurt. I knew it would take time for you to open up to anyone, especially a man you had recently met. But I felt this connection with you. I wanted to know you better.

"At the time that we met, Caroline, my wife, and I had become estranged. We were going through some difficult times, and she had become this person that I could hardly recognize. I suspected her of having an affair. She was out of the house most of the time, so much so that my sister Robyn stepped in to give me a hand while I tried to continue my business. My father was getting old and needed help with the vineyards, everything was in chaos. And when I saw you, I saw this tranquillity, this silence about you that appealed to me. After listening to your story on the plane, I hesitated and decided not to tell you what I was going through. I knew that at one point I would have to confront you, but each time, I was afraid to ruin the relationship that we had. So, I continued the lie."

Alan took a long sip from his wine. Willow thought, *What the heck,* and drank from her glass as well.

"We didn't know what was going on with Caroline, what, with her behaviour and dramatic personality changes. I couldn't recognize the woman I was married to for twenty-five years. We had wonderful daughters, Daisy and Grace, grown up by that time. I was doing what I loved, architecture, and she was an editor at a prominent publishing company. The changes weren't sudden, but instead gradual so that I didn't suspect that it was something more serious. She became impulsive, she stopped taking care of herself and the house and us. It was just about the time after… well, you know, after the incident at the gala that Caroline became seriously ill. It was just too painful. She changed, started to forget things, became a stranger to us all, when she was diagnosed with frontotemporal dementia. I always thought dementia happened in older people, but this type had no age discrimination.

"When you love someone with dementia, you lose them more and more every day. They go through different stages when they go into care and when they die. 'Rapidly shrinking brain' is how the doctors described it to me. As the brain slowly dies, the person changes physically and eventually forget who their loved ones are, gradually become bedridden, unable to move and unable to eat or drink. It was so hard to see your partner in life not recognize you, your children. I couldn't let her be by herself, so I needed a full-time nurse to look after her. She just disintegrated in front of our eyes, lost her appetite, stared blankly in front of her. She became socially inappropriate. She kind of started living in a world of her imagination. It came to a point that we couldn't take care of her at home. I reluctantly placed her in an institution that specialized with dementia. She died two years later. She was just fifty-two years old."

"Was there no cure?" Willow finally asked.

"No, there's no cure for frontotemporal disorders, and no way to slow it down or even prevent it. There are ways to manage the symptoms, but you need a team of specialists, and that's why I placed her in the institution. I had to think of our family and…" Alan stopped and looked down. "The day I saw you at the airport, it was as if I had found a kindred spirit. It just felt right. It was as if I had known you all my life."

"I didn't know," Willow said in a soft voice.

"I was going to explain everything to you, but you just ran away from me. I tried calling you, but you wouldn't answer, and I left so many voice mails, but you never replied. I sent you emails, and you ignored those too. I called Jasmine and she said that you were too depressed and didn't want to hear from me. I even talked with Francis."

Willow suddenly looked up. "Francis? You talked to Francis?"

"Yes, I did. I invited him for lunch and asked for his help, knowing how close you two were. He advised me to let you go, worrying about how you would feel once you heard my side of the story. He said that since you had been hurt so badly by your ex-husband, you would find it difficult to manage your feelings with me, and that overall, it would be disruptive to your mental health at the time."

"Francis never mentioned this to me," Willow answered.

"We promised each other to not tell you. For the best, anyway, so I stopped trying to reach you after the note I left. Are you still in contact with him?"

"From time to time. He's retired now, even though retirement has a different meaning for him. He's built himself a house on an island and lives there with his two dogs and a new lady friend. I had not seen him or talked to him since my second… second marriage, but we've recently reconnected." Willow broke off suddenly, remembering those days. The arguments she had with James about Francis. How she was forced to break contact because of how James had threatened her.

By this time, it was late afternoon, and Willow noticed that they had practically finished the second bottle of wine. Surprisingly, she felt clear-headed. "It's getting late. Shouldn't we be going back?"

"You're right, we should be going back," he replied unwillingly. They both got up. Marie came out as she heard them leaving.

"Thank you, Marie, for a delicious pizza," Willow said as Alan embraced the old woman.

"Thanks, Marie. See you soon." They both waved back at her as they got into the jeep. Roxy stayed behind. It was a silent drive, both lost in their thoughts, and by the time they arrived at the winery, the sun was getting ready to set.

Alan parked the jeep. "I have to go back home tonight."

"I understand. I'm leaving tomorrow morning too."

"But I would like to see you again. May I call you?" Alan asked.

Willow looked at him for a moment. "Of course you can."

"Good. May I get your contact information from the reception?" For a split second, they stared at each other.

"They have my phone number and email. Thank you for today. It has been most rewarding in every way."

"But you never told me about yourself," Alan replied.

"That's for another day," Willow replied, thankful that he hadn't pressed her.

"Do you want me to drop you off at your suite?"

"No thank you, the walk will do me good. Drive safely back. We did have two bottles of wine."

Alan laughed. "Don't worry." He stood there for a while by the jeep, looking at her. "I'm glad we did this."

She smiled back at him and then slowly turned around to walk up the hill toward her suite.

The next morning, when Willow got up, there was a lot going on in her mind. She looked forward to going back home so that she could sit and think about all that had happened. She knew she also had to tell Jasmine. After having breakfast and packing her things, she drove down to the reception area to check out.

"Good morning, Yvonne," Willow said to the young woman who was again there on duty.

"Good morning, ma'am. Checking out?" she asked.

"Yes, please," replied Willow as she took out her credit card.

"Ma'am, it's been paid for, and we have reimbursed your deposit as well."

Willow looked up in surprise. "What? How? There must be…"

"You are a guest of the company, and we also have a case of wine for you. I will have it delivered to your car." Yvonne reached for the phone, and as she was talking, Willow realized it must have been Alan who had arranged all this. She put away her card as Yvonne finished her call.

"Hope to see you again, ma'am, have a nice drive back. There will be someone outside to help you with the wine."

Willow thanked her and walked outside to find a young man with a case in his arms. She walked quickly to her car and opened the trunk. "Thank you," she said as the young man put it in and walked away.

She entered her car and, for a minute, did nothing. This meant, of course, that she would have to call him to thank him, and she wondered if that was exactly what Alan had planned. She smiled to herself, started the car, and slowly drove out.

She returned home late in the afternoon after picking up her dogs, who were overexcited to see her. After parking her car, she let them run around as she took out first her suitcase, then the case of wine, and brought them inside one by one. The dogs also came running in, thirsty and hungry, so she fed them and then went upstairs to change into something comfortable. By the time she came back downstairs, the dogs were sleeping, calmed down by coming home.

She looked at the case she had placed on the kitchen counter and then opened the fridge, looking for the bottle of wine she always had as a backup. There was her bottle of her rosé, so she uncorked it and poured herself a generous glass. She again looked at the case and went ahead and opened it. She thought that there might be a note or something inside— and there it was, an envelope with Alan's distinctive cursive handwriting. She picked up the envelope and went to sit at her comfortable couch in the living room. She took a sip of her wine and opened the envelope. There was a card inside, and her heart skipped a beat. *Why am I nervous? Why am I excited?* she thought to herself. *It's just a note.*

Willow,

You can't imagine what it has meant to me to see you again after all these years. I never got the chance to sort things out with you, and that had been troubling me ever since. I realized when I saw you again that I wasn't over you. Now that we've both reached a certain stage in our lives, I would like to see more of you. I have obtained your phone number from the reception, but here is mine if you care or ever want to call first. Enjoy the wine. That's what brought us back together.

Alan

Willow leaned back and took another sip of her wine. Making a gift of a case of wine was a very subtle way of Alan telling her that he knew she would want to call to thank him. She smiled wryly. That was a part of him that she always liked. Willow got up to pick up her phone from the kitchen counter and came back to sit down again. She first dialled Jasmine.

"Mom! You're back, good, how did it go?" Jasmine asked.

"You don't want to know," Willow replied.

"Why, what happened? Did something happen?" Jasmine asked, worried.

"Yes, something did happen, something big. I saw Alan," Willow replied.

There was silence.

"Jasmine? Did you hear me?" Willow asked.

"I hear you. How did you feel when you saw him?"

"He owns the winery."

"What?"

"I know, they just bought the whole estate but never got around to giving the details on their website. That's why I never saw his name," Willow said.

"How did you meet him then?" Jasmine asked.

"We literally bumped into each other. Then the next day, we had lunch and talked." Another silence. This time, Willow waited for Jasmine to talk.

"How do you feel about all this? Last time you two were together wasn't at all pretty, to say the least."

"I know. He's been a widower for the last eleven years. Apparently, his wife Caroline was diagnosed with a sort of dementia and had to be placed in hospice after we broke off. I never knew, of course. How could I? He also evidently gave up architecture and is now managing their family-owned vineyard and winery."

"How do you feel? Did you like seeing him again?" Jasmine asked tenderly.

Willow hesitated, finding it difficult to describe her emotions. "I did like seeing him again, unfortunately. I should be more in control of my feelings, I know," she finally admitted.

"Why 'unfortunately'? Maybe this time is the right time, who knows? Why don't you give it a chance again? What have you got to lose?" Jasmine said.

"That was something James said to me when we first met," Willow reminisced.

"I didn't want to bring up bad memories. I'm sorry."

"No, no, it's not your fault. I'm going to give Alan a call because he graciously covered my stay at the vineyard, and he also gave me a case of my rosé as a gift."

Jasmine laughed. "See, he made the first move. Just take it one day at a time and see where it goes. I worry about you being alone so much."

"I know you do. But that's how I ended up with James in the first place. I'm afraid of unsettling myself again, that's all."

"Well, keep me posted. And if you need to talk, please call me or write, OK?" Jasmine asked.

"I will, take care. I love you," Willow said.

"Love you back."

Willow put down her phone and thought of what Jasmine had said. *What am I so afraid of?* She took another sip from her glass and looked at her phone. She knew she had to make another phone call before calling Alan. She picked up her phone and dialled.

⤮

In another part of the world, the sun was rising over the mountains, and the sky had turned different colours of orange and purple. The sea shimmered with the soft sun rays reflecting off the water. It was very early in the morning, but Francis was always an early riser. He was standing on the veranda of his house with a mug of steaming coffee, admiring the view. His cell phone rang, and for a minute, he waited without answering. He knew it could be the call he was expecting, but somehow, he wanted to delay acknowledging it. He put down his coffee, and then removed his phone from his pocket. He glanced down and answered it.

"Hello, my dear." There were a few minutes of silence.

"You are an exceptional man. I cannot believe what you have done."

"What I've done?" Francis asked, surprised.

"A couple of months ago, we were talking, and I had mentioned my penchant for rosé wine, and you suggested I try out the rosé from Laid-Back Estate Winery." He didn't reply. "Did you know?"

Suddenly, Francis knew what Willow was asking. "Yes, I did."

"And when I mentioned to you that I was going to pay a visit to the winery, did you think that I might stumble upon him by accident?"

"I hoped you would. Did you?"

"As a matter of fact, I did. We had a long talk. Alan mentioned his talk with you way back then."

Francis paused before replying. "I thought it best that you never knew of my conversation with Alan. At the time, I believed I was doing the right thing by you in asking him to stay away. You're a very emotional woman, and sometimes, because of it, you can make rash decisions. It was an impossible situation, and you didn't need the extra burden. However, now I feel it was my fault that by separating you from Alan, I pushed you into James's arms. Willow, you're a remarkable lady and have so much to gain and give. Please release the pressure that you put on yourself all the time and be happy with what you have. You're a strong woman, and life tests us all the time."

"I wish I could believe in you. You make everything so simple."

"I just nudged you in the right direction, and this time, it worked out. I hope you and Alan can make amends for the past."

"He told me the whole story about his wife and the troubled years."

"What about you?"

"No, I haven't told him anything yet," Willow replied.

"All will work out well for you," Francis said. "Just relax, enjoy, and let life take its course. Everything will work out fine. You know that from deep in my heart, I wish you all the best, that you stay healthy, keep a good spirit, and be happy."

"Francis, you sound like you're saying goodbye."

"No. I'm in the moment and focus on what's given to me every day, deal with it, and enjoy the day as much as possible. Every day you're not full of joy and bliss is gone, will never come back—and it can't be recalled either, so let's get with the program. Do things that you enjoy and be grateful for your family and life in general. There are many people that love you and care for you, and I'm one of them.

Now, you need to choose your path and walk on it by yourself, make your own decisions. You have enough experience."

"I miss you not being here. I just wanted to share the news with you. You've played the most important role in all of this."

"The reason is that you're given a life, and you can do whatever is right for you. Alan will take care of you." Francis cleared his throat as if something was stuck, but he just knew that the longer he talked to her, the worse it was going to get. "I'm always here for you. We're soulmates and there for each other."

"My thoughts are with you."

"As are mine."

"I'll miss you."

"My dear, darling soulmate. Remember what I told you some years ago?"

"You said there was no such thing as a coincidence."

"What happens happens for a reason. That reason was you, Willow."

Francis placed his phone back in his pocket and picked up his coffee again. The sun had risen by now, and it promised to be a beautiful day. He took a sip. It took a few minutes for him to compose himself back. He turned around and entered the house.

CHAPTER SIX

Consequences

"Good morning, Mom, how are you?" Jasmine asked on the phone.

"I'm fine, just getting ready to go out and pick some veggies. How about you?"

"Ahh, busy as ever, lots of meetings today up until six o'clock."

"Oh my, are you taking care of yourself? Stay safe, please."

"Always am. So, any plans for your upcoming birthday? Sweet sixty-five?"

"Stop that. I can't believe I'm going to be officially a senior now. Anyway, I already did my travelling as a gift to myself."

"I'm so sorry I can't be there for you this year."

"I know, sweetheart, I know. I'll just open a bottle of champagne and get drunk."

"We'll open a bottle here too and say cheers over the internet. Or you could invite Alan over for dinner so you're not lonely," Jasmine casually said.

Willow hesitated before replying, "I couldn't do that. We're not that... umm..."

"You could say it's a thank you. There you go, a good excuse. You can show off your house and garden to him. I know you would love to do that."

"Come on, he owns vineyards, lives in this fantastic, renovated barn and other… He doesn't want to see my house or my garden, for that matter, I'm sure he's seen better…"

"Mom, stop it. You always undervalue yourself. Please stop this 'I'm not good for anything' stuff."

"My life experience tells me a different story."

"You told me how much you enjoy his company."

"What if he says no? I mean, if he laughs or refuses…"

"Mom! Is he that kind of man? You're not making any sense. I don't believe you from what you've been telling me about him, and what happened years ago doesn't count anymore."

"I don't know, we'll see."

"Just give him a call. Invite him for dinner. Don't tell him it's your birthday if you don't want to. That way, if he accepts, you'll know it wasn't just about your birthday."

"I don't know really, I…"

"Just call, please. Do it for me. I hate seeing you being all by yourself."

And lose my sanity? My well-being? Having to live another bad experience, as if I didn't have enough in the past? Willow thought. "I'll think about it."

"Please."

"I said I'll think about it."

"OK, Mom, you know best. I love you."

"I love you too. Talk to you soon."

How is it that when you reached senior age, your daughter started acting like your mother? She knew Jasmine wanted the best for her as she did for Jasmine. And Jasmine was right about being lonely. But she still hesitated. She didn't want to go down on a familiar path and end up being miserable. She had learnt her lesson for sure, and she could be in control at her home. How could she not be? She was becoming a senior, so what did she have to lose by inviting a charming man for dinner? And if he refused, so be it, it wasn't as if they were… what? *I think I'll just go and pick up some veggies, just to clear up my mind. That's it. I can always decide later,* she thought.

Willow picked up her basket and walked outside onto the patio. The sun was out, and she could feel the change in the air. Spring was always her favourite season. Everything started to grow back from a sleepy winter, buds on all the rose bushes, the trees pushing out their leaves to catch more of the sunlight. The grass was a plush green, and there was a slight breeze caressing the wildflowers. She had several trees in the garden and some fruit trees providing her a season of jams and jellies. The vegetable garden was on the side of the house right after the conservatory. A pebbled path took Willow straight to it.

She had several bird houses and feeders hanging from the trees, so she checked to see if there was enough feed to go around. Quails and blue jays were a favourite visitor, along with different coloured finches and sparrows. From time to time, ducks would fly in from the lake to feed. They had started coming in last autumn—first one, then two, and now they would fly in five or six. It was as if they knew when she would come out, because the minute she put feed on the ground, a group of them would fly in. There was also a pair of doves that visited. She didn't know if they were the same, but they seemed to enjoy their time in her garden. *And let's not forget the hummingbirds and butterflies, and the occasional squirrel who visits the hazelnut and walnut trees,* Willow thought. She had started to place large pots of flowers under the trees where it was difficult to plant directly in the soil, and over the years, she had added different quaint objects around them. She was always on the lookout for objects for her garden whenever she went to the flea market and thrift stores. Jasmine described it as Alice in Wonderland. And Willow thought, *I suppose I am the Mad Hatter, ha ha!*

During the summer, she would hang solar lanterns on the branches, which created an eerie fairy-like atmosphere at night. She wanted to install a small pond with maybe a waterfall feature so the ducks or other birds could enjoy themselves. She knew the birds enjoyed the bird bath she had out for them. The garden was quite large—maybe too much for a single person—but it was her paradise. This was the place that had calmed her down through and after her troubled years with James, and she had no need to go anywhere. Willow stopped midway and pulled out her cell phone from her pocket. She stared at it for a minute, then went ahead with her call.

"Hello Alan, it's Willow."

"Well, hello to you, this is a nice surprise."

"I hope this is a good time to call. I mean, if you're busy, I can call—"

"It's a good time. How are you?"

"I'm good, how about you?"

"I'm at the vineyard today."

"Oh, OK, I just wanted to ask if you would like to come to dinner this Friday?" Silence. Unbearable seconds of silence. "Look, if you—"

Alan cut her off. "I would love to, but I can't."

"Oh… all right, I understand, maybe another—"

"I would love to, but it's just that I don't know where you live." Another second of silence. "Willow?"

Oh, just trying to control the relief in my voice, Willow thought. "Of course. It's 55 Willow Drive, Sumorlan. The road is a dead end, and I'll buzz you in when you arrive at the gates."

"55 Willow Drive? Is this a coincidence?" Alan laughed.

Willow laughed back. "Yes, totally."

"What time would you like me to come, and is there anything you'd like me to bring?" Alan asked.

"How about six? We can enjoy the sunset and the garden."

"Sounds good. I'll see you then."

"Oh, Alan, I just wanted to know if there's anything that you don't like to eat or are allergic to?"

"Turnips."

"What?"

Alan chuckled.

"Funny. I'll be sure there are no turnips for dinner. See you then," Willow said.

"For sure. Bye."

"Bye." *There, done. Oh my, did I just invite him for dinner? Argh, Jasmine, you got to me there*, Willow thought.

Invitation done, Willow texted Jasmine.

Yay! Good job! I love you!

Willow sent back a heart emoji. Suddenly, she felt the need to sit down. And the first thing that came to mind was, *What would I cook?*

❧

Alan put his phone in his pocket and started walking down the vineyard.

"Who was that?" Daisy asked as she walked toward him.

"Willow. She asked me to dinner this coming Friday."

"Good on you. It's about time. I like her."

Alan looked at his daughter fondly. "I do too. She's so different now. There's something about her that I just can't figure out yet."

Daisy turned around to look at him. "Do I sense the fire rekindling again, like before?" Alan looked at her, questioningly. "Dad, I might have been young back then, but not that young to not know there was chemistry between you two."

"How do you know that? I never…"

"Aunt Robyn."

"I should have known," Alan said, frustrated. "She's always meddling in my affairs."

"Someone had to. Mom was never there for you. We could all see that."

"Come here," Alan said, giving Daisy a hug. "You were mature for your age back then. I always knew it would be difficult to hide things from you."

"Of course, I don't know how it all started," Daisy said, glancing up at him with a smile.

"Oh, no, you don't. You're never hearing that story."

Daisy shrugged. "I tried."

Alan smiled. "Willow and I have been together a couple of times, so…"

"Together?" she said, giving him a dirty look.

"It's not what you think. Anyway, we're too old for those kinds of shenanigans," Alan replied.

"No, you're not. You're a very charming, handsome man, and any woman, no matter what age, would love to be with you."

"Well, thank you, daughter of mine, but I'm not rushing this time. I just enjoy her company."

"That's a starter for sure." Daisy laughed.

"You're impossible." Alan laughed as well. "So, what do you think I should take?"

"Flowers would be nice. You said she has a garden. Maybe a potted plant, something exotic?" Daisy winked.

"Enough already, I'll take some wine."

"That'll be a surprise for sure, how original," Daisy said sarcastically.

Alan gave up with a gesture of his hands. "I'll think of something," he mumbled and walked down the vineyard.

After much deliberation, Willow had prepared a cheese plate and baked a baguette for the special evening with Alan. They could enjoy that on the patio with some wine. For dinner, it was a quiche with a salad prepared from her veggie garden, and for dessert, chocolate mousse with champagne (or bubbles, as Jasmine would call it). She could always offer espresso as well.

Since the flowers in her garden hadn't fully bloomed yet, Willow bought some fragrant lilies and placed them in the large vase on the centre of her coffee table in the living room. Immediately, their fragrance filled up the area. She looked at the flowers, remembering that Alan had brought the same kind of bouquet twelve years ago. She wondered if he would remember. She had set the table outside on the patio with her favourite china and crystal glasses. The silverware was out, the napkins nicely rolled through silver rings. She was going all out tonight. What was the point of owning things if you weren't going to use them and they'd been out of use for several years?

Willow glanced around to check how things looked. Everything was ready on the counter, the champagne and wine were cooling in the fridge, and she liked what she saw as she glanced up from the kitchen sink. She had opened the French doors leading out to the patio, and the view this evening looked spectacularly beautiful. She sighed and tried to relax. Now was the most important moment of the day. What would she wear?

Alan too was taking his time dressing. Normally, he would just throw on something comfortable, but he knew it would be important to take care of what he wore tonight. Maybe navy-blue dress pants with a blue and white striped shirt and a sweater? Willow had mentioned that they would sit outside, and it might be cool, so he pulled out his cashmere sweater. *Just in case,* he thought. He put on his boat loafers and looked at himself in the mirror. *Not bad, Alan, for a man of sixty-two.* Nice hair, longish, with grey streaks. Some tan on the face from working outside.

There was a knock on his door, and he glanced down from his bedroom to see Daisy walking in. He pulled himself away from the mirror. "Come in, it's open," he said sarcastically and, with one last look, walked down the stairs.

"Dad, you look amazing." Daisy had come to check up on him. "I haven't seen you look this well-dressed for some time now."

"I know. It's been some time," Alan said, turning around. "You like?" He pirouetted for her.

Daisy gave a thumbs-up. "So, what did you decide to take her?" She looked around.

"Wine for sure."

"Oh, Dad, why..."

"And an exotic plant. I bought her a gardenia, potted and all. It already has buds on it. I put it outside, come look." They walked out through the side door.

The gardenia was in a magnificent azure blue pot. "That's beautiful. Willow is going to love it."

"You think?" Alan asked.

"I know so."

"OK, well, I should be going. I have to find out where the house is. Never been in that part of town."

"Where does she live?" asked Daisy.

"In Sumorlan. 55 Willow Drive." Daisy gave him a questioning look, then looked at her cell phone. "It should take you about seventy minutes to get there, it says. Drive safe now. Do you want George to take you? Or I can drive you?" she asked.

Alan glared at her sideways. "I can drive. And if I can't, I'll text you."

"Promise?"

"I promise."

"Here, let me carry the pot for you," Daisy said, picking it up. They walked toward the garage.

"So, which car are you taking?"

"I'll take the convertible."

"Ahh, sophisticated and fancy, are we?" Daisy laughed.

"Something has to be." Alan laughed with her while she placed the pot in the front seat.

"Enjoy your night out. I love you."

"I love you too." He got in the car and drove out.

An hour later, Alan was in front of the gates. *Well, this is a surprise. Where am I?* he thought, staring at the two tall wrought-iron gates with an elaborate floral design at the end of the road. *Does such a place even exist?* He peered through the front window. Alan could see a huge willow tree that halfway blocked the outline of the house. A short-gravelled driveway opened onto a clearing.

There was a box with a buzzer on the left side of the gate. He noticed the small camera on top. *I guess I need to get out of the car to reach it,* Alan thought. Just as he turned to open the car door, the gates swung open slowly. He drove up the gravel driveway and stopped at the clearing in front of the house. *Are those purple shutters?*

The building looked like an elaborate English cottage, built with slate, with large French windows, and with—yes, he had seen cor-rectly—purple wooden shutters. There was a huge wisteria climbing above the front door and ivy on the sides just barely visible at this time of the year. The combination of colours was striking. He got out of the car just as the front door opened, and there was Willow, followed by three dogs that came out running and barking. The dogs sniffed him, then decided that he was all right and ran out into the garden behind.

Alan stood still for a moment. It took several seconds to catch his breath. The first thing he noticed were her earrings again. Willow was wearing the delicate earrings of small crystals that he remembered so fondly. She had put up her white hair, which always looked like it was ready to tumble down but never did. She was wearing a sleeveless long dress—*Purple to match the shutters,* Alan thought—flowing long and on top she wore a floral chiffon shirt, the colours vibrant and rich in hues of orange, with the sleeves ending at her elbows. On her feet were flats that matched her dress colour. Overall, she looked like an impressionist painting.

Alan must have stood there for a while, enjoying the vision, when Willow asked, "Sorry about the girls, they just get excited to see someone. Did you have difficulty finding your way here?"

"No, no, but what is this place?" Alan turned around, looking at the gates and the big willow tree.

"My secret garden," Willow replied. "Come on in, I'll show you around." Alan opened the passenger door and slowly took out the gardenia. As he turned around with the pot in his hands, Willow cried out, "Is that a gardenia? Oh my goodness, it is. I've always wanted one. This is amazing."

It sure is, Alan thought. *Thank you, Daisy.* "Could you grab the bottle of wine from the car?" He asked as he followed her, noticing the double garage on the side and several outbuildings in the back as the dogs rushed in after them.

ⁿⁿⁿ

"I was in the kitchen when I saw you arrive." Willow remarked as she closed the front door and looked at him. He looked incredibly handsome, even looked younger, though she noticed the extra wrinkles around the eyes and his skin that had somewhat softened over the years. He was elegantly dressed, as she remembered.

Alan looked back, and at first, Willow thought, *Am I not dressed properly? Or do I not have good taste? No, I've always had good taste, and*

I'm always very colour-coordinated, so it can't be that. Maybe the earrings were too much? She had been careful to not put on too much makeup, just some mascara and a natural-coloured lipstick. She had put on some perfume though, and now, she was anxious if it was presumptuous of her to do so.

"Here, let me get that from you." Willow reached out to take the pot from him and handed over the bottle of wine. She started walking as Alan followed looking around. After passing the small entry, they walked down into her big kitchen. She was playing smooth jazz in the background.

"This house is amazing," Alan remarked as he passed in front of the two large French doors that led out to the patio. He placed the wine bottle on the kitchen counter. They passed through the cosy living room with a big wood fireplace and comfortable couches and armchairs. The walls were full of paintings. He stopped in front of one, a painting of storks in fiery red and orange. "Amazing," Alan exclaimed, then his eyes went to the signature at the right-hand corner. "You did this?" he asked.

"Yes, there are several of my paintings among the others from my father's collection." She didn't add the thought *You never got to see them twelve years ago.*

"It's exquisite," Alan said, turning to follow her through, smiling at the lilies in the vase. There was a staircase on the side that led upstairs as they entered another living space. This one had a large TV, a comfortable couch in front, and an antique desk in the corner with a computer. Behind were bookshelves filled to the top.

"My go-to place," Willow said without turning. "The original house was smaller, but we made some additions throughout the years."

Willow passed through and turned left, where she and Alan were suddenly blinded by bright sunlight. It was her traditional-style conservatory. Plants and flowers of all sizes and varieties lay along the windowsills and on the floor. In the centre was a cosy love seat facing the outside, with two peacock chairs on the side and a coffee table with many books strewn carelessly on top. Willow removed one of the pots that was on a high plant stand and replaced it with the gardenia.

"There, it's found its place. Shall we go out?" Willow asked. "You can feel summer coming around the corner, the weather is warmer than usual this year." She walked back toward the kitchen. Alan followed her outside onto the patio, which opened onto a vast garden with tall trees.

"Would you like to walk around before we sit down?" Willow asked.

"Please, I would love to," Alan replied, and together, they went down the few steps that led to the garden, the dogs following right behind. Alan turned around to look at the house admiring the landscape.

"This is truly a treasure. It looks like it's out of a fairy tale."

"I thought so too. James, my late husband, wasn't too keen on it, but I could see the potential."

"Why wasn't he keen?"

"Oh, he said the land was too big, the house too old, and that I couldn't cope with it. He didn't like gardening or anything remotely like gardening, but he enjoyed the view." Willow continued walking.

"Here, I want to put a pond," she said, pointing, "for the birds and ducks that fly in. Maybe with a small waterfall. I like the sound of water."

"Do you have anything underground here, like irrigation or pipes?" Alan asked.

"No, I had it inspected, nothing there. It would be nice. What do you think?" Willow turned to look at him.

Alan looked at the house, then at the garden. "It's a good spot, I think. You could put a bench next to it and enjoy the view. I believe you can see the sunset from behind the trees. Where do the ducks come from?" he asked, following Willow toward the side of the house.

"I'm guessing from the lake. It started with one male, which I named Rudolph. Then a couple of days later, he brought along a friend, named him Darcy." Willow laughed. "Then one day, they brought their female friends or mates, Geraldine and Marigold. Of course, I don't know if they were the same ducks, but I'd like to think so." She walked up a couple of steps to where the greenhouse was. Next to it was a vegetable garden, all nicely planted.

"Quite the setup you have here," Alan remarked.

"Keeps me busy. My great-uncle used to say that if you play around with soil, you'll never get old. He had a green thumb, and so did my grandmother. Mom, well… Mom was the type who would cut down a tree if it blocked her view. My father liked gardening, so I guess I have the genes from both sides. I have the heart of a farmer," Willow replied, turning behind the house.

"Impressive land. Why not a pool? You have the space for it."

"James was against the idea, and after he passed away, I thought it would be too much trouble. And not only that, but expensive to upkeep."

"Don't get me wrong, but James seems like he didn't like whatever you did. How did you end up marrying him?" Willow looked up at him then with troubled eyes.

"I'm sorry. I shouldn't have said that. Forgive me." Alan said softly.

"It's all right, I sometimes ask myself that question." As they walked back to the house, Willow turned around and asked, "Are you hungry?"

"Famished," Alan answered.

"Good, I'll get things going, then. You can sit outside while I go into the kitchen."

"No, I'll join you. I want to help. But just give me five minutes, I want to look outside again."

"You know where to find me," Willow said, walking into the kitchen with the dogs. She saw him standing at the spot she had pointed out for the pond, looking around, then at the house and then behind him at the trees. He came back in a couple of minutes later.

"You have a lovely home."

"I paid a high price for it," Willow answered and instantly regretted saying it. Alan seemed not to have heard her.

"What can I do?" he asked, looking around the big rustic-style kitchen. The cupboards and design were traditional, but the appliances were high-end quality. Willow reached for the French door of the fridge to take a bottle of wine out.

Alan smiled when he saw the bottle. "Your favourite, I presume?"

"Yes," Willow said, "it's from around here, this nice winery I discovered. The rosé is exceptionally good."

"Hmm, I remember a woman saying that it was like fresh spring water with the slight scent of summer."

Willow turned around in surprise. "How do you know that?" she asked.

"You told me," Alan said.

"So, I did. Here." She handed him the corkscrew.

"What, no fancy corkscrew? I would have imagined you going for one of those fancy ones."

Willow smiled at him standing behind the counter. "I like traditional things."

Alan went out to get the glasses. "These are beautiful glasses."

"I inherited those from my parents. Most of the classic furniture and pieces you see are from them. My father was quite the collector." Alan looked up questioningly. "Both passed away."

"I'm sorry to hear about your parents."

"Don't be, it's been five years now. I do miss them, though. Now I'm the last matriarch of the family. It's just me and Jasmine."

Alan poured the wine and placed the bottle in the wine cooler she gave him. "So"—he raised his glass— "thank you for the invitation."

"Thank you for coming. Cheers," Willow said, clinking her glass against his. They both sipped. "Have a seat." She pointed toward the high stool. "I have to prepare the salad and put the quiche in the oven."

The dogs settled down next to Alan. He leaned down to pet them on the head. "That's Honey," Willow said. "The black one is Sophie, and the smaller one is Lucie." All three dogs looked up at her as she said their names. "Good girls. Now you have to wait for your dinner."

"You like to cook, I guess?" Alan said as he looked around the kitchen.

"Oh, yes. These days, I don't have to cook as much as I used to, but I enjoy baking bread and making jam from the garden," Willow replied as she put the quiche in the oven and pulled the already-washed salad ingredients from the strainer. She prepared the salad in a large bowl.

"Are those all from the garden?" Alan asked.

"Yes, everything. I've become quite self-sufficient."

He glanced at a mason jar with some sort of sauce in it. "And what's that?"

"Oh, that's the salad dressing. I like to be prepared in advance. A habit of mine." Willow took the cheese platter from the side and lifted the cover to display an array of cold cuts, as well as cheese and grapes. "I also have a home-baked baguette to go with that. The quiche should be ready in forty-five minutes."

"You baked a baguette at home?" Alan asked, surprised.

Willow just smiled. "Help me carry these out to the table." He took the platter from her hand, and she brought the bread board with the bread knife.

"I'll get your glass," Alan said and went inside.

Willow was placing everything on the table as he came back. He walked around and pulled out her chair. For a minute, Willow was startled but sat down, and Alan gently pushed her forward.

"I keep forgetting what a gentleman you are," Willow said, laughing. "Long time since I've seen anyone do that."

Alan walked around and sat facing her. "This looks amazing."

"Please, serve yourself. Here, I'll cut the bread." She slowly cut diagonal pieces and covered the rest of the bread with a teacloth. Alan leaned forward to take a piece. He popped a cube of cheese in his mouth and took a bite of the bread.

"This is good."

She smiled at him. "It's been a while since I entertained. Jasmine and Sam sometimes come and stay, but they're so busy these months, and now they're away at a conference."

"I'm the backup, then."

"No, no, of course not," Willow replied, suddenly flushed.

"I'm kidding, I'm just grateful you invited me."

They ate for a while, enjoying each other's company as they did twelve years ago.

"I'll get the quiche, should be ready," Willow said getting up.

Willow came back and placed the quiche on the trivet. "It's hot, be careful," she said, cutting a piece and placing it on Alan's plate. She sat down and watched as Alan ate.

"Is it good?" Willow asked.

"No, it's terrible, don't eat," Alan said jokingly. Willow felt relieved. They sat talking and eating as the sky gradually became darker.

"And now, it's time for dessert," Willow said, getting up. "Do you still want to sit outside? You're not cold?"

"No, no, I have a sweater somewhere here." He followed her in. Willow went to take out two small bowls of chocolate mousse and two flutes from the fridge. He looked down at them questioningly.

"I thought we might have some champagne with dessert," Willow said without turning around. She reached for the champagne in the fridge. "Here. While you open that, I'll get some candles for the table and grab a shawl." Willow came back with two glass tubes with white candles inside, as well as a purple shawl around her shoulders.

"I'll just light these and come back for the bowls."

Alan followed her with both glasses in one hand and the bottle in the other, placing them on the table. He sat down as she came out with the bowls. Suddenly, soft lights came on around the garden.

"Ahh, the solar lights came on. Perfect timing," Willow remarked, sitting down. "Jasmine loves lights of any kind. She puts them up for me."

"They are lovely. So, what are we celebrating?" Alan asked, lifting his champagne flute.

"It's my birthday," Willow replied calmly.

His hand froze in the air. "Your birthday? Why didn't you tell me?"

"I didn't want you to feel that you had to accept my dinner invitation because it was my birthday."

"And why would you think that I wouldn't accept your invitation?"

Willow remained quiet. "I'm not very good at this," she finally said.

"Not good at what?" Alan insisted.

"I've been isolated these past few years, and I think I've forgotten how to… to do this," Willow finally said, sipping her champagne. They looked at each other then. Willow hoped he would not continue in this line of questions.

"If I remember correctly, you must be turning sixty-five. Officially a senior now."

"Don't you know it's impolite to remind women of their age?" Willow said, laughing, relieved that the moment had passed without her breaking down.

"I like the white hair, though, it's quite striking."

"I first hesitated to let my hair go natural, then I saw one of my friends who had turned pure white with a pixie cut. She looked beautiful, so I went ahead with it. At first it was short, then I let that go as well, even though women my age tend to have short hair," Willow said as she started to eat.

"You're nothing like women your age, believe me," Alan said softly and took a spoon of the chocolate mousse. His eyes widened. "Goodness! My word, what is this? It's so delicious and... and..."

"Decadent?" Willow added with her spoon in her hand.

"Yes, decadent is the word I was looking for." He closed his eyes, seemingly savouring the taste.

"You look ecstatic." Willow laughed.

"I am. Please, any time, just invite me for this."

"I do have some more," Willow said coyly, noticing that he had already finished.

Alan looked up at her, then at the empty bowl in his hand. "I shouldn't," he mumbled.

Willow got up, laughing, "You should. The bowls are small, and anyway, I'll get one for myself as well, it's my birthday," she said, walking inside to the kitchen. *Why is it that I feel so comfortable with him? Why is it that my feelings haven't changed these past twelve years?* she thought. She came back with two bowls in her hand. Alan poured more champagne.

"What an exquisite taste. Your secret recipe, I'm guessing. Care to share?" he asked as he started eating again.

"Yes, there's a secret ingredient, and I'm not telling."

"I like what you've done with the place," Alan remarked, looking around as he finished off his second bowl. "Like you said, it's a secret garden. A well-kept secret."

"It was a mess when I first found the house. It had been neglected for several years when the previous owners had passed away, and the family hadn't shown enough care. I think they just wanted to get rid of the place," Willow said.

"Didn't you find it too secluded?"

"No, in fact, it was just right for us at the time," Willow replied, then worried that he might ask more questions. "How about you? Do you miss architecture?"

"A little. I miss the designing part, but not the rush to meet customer's demands. Patrick runs it now, but my younger daughter Grace works there. She likes the busy, hectic city life."

"You have only two daughters, right?"

"Yes, though Caroline had a miscarriage when she was seven months pregnant. It was a boy. It took us a while to get over that."

"I'm sorry. I didn't want to bring up bad memories."

"Don't worry, it was a long time ago. What about you? Do you miss painting?" Alan asked, looking at her.

"I do, but it's just that I don't seem to have the inspiration to start again. Maybe sometime soon."

Alan glanced at his watch. "Well, your birthday is officially over."

"Is it that late? I didn't notice," Willow replied, also looking at her watch and saw that it was after midnight. "I'm surprised the girls didn't come out." They both got up and went inside.

"Did we drink all of this?" Alan asked, surprised when he saw the three empty bottles lined up on the counter.

"We sure did. Will you be all right driving back?" Willow asked with a worried tone.

"What kind of a winemaker would I be if I couldn't handle it?" Alan answered half-jokingly.

"Alan, I'm serious. We're not young anymore. It's after midnight, and you have a long drive." *Here goes,* she thought. "You're more than welcome to stay in my guest bedroom and go back in the morning."

Alan stood still, looking at her. A few seconds passed before he answered, "Are you sure?"

"I insist. I would hate the idea of something happening on the road, and we did drink a lot, although funnily enough, I don't feel the effect yet. Maybe tomorrow morning. The guest bedroom is always made up, so you don't have to worry."

"In that case…"

"Good, it's settled, then. Let me clear the table outside."

Alan followed her. "Do you want me to take the girls out while you do that?"

"Would you? Thank you." Willow walked back in with her hands full and called out for the dogs. They came barrelling down the staircase.

"Girls, be good now and go out with Alan." Willow pushed them all outside. Alan followed down the stairs to the garden.

What have I done? Willow thought. *Inviting him to stay.* It was a spur of the moment decision, but she hated the idea of him driving with the amount of alcohol they had drunk, and besides, he had accepted to stay. She busied herself with the cleaning up so that she wouldn't think of what she'd done. By the time she had put everything away, Alan had come back in with the girls following right behind.

"All done," he said while closing the patio doors.

"Thank you for that. Let me show you to your room." Willow turned off the lights and slowly walked up the staircase while Alan followed close by. The girls rushed by them.

The second level of the house was nearly as wide as downstairs. At the top of the stairs, Willow turned right and opened a door. She turned on the lights for the large bedroom, which had a queen bed facing the windows and nightstands at each side. On one side was a wall-to-wall closet, and on the opposite side, an antique chest with a TV on top. In front of the windows was a long ottoman.

"There's an ensuite," Willow said, pointing to the door next to the chest.

"This all looks very cosy," Alan said as he entered the room.

"This is where Jasmine and Sam stay whenever they visit. My bedroom is on the other side." Willow stopped, wondering why she had said that. "There are fresh towels in the bathroom, and you should find a spare toothbrush in the drawer." Alan looked at her questioningly. "I like to be prepared," Willow said. "Good night."

"Good night and thank you for this."

She smiled at him as she closed the door. She made her way to her room to get ready for bed. She sat in front of her vanity table in her nightgown, wondering what Alan was doing. The girls were sleeping on top of her bed. *Why did it feel good to have someone else in the house? Did I invite him to stay, expecting something else? Of course not.* However, she felt good whenever she was with him, and she enjoyed the casual banter they always had with each other.

"Off you go, girls," Willow softly said as she got under the covers. The dogs got off and then promptly jumped back on again as Willow settled in. It would take a while before she fell asleep.

When Willow finally woke up, it was early, as usual. It was five thirty, sunrise minutes away. The girls were already awake, licking her face and walking over her.

"OK, OK, I'm getting up." Willow laughed and went into her bathroom. She took a quick shower and got dressed in her jeans and a sweater. She made up her bed and slowly opened her bedroom door. She peeked at Alan's door. No sound. She walked down the staircase trying not to make a sound, but the girls ran down as usual, making as much noise as possible. *Oh well, so much for quiet,* Willow thought as she opened the patio doors and walked outside. There was a soft breeze, and the sun had risen behind the trees. She walked down the steps to check on the feeders and the garden.

Last night, before falling asleep, Alan had looked at the bed and slowly lifted the covers as a scent arose from the bed. *What is that?* he thought. *It literally smells like... like sunshine. So like Willow.* He then thought of her and wondered what she was thinking of.

Her invitation had caught him off guard, and he had said yes without thinking. He sat down on the bed and texted Daisy knowing she would be worried if she saw that he hadn't returned.

Staying overnight, had too much to drink. See you in the morning. While he started to undress, he received a text.

Way to go, Dad!

I'm staying in the guest bedroom. You have a dirty mind.

Sure. Sleep well.

Alan smiled as he got into bed. It was soft and comfortable, and that scent of sunshine somehow reminded him of his childhood. He fell asleep immediately.

He woke up to the sound of the dogs. He realized he had slept soundly through the night, not waking up for anything, and he felt revitalized. He got up and walked toward the windows. He saw Willow walking with the dogs. A rush of tenderness spread through his body. He went into the bathroom to clean up and quickly got dressed. He made up the bed and walked out to find Willow. The dogs heard him before she did. She turned around with the hose in her hand.

"Good morning, did we wake you?" she asked, returning to watering the vegetables.

"Yes, and no. I usually wake up early too. It's going to be a beautiful day," Alan said, looking around. Willow turned off the water and closed the fence gate. They slowly walked back to the house.

"Coffee?" she asked, entering the kitchen.

"Yes, please," Alan said, sitting down on one of the stools. He watched her as she prepared two cups.

"Milk or sugar?"

"No, black please."

"Ahh, just like me," Willow said and sat down next to him. "Did you sleep well? I hope everything was all right."

"Amazing. You know, just as I lifted the covers, there was this scent that—"

"Oh my goodness, was something wrong? I apologize, I didn't check—"

Alan cut her off. "Stop apologizing. Why do you always assume the worst? What happened to you, Willow?" She didn't answer, but her eyes clouded over. "I was going to say that I smelled sunshine, if you can ever smell that, and it reminded me of my childhood."

"I hang out the laundry in the sun whenever the weather permits it. The sun and wind create that smell," Willow answered, clearly relieved.

"My mother used to do that at the farm, that's what it reminded me of," Alan said, sipping at his coffee.

"My grandmother told me once that while she was hanging the laundry outside, I would help her by handing the items, naming each accordingly, like Daddy, Mommy, Granny, and for myself, Cutie," Willow remarked, remembering fondly. "I was three years old then."

"Cutie?" Alan asked, smiling.

"That's what Grandma called me. Goodness, look at us remembering things like old people do," Willow said, shaking her head.

"They're good memories." They sat there looking at each other, cherishing the private moments they had shared and wanting more.

"I should be going," Alan said, getting up and finishing his coffee.

"Would you like breakfast before you go?" Willow asked.

He hesitated before answering, "I should go. Thank you for everything."

"I can make crepes, and you get to taste my exotic jams."

He looked at her then. She tilted her head to the side and was smiling at him. "From scratch?" he finally asked.

"What other way is there?" Willow replied, laughing. "Have a seat, sir, breakfast is coming up. Want another cup?"

Alan sat on one of the stools and pushed his cup forward. "You're impossible, you know, hard to resist."

"I know," Willow replied as she poured him a cup then walked back to open the cupboards.

Alan watched in admiration as Willow prepared the crepes, deftly turning them upside down and placing them on a large plate once they were done. She pulled out four jars from the fridge and placed them next to his plate. One was a dark pink colour, one lavender, one yellow, and the last a pale purple.

"What are these?" Alan asked, picking one up and looking closely.

"You'll have to guess," Willow said as she sat down next to him. He opened one and sniffed. A powerful scent reached his nose.

"Lavender?"

"Yes, that one is easy. Try the other one."

He opened the light purple–coloured one and took a sniff. "Can this be lilac?"

Willow was surprised. "You're good at this. Yes, from my trees."

Alan opened the next one and hesitated. "Do I smell rose?"

"Yes, it's rose. From my damask rose bush that I specially planted for this."

He smelled it again and reached for a spoon. He put some on his plate and tasted it. "It's fascinating. I would never have guessed. You continuously amaze me. Last one," he said, picking up the yellow one. He smelled it, shook his head, and then tasted it. "I give up. It's delicious, but I have no idea what it is."

"It's dandelion."

Alan looked at her amazement. "Dandelion? The yellow flowers all over the place?" Willow shook her head in agreement. They started eating. "You know, you should meet my brother, William. He has an organic garden, remember, and I'm sure he would be interested about this, even help you market it."

"Market it? I wouldn't dare, I make them for the pleasure of making it."

Alan shook his head. "You always underestimate yourself. You don't take the time to see your potential." He finished off his plate and drank the rest of his coffee. "I'm glad you asked me to stay, or I would have missed this treat. Thank you, but I should really be going now." He got up, and Willow escorted him to the front door.

He stopped just outside and turned to look at her. The swept-up hair, the casual outfit, the natural look, and those deep, soulful brown eyes. He knew he wanted to kiss her, yet he hesitated, sensing that she still wasn't ready for any kind of intimacy.

"Goodbye, Willow," Alan finally said, and he got into his car. Willow opened the gates and he saw her watching him from the rear-view mirror. He waved and drove off.

CHAPTER SEVEN

The Gift

*I*t was a couple of days later when Willow heard the buzzer from the gate at seven thirty in the morning. She walked to the kitchen with her coffee cup and saw a man with a hard hat standing in front of a pickup truck with several others lined up behind him.

What the hell? she thought. "Yes? Who is this?"

"Good morning, ma'am. Mr. Alan Peters sent us."

"For what?" Willow asked.

"Your birthday gift. He asked me to tell you."

"Just a second. I'm coming out," Willow said, puzzled. The dogs started barking. As she walked toward the gate, she noticed that besides the pickup truck, there were other trucks behind it, one with a bobcat, shovels, and a variety of equipment she had difficulty identifying. Several men were lingering around.

"I think there's a mistake."

"You are Willow, ma'am? And this is 55 Willow Drive?"

"Yes, and yes, it is, but what birthday gift? I don't understand," Willow replied, frustrated.

"Ma'am, we're here to build you a pond. Mr. Peters told us that you wanted a pond?" the man asked questioningly.

"A pond? Oh my goodness, a pond? You're here to build me a pond?" Willow asked.

"That's right. May we come in?"

"Just give me a minute," Willow said, walking back into the house. *Well, I'll be damned,* she thought. *I never had someone give me a pond as a birthday gift.* She picked up her cell phone and dialled Alan's number. After four rings, she was ready to give up when he answered.

"Are you crazy?"

"Hello? Who is this?"

"You damn well know who this is."

"Good morning, Willow."

"Good morning to you too," she replied sternly. "There are a bunch of men here with trucks and equipment saying they want to build me a pond. On your orders."

"That's right. I sent Daniel over. He'll get the job done."

"Alan," she shouted, "I can't accept this. It's… It's…" She was at a loss for words.

"It's what?"

"It's too much. I mean, really?"

"You told me you wanted a pond so that when the ducks visit, they'll have a place to enjoy. Right? That's what you told me?"

"Yes, but I mean… why?"

"Because I can."

"Nobody has ever done anything like this for me."

"Then they were the fools for not doing it. Look, it's my birthday gift to you. I felt bad the other day. If you don't like it, you can always return it." Alan chuckled.

"Ha! Are you serious?"

"Are you? Let me spoil you. You deserve to be spoiled." Now it was Willow who suddenly turned quiet. "Willow?"

"I'm here. Alan, I have no words."

"A thank you would be nice. And maybe another dinner at your beautiful place?" he added.

Willow smiled at her cell phone as if he could see her face. "Thank you. This is an incredible gift."

"Let me know when they finish. They're there the whole day until they finish, or else they'll come back the next day. Eight men should do it."

"Of course. I'll just tell them to start now, they're sort of waiting outside for me."

"Go and tell them to start. I'll check in later."

"Bye."

Willow buzzed the gates open and walked out the front door. The vehicles all stopped by the clearing, and the lead man she had been talking to got out. "I'm Daniel, ma'am, and if you'll show us where you want it, we'll get started. Don't worry, we'll be out of your way." The men were getting out of the trucks and unloading equipment.

"Come, I'll show you where I want it, and you can tell me if it's suitable." Together, they walked to the spot Willow had in mind. Daniel pulled out a sketch from his upper pocket and opened it to show Willow. It was a professionally sketched pond with a waterfall, appropriately placed plants, and a bench on the side. She saw that even the house had been sketched in.

"Can I take a closer look?" Willow asked as Daniel handed over the paper. A small arbour was also added in a corner of the garden, something she hadn't planned for but now wanted.

"Who drew this, do you know?" Willow asked.

"Mr. Peters," Daniel replied.

"Can't argue with that," Willow said, smiling. "Go ahead, I'll be inside with the dogs."

"No problem, ma'am," Daniel replied and went to join his men. Willow watched from the windows as the machines came in rolling and the men started digging. By noontime, they had already dug out the ground and laid out the liners. In the afternoon, she carried out some iced tea and cookies for them and watched them work until five o'clock. Daniel walked to her side.

"It's practically finished, but we'd like to come tomorrow morning so we can fill it up, arrange the landscaping around it, and of course patch things up as well."

"Of course, by all means." Willow said. She watched them leave, and as she walked back into the house, her phone rang. She saw Alan's name flashing.

"Hello, Alan."

"So, how's it going? Are they finished?" he asked.

"Practically, yes, but they're coming tomorrow morning to fill it up and finish up everything else."

"Good, Daniel will call me tonight for the update. May I drop by tomorrow afternoon to see it?"

"What a question. Do come over. We can have drinks, and you can see."

"I'll be there around four thirty. I have some work I need to finish up here."

"I'll be waiting. And Alan…"

"Yes?"

"Thank you again for this wonderful gift. I'm forever grateful."

"I'll keep you to that promise. See you tomorrow."

Willow placed her phone on the kitchen counter and sighed. *I'm going to get into trouble again,* she thought. *I'm getting caught up in my emotions.*

The next day, Daniel and his men came in early again. Willow noticed from the window that this time, they had come with some plants and an arbour as well.

"What are these, Daniel?" Willow asked, walking outside. There was an array of some beautiful plants and decorative grasses. The arbour was white with intricate trellis designs on each side.

"Mr. Peters said that these would be perfect for the place. You must have seen them on his design," Daniel responded as the men started placing them on the ground. "Any objections for the placement of the arbour?" he asked, showing the graphic design.

"No, no, go ahead, it's all very beautiful. Leave the plants for me, I'll plant them." Willow stood around and watched as they installed the arbour, admiring the result.

"Would you like to turn on the water?" Daniel asked, smiling.

"The initiation ceremony." Willow laughed and walked toward the tap. Water started gurgling from the small waterfall and started to fill up the pond.

"We'll do the cleaning up, and our job will be done here, ma'am," Daniel said as they gathered up their equipment. Just at that moment, she noticed Alan driving through the open gates in a pick-up truck. He waved.

"Daniel, give me a hand here, will you?" Alan shouted. Willow walked toward him and saw that he had a bench in the back of his truck. It was a beautiful cedar bench with a back carved in a floral design. She looked up questioningly at Alan.

"Well, you need something to sit on to enjoy the pond, no?" Alan said as Daniel and another man picked up the bench. They all walked back to the pond.

"Where would you like it?" Alan asked.

"You go ahead and place it wherever you like," Willow answered. She watched as Alan pointed and the men placed it diagonally so, once seated, she could enjoy the pond and the landscape at the same time.

"Come and sit and tell me if you like it here," Alan told Willow. She walked over and sat down. It was the perfect spot. Alan walked with Daniel back toward his truck while the men slowly left. Willow saw Alan closing the gates, and he returned to sit next to her. The water gurgled on while the pond filled up.

"Do you need a hand with the plants?" Alan asked as he stretched his legs.

"I can do it, no need to get your hands dirty," Willow replied as she got up and walked to the edge of the pond. Alan came beside her.

"I come from a family of farmers, so I don't mind my hands getting dirty. Give me a shovel," he said, pointing toward the tools Willow had brought out.

Together, they placed the pots according to the design, and then each started digging and planting.

"Why are you doing all this?" Willow asked from where she was kneeling, brushing aside strands of her hair. She turned to look at him. Alan was expertly planting each pot, oblivious to the fact that Willow had stopped to take in a glance at how his wavy hair had grown long and curled up around his neck, how his face was tanned from working outside. She looked at his arms, the muscles moving as he worked. He hadn't shaved in a couple of days, and the stubble made him look… *Sexy would be the word,* she thought.

Alan suddenly turned to look intently, and Willow felt her heart beating fast as he smiled. She noticed that his eyes had again turned from green to blue, just like she remembered twelve years ago on the airplane. Alan was looking at the vein she felt throbbing on her neck, and she felt this incredible urge to rush over and kiss him. She quickly looked away.

"Why?" she asked again after a while.

"Because I want to bring a smile to your eyes. I want to help ease the pain that you're trying so hard to hide."

Willow's head swirled around. "How… How… What do you mean?" was all she could say.

"Somebody or something has hurt you deeply, and you have this facade that you present to the world. You keep a curb on your feelings. You don't open up. You don't share."

Willow didn't respond. They both stood up in silence and watched the finished job, each silent in their individual thoughts.

"I think it's filled, what do you think?" Willow asked, peering into the pond.

"Yes, quite so." Alan watched as she turned off the tap. She looked around, then turned to smile at him.

"How about that drink?" Willow asked.

"No better time. You want some help?"

"Stay. I'll go in and prepare them. Enjoy the view. After all, it's your creation." She smiled and walked toward the house.

Once inside, Willow rushed to the bathroom downstairs and looked at her face. She had barely held on out there, her feelings for Alan overcoming her mind and logic. She looked flushed, so she splashed some water on her face and looked up again at the mirror. "Get a hold of yourself, woman," she said to herself, then walked back into the kitchen to prepare the drinks.

"This is nice," Alan said as he sipped on the gin and tonic that Willow had brought out. She didn't respond. He turned around to look at her. "I like being with you. Just coming here and sitting, watching your wonderland garden brings me peace. It's been a while since I felt like this."

"I like you being here as well. You're most welcome to come visit anytime." Willow smiled.

"About that." Alan said, placing his glass on the grass. "I want to invite you to our annual family barbecue this Sunday. It was a tradition started by my mother. She wanted the whole family together at least once a year. Robyn carries on the tradition. It'll be fun, and you'll get to meet everyone."

For a moment, there was just the sound of the waterfall nearby. Willow suddenly became very aware of the sound.

"What do you say? I also want to invite Jasmine and Sam. Think they can make it?" Alan asked.

"I don't know, they're usually very busy," Willow replied.

"Do you mind if I call her?"

"Of course not, by all means. Here, let me give you her phone number."

Alan handed over his phone as Willow entered the number.

They sat there for a while, enjoying their drinks and the scenery. Alan didn't stay for dinner, and Willow waved as she closed the gates after him, watching him go.

Suddenly, the house felt empty, even with her dogs.

∽ℰℰ∾

Willow woke up at her usual time and walked to the windows to look outside. Two ducks were in the pond sleeping. She smiled and grabbed her phone. She sat on her bed and texted Alan.

Have visitors this morning sleeping on my pond!

Who are they?

Rudolph and Marigold. I'm sorry, we're supposed to be grown-ups, I shouldn't be texting you this early. Sorry, did I wake you up?

That's a lot of sorry. No, you didn't, and why not?

Why not what?

Text. Because we're grown-ups? Enjoy the moment, Willow, and keep me updated of new arrivals.

Willow looked at the heart emoji Alan had sent with his text. It was just an emoji, but suddenly, it felt like something more to Willow. *I'm acting silly. Like a young girl,* she thought as she dressed and went downstairs. She let the dogs out, and of course, the ducks flew off when they heard them running. She made herself coffee and then walked outside to sit on the bench as the dogs ran around, playfully chasing each other. The sun rose on another beautiful day.

Her peace was disturbed by her phone ringing. She looked at the screen and saw Jasmine's name.

"Good morning, baby girl, you're up and early."

"Good morning, Mom, how are you? How is the pond going?"

"Oh, they finished yesterday, it's beautiful. You must come and see."

"Actually, that's why I was calling. Alan called me last night and invited me and Sam to his family barbecue this Sunday."

"I know. He was here yesterday, and he invited me too. I know you guys are busy, so no worries, I'll tell…"

"We would love to come, I said yes." Willow was suddenly silent. "Mom, are you there?"

"Yes, it's just that… I'm surprised you're coming."

"We want to come so that we can meet this man that seems to have a special effect on you, as well as his family."

"Jasmine!" Willow replied in shock.

"I'm kidding! But yes, we're curious, so we'll come in on Saturday and leave early Monday morning, if that's all right with you."

"Sure it's OK, it just means a lot of driving for you, that's all."

"Nah, it's just three and half hours, and we're two drivers, so we'll see you on Saturday."

"Love you." Willow said. She had just put her phone down when it rang again. She looked down to see Alan's name flashing.

"So, we're over the texting, is that it?" she jokingly said when she picked up.

"It takes up too much time. Besides, I like to hear your voice." Willow smiled at the remark. "You're smiling, aren't you?" Alan asked.

"No, I'm not," Willow replied, trying to sound normal.

"You can't fool me. Anyway, the reason I'm calling is that I talked with Jasmine last night, and they're coming."

"So I've learnt this morning."

"You know the way, right?"

"Yes, I do. Can I bring anything?"

"Just yourself. There'll be too much food and too much alcohol, believe me. Be prepared."

"What time shall we come?" she asked.

"Anytime. We start off early here at the farm. Oh, and bring the girls as well. They'll have fun with Roxy and the other dogs."

"Look forward to it. Thank you for the invite."

"Until Sunday," Alan said. Willow looked at the phone in her hand, then around her. *Meeting the family,* she thought. *That should be interesting.*

∽୧ℰᴐ

It was eleven o'clock in the morning come Sunday that Willow arrived with Jasmine and Sam and the three dogs at the farm. Willow saw that there was already quite a crowd with other dogs and children running around. There was a large barbecue going full blast, and a long table had been set up near the gazebo where Willow and Alan had previously eaten. Alan turned around from the barbecue when he heard their car. He handed over the tongs to the man next to him and came running over.

"You made it," he said, smiling, and kissed Willow on the cheek. She was taken aback by the gesture. "Hello, Jasmine, it's been a while," Alan said shaking her hand. "And you must be Sam."

Willow's dogs had already taken off running after Roxy and her canine friends.

"Welcome to family chaos, please help yourself to a drink," Alan said, pointing to the iceboxes and the table with wine. "Come, let me introduce you to Robyn. Please feel free to mingle." Alan took Willow by the arm.

"Willow, this my sister, Robyn. Robyn, this is Willow's daughter, Jasmine, and this is Sam, her husband." Willow looked at the woman she had seen at the winery with Alan. Up close, she noticed the similarities between brother and sister. They both had the same warm smile and green eyes.

"Pleased to meet you," Robyn said. "Do you mind if I borrow Willow? Come, let's get a drink and sit down." She picked up two glasses of wine, walked down toward the river, and sat down on a tree trunk.

"You know, I've known about you since the day Alan saw you at the airport twelve years ago." Willow turned to look at Robyn with astonishment. "Yes, I'd called him that day, and I was the one who suggested that he go and buy a book so that he could sleep on the plane. He later called me when he got home, and we talked about you. He sounded so excited. I hadn't heard him like that for a while. I know you found out about Caroline in the wrong way and Alan never forgave himself for that, even though I'd insisted that he come forward with the information." Robyn stopped to take a sip from her glass. "He's lucky to have found you again. It's been a while since he has been happy and I—I mean, the whole family is grateful."

"I should be the one to say I'm lucky to have found him again, although our lives have changed, and we're different people now. Like they say, with age comes wisdom," Willow said.

"He's the leader of our gang now. My husband, Christopher, and I live here. As you know, I'm the winemaker, and Christopher is into craft beer, so we make quite a team." Robyn laughed.

"Do you have kids?" Willow asked.

"Four, three boys and a girl. They're all grown up now, of course, and I have six grandchildren. You'll see them running around with the dogs. My three boys—you saw one of them with Alan when you came in—they're all married and live close by. They work at the vineyards with us. My daughter is still living with us, and she takes care of the horses and offers riding lessons. Then there's our youngest brother, William, who lives down by the river with his family. He has five kids, some of them working, some of them still at school."

"I must say, you have quite a large family. I come from a very small one. Our family gathering wouldn't have been more than six back then, and now it's just me and Jasmine," Willow said.

"She's quite striking, your daughter."

"Thank you. They don't want any children, so I'll miss out on being a grandma."

"Come here anytime and you can play with ours," Robyn said, getting up. "So there's a little family history for you. I'm sure Alan will fill you in with the rest. I should get back into the kitchen and check on the food."

"Anything I can do?" Willow asked as they walked back.

"No, enjoy yourself, I'll be with you shortly." Robyn left and Willow looked around to see Alan talking animatedly with Jasmine and Sam.

"What has Robyn been telling you? I hope nothing bad?" Alan asked as Willow joined them.

"It's a secret. What have you three been talking about?" Willow asked.

"Sam here has been telling me about the foundation he and Jasmine are planning to set up. I told them I might be of help. Have you met anyone else?" Alan asked.

"No, but there are so many of you that it's going to be difficult, I'm not used to big families," Willow said.

"I'll be quick. Come on, let me introduce you to the gang." They walked around together, Alan introducing them to everyone. After a while, Willow had difficulty following the names. The children were chasing each other, and the dogs were running after them in a wild pack. The smoke from the barbecue filled the air, and Willow realized she was hungry.

Finally, Robyn came out ringing a bell, and everyone settled down. It was a festive event, everyone talking at the same time, food served from one plate to another. Alan had a big tray full of barbecue that he planted on the table, and he sat down next to Willow. Willow looked around and at one point became envious of the joyful interactions of the group. Jasmine saw her and smiled, cheering with a glass of wine.

"Are you OK?" Alan whispered.

"Yes, just overwhelmed a little. You have a great family," Willow said.

The lunch continued for over three hours with people mingling around, the barbecue still going on strong until everyone was full. Willow got a chance to talk with Daisy and her partner, Ivy, and she saw Jasmine and Sam talking with Alan's brother, William. Alan's youngest daughter, Grace, and her husband, Mark, arrived late due to their delayed flight.

"Sorry we're late," Grace said, bending to kiss Alan on the cheek. Everyone made space for them to sit down.

"Before we sit down, we have some news we would like to share," Grace said as Mark stood next to her. Everyone looked up expectantly.

"There will be a new addition to the family in seven months." No one spoke.

Alan stood up. "Are you saying what I think you're saying?" he asked hesitantly.

"Yes, Dad, you're going to be a grandfather." Grace smiled at him as everyone stood up, shouting and congratulating. Willow looked at Alan and saw how emotional he had become. Willow held his hand and kissed him on the cheek.

"Congratulations, Grandpa," Willow whispered in his ear. Alan turned to hug her.

By five o'clock, the children had grown tired, and the dogs were panting under a tree. Willow helped clear the table with the other women as the men gathered around the barbecue to clean. She glanced at her watch and saw that it was coming to six o'clock and went to find Jasmine and Sam.

"My father is showing them his home," Grace said when she saw Willow looking around.

"Thank you. Congratulations again, do you know whether it's a boy or a girl?"

"It's a boy."

"Have you picked a name yet? I know it's still early," Willow asked as they waited.

"Mark wants Robert, but I'm thinking Simon."

"Strong names. You're an architect like your father, so he tells me," Willow replied.

"Yes, I work with Patrick since Dad left. Ah, there they are, coming out." Grace pointed, and they started walking to meet them.

"Like you said, Mom, it's amazing," Jasmine said. "Just love it."

"We should be going. Jasmine, could you get the girls?" Willow said. "Alan, it's been a wonderful day, thank you so much for inviting us."

"Our pleasure," Alan said, walking with them to their car. Robyn and Daisy waved from afar, but William came along to send them off.

"Once again thank you," Willow said turning to shake William's hand.

"Don't let her get away this time," William said looking at Alan. Willow, caught off guard, didn't know what to say.

"I won't," Alan replied as he continued to look at her. She gave him a smile then and waved goodbye as she got into the car.

∽℮∾

The next day, Jasmine and Sam returned home. Before she got in the car, Jasmine turned to Willow and said, "He's nice. He's so different from Dad and certainly from James. He really likes you," she added.

"I don't know what to do. I'm so afraid of doing something wrong like last time," Willow replied.

"Maybe this time you should just enjoy each other. It's obvious there's chemistry between you two."

"You think?" Willow asked.

"I know so." Jasmine gave Willow a hug. "I'll let you know when we get home. I know you worry when we're on the road."

Willow waved, watching them leave in their car.

"Come on, girls. You must be tired as I am," she said to her dogs, and she walked inside.

CHAPTER EIGHT

Serenity

Willow was pleasantly surprised when Jasmine called two days later. "You're spoiling me, baby girl, how are you?" she asked as she was walking outside.

"We're good, how are you doing?"

"I'm fine, is something the matter? You don't usually call this soon."

"Something came up and Sam has to go to a conference out of the country, and I thought I might come over and stay a week or ten days and work from home. And I mean work, so Mom, feel free to go ahead with whatever plans you have."

"That's wonderful news. I don't have any plans, I'm just thrilled. When are you coming?"

"I thought I might drive down the day after tomorrow, if that's all right."

"Perfect. I'll be waiting. Please drive safely."

"Mom," Jasmine said in an exasperated voice.

"I'm sorry, I know I'm being a fussy mom again."

"All right then, I'll see you soon. Love you, Mom."

"Love you." Willow, suddenly excited at the prospect of seeing her daughter again, got up and walked back in.

Later in the afternoon, Alan called, "How are the ducks?"

Willow laughed. "They're OK until the girls run outside and frighten them away. It'll take some time for them to get used to each other, I guess. How are you?"

"Running here and there. I wanted to ask you something."

"Sure, go ahead, what is it?"

"I'm going to visit a friend's vineyard on Friday, and it's a beautiful place. I think you'd enjoy it. Won't you come along?"

"Oh, I'd love to, but Jasmine is coming over on Thursday to stay for a week or so."

"That's great news, but she's a big girl. I'm sure she can manage for the day, no?"

Willow hesitated. *Jasmine had said she would need to work,* she thought. *Just for the day wouldn't be a big deal, would it?* "Will we be gone for long?"

"We'll come back late afternoon, I promise. I would love your company."

"All right then, I'll come."

"Good, I'll pick you up at nine in the morning."

"I'll be ready. Thank you, Alan."

"My pleasure."

∽∾

Willow spent the next day preparing Jasmine's favourite foods while waiting for her arrival. Jasmine came in early afternoon. They spent the day talking, and Willow told her about Alan's invitation.

"I hope you don't mind?" Willow asked.

"I told you, I need to work, go and enjoy yourself. Now sit outside while I unpack, and when I'm finished, I'll bring you a glass of wine."

The next morning, Willow was getting ready while Jasmine watched.

"Jasmine, why don't you open the gates? Alan will be here shortly."

"Sure," Jasmine replied, jumping down from the bed and walking downstairs. She buzzed them open and walked out, the dogs following close behind. Willow was checking herself in the mirror when she heard a car pull up in front of the house. She heard Alan and Jasmine talking and the dogs barking. Willow walked slowly down the stairs toward the front door just as Alan came in. She always felt a thrill seeing him. He took off his sunglasses and gave her a kiss on the cheek.

"Jasmine is with the dogs, she said she'll come back in five minutes. We'll leave then."

He turned around in the kitchen and looked at her. Something was different, Willow felt, and she looked at him quizzically.

"So which vineyard are you taking me this time?"

"Vineyard? Oh, yes, vineyard. This one is a bit far away, but the view is spectacular, it's very private. I think you'll enjoy it."

Willow looked at him questioningly. "Do you think we'll be back in the afternoon?" she asked. "Maybe we can have dinner here with Jasmine."

"We should be back before six. Sure, I'll stay. I'll let Daisy know, she worries if I'm not in touch." Alan walked outside with his cell phone. Willow went to pick up her jacket and bag from the armchair when Jasmine came inside, the dogs rushing past to their water bowls.

"Ready to go?" Jasmine asked.

"Do you think something is wrong, Jasmine?" Willow asked. "He seems different this morning. Preoccupied, even."

"No, why?" Jasmine asked.

"I don't know, it's just that…"

"Shall we go?" Alan peeked from the front door. "I just talked to Daisy. Everything is settled." They all walked outside. Alan went to open the passenger door.

"Ever the gentleman." Willow said, smiling. "See you, Jasmine." She waved.

"Enjoy your time, don't worry about me." Jasmine waved back.

Why would I worry about her? Willow thought.

It was a nice summer day, and the sun was shining bright. Alan had put the top down on his car, and Willow could feel the wind in her face. *So much for the hair,* she thought.

"So, where are we going?" Willow asked. "How far is it?"

"Should take us about two hours," Alan replied, glancing at her. "We'll take the highway. It'll be faster." He pulled into traffic. Soon after, they were driving fast on the highway. As Willow glanced at the scenery passing by, she noticed that he had turned into an exit.

"This is the way to the airport," Willow suddenly realized. "Why are we going to the airport?"

He just smiled and continued until he stopped in front of one of the hangars adjacent to the airport. A woman carrying a folder was walking toward the car with a man following close behind.

"Good morning, Mr. Peters, ma'am," the woman said, looking at Willow. "Everything is ready for you in the folder." She handed it over to Alan. The man following her had come to the car and was opening the trunk. Alan walked around to her side and opened the door.

"Come on, Willow, follow me," Alan said holding her hand. Willow looked down at his hand and then at his face.

"Alan, what is going on?" Willow turned around to see that the man was carrying two suitcases, one of which looked familiar. "Is that my suitcase?" She pulled away her hand and stopped walking.

"Sally, you go ahead. We'll be right there," Alan said, stopping as well.

"Yes, sir," Sally said, joining the man and walking through one of the hangar doors.

"Why do you have my suitcase? How do you have my suitcase?" Willow was getting angry now.

"Jasmine."

"Jasmine?" Willow was at a loss for words.

"She helped me organize this surprise."

"What are you saying?" Willow finally said.

"I want you to come away with me for a couple of days. There's a place I would like to show you." Willow felt spooked. "Look, take it as just an invite from a friend. No obligations, nothing expected, just some time away from here."

Willow's thoughts were running around in her head. "You know I'm not good at relationships," she said.

"I know. That's why I said no obligations, no expectations. We'll be gone just for a couple of days. Jasmine is going to take care of your house and the dogs. She also packed your suitcase."

"How? What? How did she know what to put in it? Really, this is just too overwhelming. And how did you keep this a secret? When did you plan this?"

"Look, I'll tell you everything, but we need to go. The chopper is waiting."

"Chopper? What chopper?" *I'm blabbering,* Willow thought to herself.

"We're taking the corporate chopper. It's faster, just bear with me." Alan took her hand again, and they walked toward the hangar door. Once inside, Willow saw the chopper. Sally was waiting by the open doors. The pilot nodded a salute, which Alan acknowledged.

"Have a nice trip Mr. Peters, ma'am," Sally said.

"Thank you, Sally. You go in first, Willow," Alan said as he slid the door open.

Willow climbed in, still in a state of shock. She sat down on the seat next to the window, and Alan sat across her.

"Hi, Chris," Alan said, putting on the headphones. "How's the weather for the trip?" Willow put on the headphones Alan handed her.

"All clear, should be no turbulence."

"Good," Alan replied, "let's go." He slid the door closed, and Willow could hear the rotor blades start.

"First time in a helicopter?" Alan asked upon seeing the worried look on Willow's face.

"Yes, it is," she replied.

"Please fasten your seatbelt. You'll feel a bit strange as it lifts off, but then it should be all right."

"I can't believe all this. I've never been surprised like this in all my life."

Alan smiled. "I know. Jasmine told me."

"What else did she tell you?"

"That you liked surprises. Pleasant ones, that is, but you always somehow guess beforehand. Looks like this will be your first time. I started planning this with Jasmine at the barbecue party. I was thinking about it for a long time, and her being able to get away and stay gave me the opportunity. I did get her approval."

"I'm sure you did. There'll be a reckoning when I get back. When do we get back from wherever we're going, anyway?"

"A couple of days," Alan mumbled. Willow leaned back in her seat and looked outside. *Well, this is a hell of a surprise,* she thought. *Nobody has ever done something like this for me. I'm anxious yet happy at the same time—how that can be? Flying on a corporate chopper with a charming man to somewhere unidentified. I mean, who does that?*

"I didn't know you owned a chopper," Willow finally said as they gently lifted into the air.

"It makes travel easier. I don't like traffic. We also have a corporate plane for long distance."

"So, where we're going is a short distance then?"

"Good, you're laughing. For a minute there, I was afraid you were mad at me."

"How can I be? I'm being flown to… who knows? I trust you and Jasmine to be sure that I'm going to enjoy this. I may be too old now for surprises."

"Too old? No one is that old, especially for surprises."

"So, how long will we be flying? Willow asked, trying to guess where they were going. *I wonder what Jasmine packed. I was unprepared, so was she able to think of everything I might need?*

"What are you thinking? You're frowning." Alan asked.

"Just thinking if Jasmine knew what she needed to pack for me."

"Well, I told her where you were going, so I'm guessing she packed accordingly."

After about an hour, Willow heard a crackling sound and the pilot's voice.

"Mr. Peters, we should be there in about half an hour. We'll be approaching from the right, so you should be able to get a clear view."

"Thanks, Chris," Alan replied and leaned to look out the window.

"What are we looking at?" Willow asked as she too leaned forward to the window. It was then that she saw the island. As they flew closer, she saw houses and roads among lush nature and several beaches. The chopper started to descend, and she got a closer look. They were approaching the edge of the island, and suddenly, it was in full sight. A magnificent modern house lay atop a cliff, as if it belonged there, so incorporated was it into the natural lines of the land surrounding it. She might have even missed it if the chopper hadn't been hovering low. A sleek design for sure. The cliff dominated a small cove and beach down below with a reciprocal cliff on the other side, like a crescent moon.

Willow looked up questioningly at Alan. "Is that Serenity?"

It was Alan's turn to be surprised. "How do you know that?"

"You showed it to me the first time we met on the airplane, don't you remember? I asked you to show me some of your designs, and this one was something you were working on for yourself. You said you wanted something special. Something close to your heart."

"You remember all that?" Alan asked.

"Of course I remember. My problem is that I never forget." Willow smiled.

They passed over the hilltop, and right behind, Willow saw the town and marina with a small airport toward which they were flying. The sea was sparkling, and it was a glorious day. Willow suddenly realized that she was looking forward to this impromptu holiday.

They landed in a corner of the airport where several small aircrafts were already parked. A jeep drove out to meet them. Alan slid the doors open and helped Willow out.

"Thanks, Chris, see you in a couple of days." The pilot acknowledged him by giving him a thumbs-up.

The elderly driver of the jeep got out. "Welcome back, Alan."

"Nice to be back, John. It's been a while. Everything ready as I asked?" Alan asked as he and John put the luggage in the back of the jeep. The chopper lifted and left in a swirl of wind.

"As you requested. Let me know if you need anything," John replied. He smiled at Willow as she got in with Alan.

It was a twenty-minute drive to the house, and Willow enjoyed the narrow, winding road that climbed the hilltop among some beautiful properties. Alan drove expertly, manoeuvring through until they reached the top. As the road turned left, he turned right to reach a tall fence with a gate. He punched in some numbers on the box by the side, and the gates automatically opened.

Once they passed through, the gates started to close, but Willow was distracted by the amazing landscape as they travelled on a paved road surrounded by very tall, dense trees. She could see the sea from between the branches, and for a moment, she was disoriented as to where they were—when suddenly, the area cleared, and they reached the edge of the cliff. A short banister created a perimeter around the area. Alan parked the jeep and got out.

"Come on, let's go in first. I'll bring in the luggage later."

Willow followed him and saw that there were wide steps leading down to another precipice into which the house was built with minimal impact on the surrounding land. They went down, and Alan opened the door.

"You go in. I'll leave you with your first impression while I get the luggage."

Willow didn't offer to help because she suddenly found herself in a living room with picture windows framing a large terrace with a dizzying view of the ocean below. She walked in slowly, noticing the open kitchen on one side and the living area with a big fireplace. On both sides of the fireplace were bookshelves and a section for vinyl records and a record player. She passed them to reach the sliding doors and pulled them open to go outside and was immediately greeted with a scent of the open air and sea. Once on the terrace, she had the impression of being on top of the ocean with an amazing panorama. She saw that there on the side yet again was another level below the one she was standing, with a natural looking pool and a small waterfall above it. The tiles of the pool were a deep dark blue with grey flagstones around it, and the surrounding natural green habitat made it look like something out of paradise.

The terrace itself jutted out toward the ocean, and she saw that the natural landscape was, as she saw from the chopper, in a crescent-like shape with an opposing cliff at the end of the cove and beach. She glanced around where she was standing and saw the comfortable-looking lounge chairs and couch. She noticed a dining table next to the barbecue in the corner. Overall, it was breathtaking, and Willow was overwhelmed. She walked back in.

"How do you like it?" Alan asked as he brought in the suitcases and closed the door. Willow turned around her eyes, brimming with tears.

"What is it?" Alan asked, worried.

"It's just that… Alan, you've created a masterpiece here. It's just out of this world I have no words to describe the beauty of it. The house, the landscape, the materials... you've poured out your heart here," Willow said.

Alan quickly walked to her side. "I did pour out my heart in this place," he said. "Here, I'll show you around." He walked back toward the entrance with Willow following and opened a door on the left. It was a big bedroom with a king-size bed and nightstands. There was a vanity table and a hidden closet with an ensuite on the side. There were floor-to-ceiling windows here as well, with a magnificent view of the ocean and a small balcony.

"Do you like it?" Alan asked. Willow didn't reply, immediately looking at the bed. "It's your bedroom, Willow, mine is on the other side." Alan said softly. Willow looked up, surprised but somewhat relieved. "Like I said, no obligations." Alan walked out toward the other side and opened a door. Willow glanced in and saw that it was a similar bedroom, maybe larger and more masculine in decoration.

"Mine." He smiled awkwardly. They both walked out again into the living room with the open kitchen. Alan walked up to the fridge and opened the door. Willow saw from behind that it was fully packed. Alan then proceeded to open the wine fridge and Willow saw that it too was full.

"What do you say we both unpack and get comfortable, and we can have a drink on the terrace to watch the sunset?" Alan asked.

"Sounds good," Willow said. "See you in a bit."

"Just before you go, we're off-grid here. There's no internet, and the reception for the phones here is, well, challenging. I do have a satellite phone for emergencies, and when we go into town, the phones will work. However, don't worry—I asked Chris, our pilot, to have my office call Jasmine to say that we've arrived safely, and if Jasmine ever needs to contact us, I did give her the number for the satellite phone and John's as well."

"You've thought of everything, haven't you?" Willow said, smiling. "Thank you for making me feel comfortable." Then, she walked into her designated bedroom and closed the door.

Willow sat on the bed and looked around. On one hand, she was relieved that she had a bedroom to herself, and on the other hand, she worried that Alan had done this because he wasn't interested in her in that way. But then she thought it could be that he showed respect to her by not insisting on sharing a bed because frankly, they hadn't approached that question in their relationship. They hadn't even kissed yet or become intimate in any way. Even still, she didn't understand why she was bothered, but now wasn't the time to deliberate on the reasons.

Willow got up and started unpacking, looking and wondering at the choices Jasmine had made for her. She decided to change into her favourite lounge pants and a tunic over it. She tidied up her face and hair and walked out to find Alan waiting in the kitchen area. He glanced admiringly at her.

"What would you like? A cocktail or wine or something else? The bar is full."

"Maybe a gin tonic if you have it," Willow replied.

"Of course I do," Alan replied. "It is your favourite." Willow sat on one of the stools on the other side of the counter while Alan prepared the drinks. "I don't forget either. You said it on the plane, twelve years ago," Alan replied. Willow shook her head. He prepared the drinks quickly and, after adding a slice of lime, picked up both glasses.

"Follow me." He walked toward the terrace.

"I noticed that there's another level down?" Willow asked, turning around to Alan, who had approached her.

"Yes, there are a few stairs to reach the pool and my office, then there's an elevator that goes down to the beach area and the dock. We'll do that tomorrow, if you like," he replied. Willow stood up and gazed at the panorama.

"You couldn't grow old here," she said softly. She walked back to the lounge chairs where Alan had placed their drinks on the table between. She sat down and leaned back. The sun was going to set behind them, but it was already casting shadows and creating magnificent clouds of red and pink. Alan settled down as well and grabbed his drink.

"Thank you for coming," he said and lifted his glass in a cheer.

"You left me no choice. Why did you bring me here? Willow asked as they sat.

Alan didn't answer immediately. "I thought you would understand," he finally replied.

"What do you mean?" asked Willow.

"I believe friendship is one of the greatest gifts one can offer at our age. True friendship, no judgements. I know I'm asking too much when I say I want your friendship. Why trust me? is a good question you're asking yourself. I want you to know that I'm here for you, and I'm a very good listener. I just want to know what happened to you. You look like a wounded animal sometimes, especially with your eyes." Alan stopped talking and looked at her, waiting patiently.

"Why here, though? Why fly out to this place? Not that it isn't beautiful—I love it—but I feel there's another reason for it."

"I brought you here because this house has a special place in my heart. I started to build this house about the same time when we met and then separated. Then, Caroline fell seriously ill, and I had to place her in an institution. I was just about to go crazy with what was happening in my life, and this was a release for me. Something I'd always wanted to build ever since I bought the land several years ago. It was a challenge, getting the design to work, collaborating with engineers and workers, flying in and out. Sometimes, I would curl up in a hammock among the trees and watch over the work. Once I finished, I realized that I had built a sanctuary—or Serenity, as you called it—for myself. Sometimes, Daisy or Grace would join me, sometimes Robyn, but it's no place for small children or young people, so gradually they left it for me, realizing what it meant to me.

"I closed the place after Caroline became too ill. It was just too painful. It was only after she passed away did I escape back here to bury myself in my grief. My stay here at that time helped to heal me and to accept the realities of life, but I had to continue to live, for my children, for my family that I love, and most of all, for myself. This was ten years ago."

"I'm so sorry, Alan," Willow said, understanding the pain he had gone through.

"Don't be. I brought you here because we're far away from our normal life. It's just you and me and no one else to pass judgement," he replied. "This place might help you talk to me."

"Why do you insist I tell you about my past? What is it you need to know?" Willow asked.

"Tell me, have you ever talked about what happened to you with anyone, maybe your daughter?" he asked.

Willow hesitated. "No, I haven't told her all the details. She was witness to several incidents, but I never told her all that happened. Why bother her with something she couldn't solve? And anyway, it was my own mess to deal with. I didn't want to burden her with my problems."

"Much good that must've done you," Alan remarked.

"Did you talk with anyone about your problems? Caroline and all?" Willow said.

"Yes, I did. I had Robyn, my parents, and my brother to help me deal with... with all that happened. I couldn't have made it through without their help," Alan admitted. They sat in silence for a few minutes, both looking at the horizon, deep in their individual thoughts. Willow glanced at the glass in her hands and finished off her drink.

"Want another one?" Alan asked softly, draining his glass as well. Willow glanced at him. "Coming up," he said, getting up and going inside.

Willow pulled up her legs under her on the chair and leaned back, gazing at the ocean. *Should I finally tell him what happened?* she thought, hesitating but understanding that he was doing her a service by asking her to talk. Maybe in this way she could get rid of the awful memories and stop punishing herself by always remembering them. The fact was that until now, she had nothing to look forward to, and she had accepted the reality that she would be alone for the rest of her life, a promise she made herself to protect herself from getting hurt again. Twice was enough in a lifetime.

"Here you are," Alan said, handing her the drink. "Are you cold? It sometimes gets a little chilly in the evenings."

"No, I'm fine, thank you," Willow replied.

Alan sat down beside her, leaning against the corner of the couch and facing her. "You look troubled," he remarked.

"No, I was thinking over what you said just now, and you're right. I should talk. I need to talk at some point."

"I promise I won't judge you. I'll just listen, and if you want my take on it, I'll tell you when you finish. Agreed?" Alan asked.

Willow hesitated. Her life experience had taught her not to trust anyone, and she really didn't want to get hurt again. What good would it bring her to share her story with Alan? Why should she share it with him? There were things she hadn't told anyone, not even Jasmine, who was her closest friend. But then again, what could she lose if she did tell him her story? He'd said no judgement, and maybe it was time for her to get the burden off her shoulders. Time to relieve the stress that she always felt coming and going depending.

"We don't have to do this tonight. Why don't we just enjoy our drinks and the view, and maybe tomorrow you'll think about it?" Alan said.

Willow, grateful for Alan's offer, said, "We'll talk tomorrow," smiling at him. By the time they finished their second drinks, dusk had finally settled in, and Willow noticed that soft lights had come on throughout the terrace.

"Shall we go in?" Alan asked, finishing off his drink. "I'm getting sort of hungry."

"Let's," Willow said, getting up. As they both walked inside, she noticed that lights had come on around the pool area as well. "That pool looks so inviting, I love how you've created a mystical atmosphere."

"It's heated, so you can enjoy it anytime," Alan replied, walking into the kitchen area. He opened the fridge and peered inside. "I asked John to do some shopping for us, just necessities until we can go and do it ourselves," he said, turning around.

"What are our options for tonight?" Willow asked. "I can cook something."

"No, we just got here, and I don't want you cooking on your first night. How about an antipasto plate like the delicious one you prepared at your place? We've got some cold cuts and cheese, and there's a fresh loaf of bread, maybe garlic bread, and we can make a salad as well?" he asked.

"Sounds great, let me help." Willow got down from her stool and went to the other side of the counter while Alan took everything out of the fridge.

"I'll do the salad." Willow said. As she moved behind Alan to reach the sink, she brushed up against him inadvertently. She noticed his body tense as he stopped what he was doing and deep inside she was pleased at the effect she had on him. Willow moved to his side and started washing the cherry tomatoes and salad, so Alan got busy slicing and preparing the plate.

"This is nice," Alan commented.

"Yes, it is," Willow answered as she placed the bowl on the counter. Once finished, they sat opposite each other as they ate.

"Do you come here in the winter as well?" Willow asked.

"Sometimes, but I prefer it when I can sit outside. Preferably not in the snow," he added.

Later, they sat on the couch, and Alan described how he built the house and the problems that came with it. Willow listened, watching his face become animated as he talked. Without realizing it, time flew by, and when she glanced at her watch, she saw that it was coming to midnight.

"I think I'll retire. It's been a long day," Willow said.

Alan looked at her. "Of course. Sorry for talking so much, I just get caught up in it."

"No, no, I enjoyed listening," she said, getting up. "Good night, Alan."

"Good night, Willow."

∽e∾

Next morning, Alan woke up to the smell of coffee. *Willow must be up,* he thought as he yawned and got out of bed. He peeked outside from the window. It was a beautiful day with a few clouds. He took a shower, then got dressed.

"Good morning."

Willow was standing outside on the terrace with a cup. "Good morning," she replied, turning around.

"You went for a swim?" Alan asked, noticing her hair was wet.

"Oh, yes, I couldn't resist. I got up early to watch the sun rise, and the pool looked so inviting." She sat down on one of the lounge chairs.

"I'll grab a cup and join you," Alan said, walking up to the kitchen. As he poured his coffee, he glanced at her. *She looks relaxed,* he thought. *That's an encouraging sign.*

"This coffee is good," he said when he came back and sat down next to her.

"You had doubts?" Willow asked, smiling.

"Not really. What do you say we go into town this morning and do some shopping? It's a market day, and…"

"Markets? I love markets, let's go." Willow practically jumped up from her seat.

"All right, all right. Let me finish my coffee." Alan hadn't expected that reaction but was pleased that he'd suggested it.

"Is it a food market, or do they have other exciting stuff?" Willow asked later as they walked toward the jeep.

"They have other exciting stuff," Alan replied, laughing. "You're a funny woman, you know that? I haven't seen anyone get this excited over a market."

By the time they made it into town, it was bustling with people. Alan managed to find a spot to park. "Do you first want to stroll through the exciting stuff or go to the food market?" he jokingly asked.

Willow glared at him. "The exciting stuff."

"All right, then," Alan said, grabbing her hand. Was it the thrill of being in a market, or was it her hand that was holding his tightly that made him feel giddy with excitement? Alan thought as they walked.

"This is where the exciting stuff is," Alan said as he pointed down the long aisle. Willow started walking slowly, glancing from one side to the other. It was a colourful sight. He watched Willow as she shopped around, picking up a scarf or trying on hats, when a jewellery stand caught her eye. She bent down, and from among the many items, she picked up a pair of sparkling earrings. It was made of tiny crystals that were strung on a small hoop, and in the sunlight, they shone in shades of purple and blue.

"May I try them?" Willow asked the young woman behind the stall.

"Of course. Here, let me give you a mirror."

"What do you think?" Willow turned to ask Alan.

"Sold."

"Are you sure? They're not... too much for a woman my age?"

"You have to buy them," the young woman said. "They're your colours, the colours of your aura."

"My aura?" Willow asked as she took them off and handed them back.

"Yes, you have an aura about you. Purple is the colour of royalty, and you are royal," the young woman said as she placed the earrings in a small bag.

"Hear that, Alan? I'm royalty." Willow laughed as she handed the money over.

"I always knew it, princess." Alan said.

"Princess?" Willow quizzically asked. "Please, more like a duchess or even a queen. Thank you." Willow placed the earrings in her bag. "I love markets."

"Now I see why."

They continued walking. At the end of the aisle, just before the food section, he noticed that Willow saw a stall that sold fabrics and dresses. Of the many that were hung up on a string, one seemed to catch her eye. It had an elaborate design with what looked like flowers and peacock tails and birds of paradise intricately woven into each other so that from a distance, it looked like a kaleidoscope of vivid colours.

"May I see that fabric?" Willow asked the old man sitting in the chair right underneath, pointing.

"It's a dress," the old man replied while pulling the fabric down with a pole. It was then that Alan noticed that what he had taken as a piece of fabric was indeed a dress that was folded up. The fabric itself was silky and as Willow held it up, he saw it was a kaftan with a V-neckline, the kind of dress that you just pull over yourself.

"It's a little fancy for my taste, but I love the colours and design. Where would I wear it? Willow asked Alan, "I can't work with this in the garden, maybe wear it as a nightgown?"

"It's beautiful," Alan said from behind her.

"I know the design is beautiful, but where would I wear it? It's not that practical, and it's definitely nothing to garden with."

"Wear it at home when you're relaxing. A nice, chilled glass of wine, curled up on one of your chairs…" Alan winked. He could see Willow think about it.

"No, I'll pass, thank you," Willow finally said, handing it over to the old man. "Too fancy for me." She continued to walk down.

Alan followed up, "You don't know how to spoil yourself, do you, Willow?"

"No, I don't, and if I do, it's very rare. Habit, I guess. I'll think about the dress for a bit, but then I'll move on, don't worry. Come on. What are we buying as food?" Willow asked, changing the subject.

They shopped for fresh fruit and vegetables, and by the time they had finished, the market was overcrowded. "Let's go buy some cheese and cold cuts and maybe something for the barbecue," Alan said as they walked out of the market area into a side street lined up with several shops. Alan walked into one of them, busy again with customers.

"Why don't you buy whatever you want here? I have something to do, and I'll meet you here, all right? Give me ten minutes," Alan suddenly said and left.

The little shop was crowded, and Willow struggled to pass the people standing around looking at different shelves. It seemed to be a popular place. She approached the cheese and delicatessen counter and placed her shopping basket on the floor.

It was then that she heard a man's voice. "Willow?" She turned around upon hearing her name. "What are you doing here?"

Willow was speechless. Her ex-husband Philip was standing in front of her wearing shorts and sandals, suntanned and looking very healthy.

"I would like to ask the same question to you," Willow finally responded.

"Oh, I came down with some friends who have a boat. We're going out to sea tomorrow morning for a couple of weeks. You know, diving and stuff."

"I am sure you are." Willow turned around as the salesman handed her the cheese packages. "I have to be going," she said, picking up her basket.

"You haven't answered my question," Philip persisted.

"What question?"

"What are you doing here? I heard that you remarried."

"Yes, and now, I'm a widow," Willow answered while fiddling with the packages in her basket.

"Here you are. I've just ordered the wine cases to be sent over, and—" Willow and Philip both turned to stare at the beautiful young woman who stopped talking suddenly and looked questioningly at Willow. "Darling, we need to go," she said, leaning up to kiss Philip's cheek.

Willow just stood there. "Hi, I'm an old friend. I don't think I've met you," she said at the young woman. Suddenly, Philip became reserved, but before he could intervene, the young woman replied.

"Hi, I'm a diving buddy of Philip's. Candice." *Sure you are,* Willow thought, shaking the hand that Candice extended, still reeling from the encounter while glancing sideways at Philip. He had a strained face but refused to say anything. Willow felt her whole body shaking with anger but tried to stay calm.

"Are you all right? You look kind of fazed," Candice said.

"It must be too much sun, I guess. I need to…" said Willow when suddenly, Alan was by her side, grasping her strongly by the waist and bringing her close to his body.

"There you are. I've been looking all over for you." Alan smiled down at Willow and kissed her fully on the lips. Caught off guard, Willow was flustered and panicking. Alan turned around to face an astonished Philip and a bemused Candice. Meanwhile, Willow was struggling with the fact that Alan had kissed her, let alone in front of her ex-husband. There was an awkward silence while Alan kept her tight by his side, not letting go of her waist.

"So, you've met old friends," Alan said. The silence continued. Willow was trembling in his grip.

"And you are?" Philip asked finally.

"A new friend." Alan smiled.

"We must go. I still have some shopping to do," Willow said, trying to disengage herself from Alan, but he held on strong. Philip was just staring at her, seemingly trying to understand. Candice slowly shook his arm.

"We should be going too. Pleased to meet you. I didn't catch your name."

"I'm sure he'll tell you. Goodbye, Philip," Willow mumbled and turned away, slipping from Alan's arm with a strength she didn't feel. Alan was still as he watched the couple leave.

"That was your ex, wasn't it?" Alan finally said.

"How did you know?"

"Your body language."

"I can't thank you enough for coming just at the right moment, although I wish he hadn't seen you," Willow replied.

"Why?"

"I don't know. I don't want him to think that…"

"The woman with him. Was that your…"

"No. This one is new."

"All that is over now. Come on, get over it," Alan said, taking the basket from her hand.

"It hurts, you know. Suspecting but never being able to confirm."

"Suspect what?"

"All those phone calls that he would take out in the garden. Not being part of the group that went diving just because I didn't dive. It's just that I never imagined he would have the time, or that anyone else would... you know... be with him."

"And this makes you feel bad?"

"Yes. I mean, it did."

"That's why I wanted him to see me. I saw the pair of you talking, so I waited for the right moment."

Willow turned around to look up at Alan. "You did that on purpose?"

"Yes, because I know being a guy, he would feel superior to you with a beautiful young woman beside him, and there you were, feeling sorry for yourself."

"No, I wasn't," Willow said defiantly.

"Oh, yes, you were. So, I wanted him to see me. The splendid specimen that I am."

Willow burst out laughing. "You're impossible, you know."

Alan smiled and said, "Have you finished shopping here? I thought I might go and buy some steaks for a barbecue, what do you say?"

"Sounds good. I still have some more shopping. What do you say we meet at the jeep?"

"Will do. Be careful now, we don't want you meeting anyone else from your past."

Willow gave him a stern look. "What do you mean?"

"I'm joking. See you in a bit," Alan said and turned to leave. Willow watched him go, silently thanking him for saving her from the awkward situation with Philip. *So, he now has someone new,* Willow thought as she continued with her shopping.

Once finished with the shop, she exited toward the market, which was in full swing. She walked by the fabric stall again to see the dress but noticed that it was gone. *Just my luck,* Willow thought, shrugging her shoulders. *I should've decided when I saw it.* She continued walking and saw a flower stall with beautiful fresh-cut flowers. She bought a bunch of colourful wildflowers and a bunch of anemones with purple hues.

When she arrived by the jeep, Alan was already there, waiting for her. "Those look beautiful," he remarked. She placed everything in the back seat and noticed several packages. He opened the passenger door for her.

"Did you find what you were looking for?" Willow asked as they drove off.

"I sure did," Alan replied.

Once home, they placed everything on the kitchen counter. Willow looked around for a vase for the flowers.

"Take a look in the cabinet under the records, there might be something there," Alan said when he noticed her searching look.

"Got it," Willow said as she pulled out a long glass cube vase. She carefully arranged the flowers as Alan looked on.

"You have a beautiful way of arranging flowers," he said, smiling. She smiled back and placed the vase in the centre of the coffee table. Alan was putting most of the shopping in the fridge when she noticed there was a package left on the counter.

"You forgot this," Willow said. When she picked it up, she noticed it wasn't food. She felt through the paper, then looked up in surprise. "You did not" was all she said.

"I most certainly did."

She ripped it open to find the dress she had admired, the silky fabric slithering through her fingers. "Alan."

He looked on affectionately. "That dress belongs to you. I knew it the moment you picked it."

Willow then came over and placed a gentle kiss on his cheek. "Thank you."

"You're very welcome. I hope I'll get to see you in it," Alan said as Willow walked to her bedroom. Once inside, Willow closed the door and sat on the edge of the bed. She looked at the dress in her hand. *It is really very beautiful,* she thought. *I never would have imagined him buying it for me.* She got up to hang it in the closet. *He'll be expecting me to wear it, but not tonight,* she thought. *Not with all that happened.*

Maybe tonight was a good time to have that talk with him, because she noticed that they were getting comfortable with each other. And that kiss Alan had given her. She smiled to herself. *That was some kiss,* she mused. Was it a promise for better things to come? Willow shook her head. *Come on, woman, behave. Not again. You promised yourself. Not again.*

She came out to find Alan still in the kitchen seasoning two steaks. He looked up when he heard her come in. "I thought we might eat early since we skipped lunch. Enjoy the sunset." She noticed that he seemed disappointed that she hadn't worn the dress.

"Those look amazing. Can I help in any way?" Willow asked.

"We have potatoes. Would you like baked potato along with the steak? And maybe a salad?"

"I'm hungry already, I'll get to it. I'll also set the table outside."

By the time they finished the preparations, the sun was getting lower over the horizon. Alan was busy at the barbecue, and Willow was checking the table she had set. She went back in to open a bottle of red wine and poured it into two glasses. She picked a small, clear glass, filled it with water, and placed three or four flowers into it from the vase. She brought it all outside and placed the small glass on the table, then turned to offer Alan a glass of wine.

"Thank you, these should be ready in about half an hour," Alan said, turning around at the table Willow had set. She noticed him looking at it. He looked at her then and said, "Cheers."

"Cheers," Willow replied and leaned against the terrace rail, watching him work the barbecue. "The smell is intoxicating and the evening beautiful," she remarked, taking a sip from her glass.

"Are you OK after what happened today?" Alan asked.

"In fact, I am. And I might even be ready to have that famous talk you've been waiting for."

Alan stood still with the prongs in his hand, unsure of what to say. "Whatever makes you comfortable."

"I know. We'll see." She moved toward the table and sat down.

By the time they finished their dinner, the sun had set, and the terrace lights had come on. Alan cleaned and closed the barbecue as Willow took the dishes back into the kitchen and placed everything in the dishwasher. He moved the half-empty bottle of wine and their glasses to the comfortable lounge chairs.

"I thought we might sit here. You're not too cold, are you?" he asked.

"I'm fine, thank you," Willow said as she sat down. "That was some meal."

Alan poured the rest of the wine into their glasses and leaned back casually. They sat in silence, both lost in their thoughts. He was waiting for Willow to make the first move, as he could clearly see her hesitating whether she should tell him her story. She suddenly laughed, and he looked at her, curious.

"I was just thinking that I should be brave and tell you my story, then I remembered. My friends thought me brave. For what? For ending a thirty-year old marriage and trying to start a new life after fifty? Was that bravery? No, it wasn't. There are so many brave people in the world that I would be ashamed to call myself brave. But nevertheless, people continued to tell me I was. Which scared me, really, because then I started to think, *Did I do something wrong? Or daring? Should I be scared? Am I crazy to act like this?*" Willow paused, looking at Alan, who said nothing.

"No, I wasn't. Because I knew that when they said brave, they meant that they themselves did not have the courage to do what I did—leap into a new life without looking back. They were the ones who were scared. Why? I guess because with change comes a certain risk. You might make a better life, or you may not. It's a risk. I know that."

When Willow stopped speaking, Alan remarked, "The truth is, you create opportunities for yourself. A second chance in life. The life you had previously was dominated by others and what they thought about you. You lived a life according to their rules and what you thought was the right thing to do. And the result? You lost your soul. You became another you. An image, a reflection of the people and the world surrounding you. You acted as you believed it to be correct. You believed in people, you trusted friends. Worse of it all, you thought this was the best you were going to get out of life. You were afraid of change."

"Exactly—well, no, I wasn't afraid of change. However, you're right about the rest," Willow replied.

"Go on, sorry. I had to cut in there."

Willow continued, "I was very much alone during my teenage years. I never had dates, never went out with friends. Books were my only friends, and so was painting. I got married at the young age of twenty-three, having fallen in love with the first man that showed me any kind of affection. Imagine this, Alan. A young woman gets married. She's excited, hopelessly in love, with dreams of a life lived happily ever after. Whereas the young man to be her husband is a man who has made his choice, thinking that he might be in love, believes he has found the suitable wife that will bring him honour and happiness, having a similar background as his, who is present-able, knowledgeable and, most of all, is in love with him." Willow paused to take a breath, then continued. "They're regarded as the perfect couple, coming from prominent families with high connec-tions." Alan became very still, and Willow paused. "Do you want me to continue?" she asked.

"Please."

"My greatest mistake was that I knew I was substituting a shadow in his life—a shadow of a young woman, his great love—yet I still went ahead. They had met while students at the university and fell madly in love. In fact, Philip was her first lover as he was mine. But when Philip had to go away for a year to study, she betrayed him with his best friend and then confessed on his return."

"So, she broke his heart, and he left her," Alan said.

"As stories go, yes," Willow replied. "I thought I could make him forget her, and I tried hard, even when I found the love letters hidden in a drawer in our first year of marriage. It was tough going during those first years. But I was in love, and I pretended not to see. I forgave him for the little things that hurt me. I forgave him for the way he treated me. I forgave him for a lot of things. I forgave him until I lost track of who I was and who I had become."

"Maybe he shouldn't have married you." Willow looked up as Alan stared into his glass and refused to meet her eyes. She took a deep breath. Alan's hand trembled slightly as he sipped his wine.

"I married Philip because I fell in love with him. He was the first man that ever kissed me, a virgin with no experience, but over the thirty years that we were married, I thought we had a good life. For the first twenty years, at least. Then, things changed. He became argumentative at work, unsatisfied with his job, quarrelling with his superiors, travelling a lot. Suddenly, it was him who knew best.

Nobody could challenge him on his ideas. Nobody was good enough for him. I was hoping for several children, but when Jasmine was three, he said, 'I don't want any more children,' and suddenly, my life became empty.

"He got angry because Jasmine wouldn't go for a master's degree, finally resulting in a faltered and failed relationship with her, for which I have never forgiven him or ever will. For him, I wasn't educated enough because I had graduated from a fine arts academy…"

Alan stared at her. "You can't be serious" was all he said. Willow ignored the remark.

"I wish I knew what was going on. We went on a holiday for a week, trying to patch things up between us, but he was never the one to communicate. For me, it was all very romantic, but it was the last time we made love. After that, we came back to our house, and he accepted a job in a different city. Against my will. He stayed away for a year. He came up occasionally, but only for the laundry and home-cooked food, and we gradually drifted apart. That was the year I went into menopause."

Willow gazed out at the ocean. "Do you know how lonely I felt? I was going through this difficult stage. I was emotionally distraught. I felt unloved, ugly, fat, and insecure." Willow got up from her chair and walked into the kitchen to get some water. Alan followed her with his eyes but didn't say anything. Willow came back with a glass and a new bottle of wine and settled down once again. Alan opened the bottle and poured.

"I felt so rejected and alone. And then one day, he quit that job and came back as if nothing had happened. By then, we had separate bedrooms and continued to live the charade that our marriage had become. Not once did he try to kiss me or touch me, and I lost interest, gradually believing that this was the way it was. This went on for about seven years before the divorce."

"Didn't you ever ask why?" Alan remarked.

"How could I? Would you? Would you ask someone why they don't want to kiss you or touch you or make love to you? Could you make yourself ask? I couldn't. I couldn't lower myself to that level. So, I said to myself, 'Fine, if he doesn't want me, I don't want him.' I punished myself. And after thirty years of dedication, I ended up learning that my husband was cheating on me. With my best friend and colleague that was working with me at my company. The shock, the humiliation, the hurt. After the divorce, I learnt that there were many others before her throughout our marriage.

"I know men go through a midlife crisis, I understand that. But when you think of all the effort and support a wife has given him over the years to make him successful, all the effort she puts into taking care of the house and children—the fact that it can be brushed off with a younger woman is hurtful. My whole youth was spent in that marriage, years that I can never get back. Women go through far more crises. Funny thing, though—my friends told me that when he learnt that I had found out, he said I should be happy because he was with someone I knew. What a notion, to even think of it." Willow paused, glancing at Alan and then at her glass.

"And then I met you," Willow finally said. Alan was at a loss for words. He now understood some of the things that at the time had seemed strange to him. Especially the way she had reacted the first time he had touched her.

"When I first met you, I thought I had another chance. I thought that I could start living again, that there was hope for me. Life had a new meaning. I felt young again. You made me feel young again. For a while, at least. Then I was left alone, again." Alan looked up at her.

"After you, when I fell in love, or thought I did, I got married on top of it. And all that happened with that marriage, I think that's what broke me in the end. I always believed that I was born at the wrong time and in the wrong century." Willow looked up at him, trying to control the tears.

"I never meant to bring up bad memories," Alan said. "But I want to know what happened with your second marriage."

"You want to know why I'm sad and hurt? Wounded?"

Alan just looked on.

"I had gotten out of a thirty-year marriage, being betrayed by a husband who cheated on me with my best friend. And then, once I thought I was free, I put myself into another cage." Willow paused. Alan waited quietly.

"It's an embarrassing story at start, and I still have difficulty admitting how stupid it was. Brace yourself. It was about the time that we had our fallout, and I was struggling in my new life after the divorce, and then you. My feelings were raw; I was deeply hurt, frustrated, lonely, and afraid of what the future held for me. I had no friends in my new life, just a few acquaintances from my yoga class." Willow looked up at him. "Yes, I went to yoga classes to get rid of stress, upon Jasmine's insistence. You know how persistent she can be. Then one day, she said, 'You should start dating.' My first reaction was 'Don't be stupid, me, dating? I've never dated before in my life. I wouldn't even know how to go about it,' but, Jasmine being Jasmine, she got the better of me, and she signed me up on an online dating site.

"She wrote all the information and even selected the photos I should post, and I went along with her just for fun, with no intention of ever doing anything. It was funny to see the matches the site had found that would be suitable for me every morning, and I laughed or got shocked by some of them. I didn't even respond to any emails that I received or even read any of them. It was a trial run for three months, so for a while, I had my entertainment cut out for me. I would never go out or even communicate with any of them because like I said, I had never dated before and was unfamiliar with the process. I would joke about it to Jasmine, who of course was not amused. She said, 'Look, Mom, I just want you to have fun, go out with someone. I'm not asking you to go to bed with them.'

"I think it was the last week before the end of my trial period. That morning, I sat at my computer and looked over the daily matches when I saw James's photo. What caught my attention was his smile and intelligent looks. He was handsome, twelve years older than me, and retired, but what was interesting was that instead of a story about himself, he had written a riddle and was curious to see if someone could solve it. It was a quote, and he wanted to know who said it and in what context. Now, me being a history buff, I knew the quote to be from Cicero, and the context was war. So, I wrote back the answer and asked a riddle of my own.

"This is how our correspondence started, and after a week of this, he said, 'We have to meet,' and I agreed. He suggested the bar at one of the famous hotels in town for a five o'clock meeting. You can imagine my anxiety. Jasmine prepped me up with 'Mom, you just go and have a drink, don't go anywhere with him, certainly not to his home, and come back. If you need anything, give me a call.' Not much help that was to me, but I braved myself and got dressed and took the subway downtown where the hotel was.

"As I emerged aboveground and started walking, I noticed a tall man walking in front of me and realized it was James. I recognized him from his photos. I slowed down, and to make certain, I followed him until I saw him enter the hotel. I was early, so I walked around the block and entered the hotel on time and walked to the bar. There he was, sitting in a corner table, with a waitress next to him, when he saw me walking. He stopped and got up as I approached him.

"James?' I asked hesitantly. 'Willow,' he said, smiling. We sat down. 'What can I offer you?' he asked, as the waitress was still waiting. 'I'll have a glass of Merlot, please,' I replied. He looked pleasantly surprised and said, 'I'll have a Pinot Grigio.' We settled down after the waitress had left. Like I said, the attraction was mutual, and we talked about our families, our hobbies, and things in general, and we ordered another round of wine. His first marriage had lasted fifteen years with no kids, but they fell apart over the years and finally divorced. He was single for the last eight years.

"I glanced at my watch, and it was coming to seven o'clock when he said, 'Are you spoken for dinner?' I thought that was the most romantic way of asking me, so I accepted, then told him I needed to use the washroom. Once there, I texted Jasmine the details and said I would be home after dinner. She was jubilant, of course. James and I walked to the restaurant, and as we sat at our table, he looked at me and said, 'I will marry you.' You could imagine my surprise.

"I didn't say anything, but once I came home alone that night, I reviewed the whole meeting. Deep down, I felt happy and beautiful because such a man had shown interest in me. It seemed we had many things in common, and both of us, being intellectuals by habit, communicated well. Or so I thought.

"Two weeks later, he again asked me to marry him, and when I hesitated, he said, 'What have you got to lose? Only time at our age.' So, I said yes. Everyone in my family was caught off guard. Jasmine and Sam were troubled, but they agreed since they saw me happy, and just two months later, we got married. He told me he was fascinated with me because I was so different from the other women he had dated, with my social habits and intelligence and all. As for your question about a good and joyful marriage, I wish I could say yes, but in fact, it turned out to be an abusive relationship." Alan looked up in shock.

"Abusive? You mean he hit you?" Alan asked in a menacing tone.

"Not physically, even though at first, I was afraid it might turn into that. But it was all emotional. He played on my emotions and said the most awful things about me, my family, my... truth be told, there were times I wished him dead because he hurt me so much. We had moved into a rental apartment recently, but he wasn't happy with it. He got drunk one night and took a broom and started banging on the roof of the living room because he heard the neighbours upstairs making noise. I tried to stop him, and that was when he pushed me. I thought he might hit me, and I was so lost and afraid that I rushed out of the apartment, grabbing the car keys and going down to the garage. I sat in the car, trembling, with nowhere to go, when he called me on my cell phone and said that if I didn't bring back the keys to the car in five minutes, he would call the police and tell them I had stolen it. The car was his.

"So, I came upstairs again to see that in that time, he had emptied my closet and things and put them in garbage bags by the door. Everything that belonged to me. I dragged them inside. I walked into our den to see that he had taken a hammer to my desktop computer and destroyed it. All my cables were cut in half in the garbage bin in the kitchen."

Alan looked up to see the tears flowing down Willow's cheeks. "You don't have to go on, please," he said softly. Willow sniffled and shook her head.

"I might as well go through this once and for all."

He walked inside and came back with a box of tissues, handing it to her.

"Thank you." She blew her nose and took a deep breath.

"He locked the doors to the bedroom, so for two weeks, I slept on the couch in the living room and used the second bathroom as a dressing room. A couple of days later, it was as if nothing had happened. But I knew he was smouldering inside. One day, he came back with a black hoodie, went downstairs to the garage, and slashed the tires of the neighbour's car. I had difficulty recognizing the man I had married. I was regretting my impulse, blaming myself for the position I had put myself in. I thought of divorcing him, but from the very beginning, he said he would never divorce, so I should forget about it.

"We later moved to another place, and he continued to pick quarrels with the neighbours there too, even with the management, until one day a police officer showed up at our door about complaints made against him. That was when I decided we had to get away from the city, and we moved to the house on Willow Drive. We had a different opinion of what we were looking for in a home. He wasn't the type to help around the garden. He couldn't understand why I fell in love with an old house with a large garden and many trees. We had a good deal with the owners, so he said, 'All right, here's what we'll do. You buy the house with your inheritance, but I want my name on the deed. I'll buy an RV and put your name on it.' He knew I had just about enough to pay for the house after my parents passed away, and I would have some left over, even though he was the one with money. He was quite paranoid about that too, thinking everyone, including me, was after his money. I had had no objection to signing a prenup when we got married, but there you go, he was who he was.

"I went ahead and bought the house with my inheritance from my parents since I didn't want it to go to waste on a condo or part of a complex. I wanted it to be like an estate, honouring my parents and something to leave behind to Jasmine. You know, I felt I hadn't done enough for my family, and in this strange, romantic, ancestral way, I felt that the house and property would be nice. I fell in love with the place because of the land and the many trees and the old cottage style. The problem was, I could envision what I could turn it into, and James never could.

"Meanwhile, he continued to become paranoid of everyone that I loved—my friends, my parents, even Jasmine and Sam. He picked a quarrel with Sam and forbade him to come visit. He broke off all communication with my parents, so we never went back to see them. He picked a quarrel with Jasmine, and at one point he asked me to ask her to leave while she was visiting. I became afraid that he would harm her, so I asked her to go. She understood, but it was one of the most difficult things I had to do in my life.

"That was the final straw. By that time, we had our separate bedrooms, and I spent my days crying in secret, huddled in a corner so he wouldn't hear me. I just didn't know what to do, how to go on. I didn't know what he wanted, really, because he hated it everywhere. I just couldn't believe that a person could be so cruel, so mean, so devious, and so paranoid of everyone.

"Once we moved, the fights went on, more bitter than ever. Every other month, he would say, 'Let's get divorced,' and ask me to buy his stake in the house, even though he hadn't paid anything for it. He knew I was cornered. Every day I would wake up and wonder what kind of day it would be, peaceful or fighting. I lost sense of who I was, and I would look at the miserable woman in the mirror that was me. I was ashamed because I'd distanced myself from my parents and friends. I was too ashamed to admit I had done a major wrong to myself and to everyone that loved me, so I repented for my mistakes by suffering under James." Willow took another tissue from the box and wiped her eyes. "I must look a mess," she said quietly. Alan was just too emotional to say anything, refusing to look at her.

"Then one day, he got ill. When I went to check up on him one morning, I noticed that he was delirious and could barely stand up. There was an awful smell, and I noticed that he had defecated in bed. I sort of dragged him into the bathroom and tried to clean him up, but he was just mumbling and falling to the floor, saying he wanted to sleep. So, I called the paramedics, and they came and cleaned him up and took him to the emergency at the local hospital. Like a robot, I cleaned up after them, opened the windows, changed the sheets, did the laundry, all automatically, trying not to think of what had happened or was going to happen.

"I later went to the hospital to find him propped up in bed with an IV drip. He was conscious, a little wary of the hospital since he hated them and doctors too. I talked with the surgeon, who said that they wanted to keep him overnight and do a colonoscopy the next day with some more tests. James wasn't happy but didn't resist. Long story short, he stayed four nights, and on the last day they diagnosed him with stage four colorectal cancer that had already metastasized to his liver and lungs.

"Once diagnosed, James decided he didn't want any kind of treatment whatsoever. He even refused to have more tests done or have a MRI, nothing, so we didn't have any idea how much time he had left. I knew any suggestion or encouragement would fall to deaf ears, so I gave up. At that point, chemotherapy and radiotherapy would have just extended his life by maybe a couple of months or a year, but there would be more damage done to his body. He was a proud man, and he kept saying that he had done everything on his bucket list and that it was time to go.

"James had no family, no children. Just me. Our family doctor put him on palliative care so I would have support and indicated that James was a candidate for dying with medical assistance if he so requested, which he promptly did without hesitation. He even decided that he wanted to die on his birthday, which was six months away. I thought it morbid but understood why he had chosen that date. He said, 'I was born on that date, and I shall die on that date.' Morphine became his best friend, and in increasing doses. I was the caretaker, the nurse, what have you, and I would also take care of the house and the dogs and everything else while he rested. He would sometimes come down and sit in the conservatory, enjoying the sun and watching me work.

"Gradually, it became harder for him, and with the loss of appetite, there was no point in setting a table. I would carry up his tray for breakfast, lunch, and dinner. If he ever did venture to come downstairs to sit with me or watch TV together, it would be for an hour or so, then he would retire to his bedroom. He had all the comforts there. It's hard, as you saw with your wife, to watch a person slowly disintegrate in front of your eyes. The loss of weight, colour, and strength became evident, and that tall, proud man shrivelled to a bony ghost of his previous self.

"James saw it himself. Of course, I didn't mention anything. He became kinder and softer toward me, finally admitting that he had wronged me in the past and that many decisions I had made were in fact good decisions and that he was wrong to judge me for them. He diagnosed himself as bipolar, which I thought made sense remembering past incidents, but it was too late for all that now. He had wasted his time and mine by being angry and cruel. As for me, I just felt pity and sadness to see a human being going to waste in such a manner.

"After the six months had passed, he was feeling good and decided to postpone dying and instead celebrated his birthday in October. However, come the following springtime, the pain became just intolerable. The doctor said to give him as much as he needs to make him comfortable, which led to him sleeping a lot, but never without pain. He had difficulty going to the bathroom or to wash himself but refused my help, deeming it too humiliating for him. Many times, I stood outside his bathroom door and waited until he finished whatever he was doing and helped him back to bed. My life had also stopped and only revolved around caring for him and doing the basics around the house. He couldn't even bear the dogs, who were young and always excited to see him; it was just too much for him to handle, even sitting down.

"One day in April, I brought his breakfast to his room, and he looked up at me and said, 'Enough is enough. I can't take it anymore. Arrange everything for this Sunday, please. There's no point in continuing this charade of a life. It's not fair to you.' And I replied angrily, 'Don't you ever decide to do this because of me, ever. You do it if you want to, but not for me, or as a matter of fact, for anyone else.' James looked at me with gaunt eyes. 'Look at me, Willow. I'm in constant pain. I have no appetite, have no desires, no strength. I'm not the man I once was, and besides, what's the point? I've done all I wanted in life. Please understand me and arrange it for this Sunday,' he said, looking at me, and I could see that he was sincere. 'Very well,' I said. 'I'll arrange it if they're available.'

"James was an organized man, so prior to all this, he had had me arrange all details with the lawyer, banks, and even the funeral home. He wanted to be cremated and his ashes scattered over the ocean. I had never gone through such a process, so frankly, I was terrified about it all but didn't show it to him. Everything worked out with the doctor and funeral home, and we arranged his death on a Sunday morning. We continued to live the next couple of days as if nothing had happened, and come Saturday night, we had dinner in his bedroom and watched one of his favourite movies with the dogs curled up on his bed. I glanced at him from time to time to see how he was feeling or thinking, but he was in so much pain that I decided not to say anything. I had a hard time coping with how a person could choose to die or know that they'll die, but then, I wasn't the one in pain and discomfort, so I had no right to judge.

"I'll never forget the next day. I get goosebumps even now, talking about it to you. I didn't sleep at all, and when I went to check up on him early in the morning, he was already awake. 'What do you think I should wear?' was what he asked me, and for a minute, I stood there in silence, trying to come up with an appropriate answer and thinking about whether it mattered, really, and about how awkward this was. 'Whatever makes you comfortable' was all I could reply, and I helped him get dressed. 'I'm not hungry, but I'll have a cup of coffee with you downstairs in the conservatory,' he'd said.

"I took the dogs to day care and came back in an hour, and we went downstairs. I sat him on his favourite armchair facing the gardens. The nurse was the first to arrive, and while she was fussing around with syringes and vials, James told her about some of his adventures as if it was the most normal thing to do. And I sat there, watching, trying to fathom what was about to happen. I had never seen a person die—or even a dead person, for that matter—and I didn't know if I had the strength to go through the whole process without breaking down. That was the last thing I wanted, so I willed myself to remain calm.

"The doctor arrived a little later and asked him if he was still willing to go ahead, since they must always ask before the procedure. 'Let's get it done, doctor' was all James said, but I noticed he wasn't looking at me, and I realized there would be no last words or good-byes between us. Was it because he didn't want to cause me more pain, or was it because he just wanted to cut it short? I never knew. After all, what could be said for a tumultuous eight years of marriage? I held his hand—more a comfort to myself than him—and he just looked on as the doctor inserted the syringe.

"In a minute, he was gone. I felt the strength go from the hand that I was holding, and I looked up and saw that his mouth was open, but his eyes were closed. I looked at the doctor with questioning eyes. 'He's gone,' he said softly, and I felt the hot tears in my eyes. They packed up their things and left me alone, wishing me condolences. I called the funeral home, and they said they would be there in an hour, so I sat there in the conservatory with James, who was now without pain. And I just cried. Cried for the troubling years we had, cried for the death of a person that I once thought I had loved but came to hate, then accept, and I cried for the selfish relief and for the lonely years waiting ahead for me.

"The funeral home personnel arrived, and they asked for privacy as they prepared James to take away. I watched the black body bag on the stretcher bed as they rolled him out of the house and left. The house was silent, and I realized I had to go and pick up the dogs, so I did that. Then when I got home, I called Jasmine to tell her the news. I poured myself a long drink and sat down to think and reorganize my brain. *He must have been really in a lot of pain to do this,* I thought, because like I said, I had difficulty understanding how a person could want to die.

"I know James loved me in his own way, but the damage was done. When he fell ill, I'd accepted to take care of him, atoning for the mistakes I'd made in my life. Because of this, he left me financially secure so that I didn't have to worry about my own future after him. It was his way of showing he cared.

"Funny how efficiently things run after someone has died. The funeral home and the lawyer took responsibility and completed all necessary details. I went to pick up the urn once the cremation was done, and when they handed it over, I found that it was so heavy. To think I was holding the ashes of a human being was weird enough. I couldn't bear to see it, so I put it in his bedroom until I was ready to scatter them, as he wanted. Luckily, Jasmine and Sam came over for the holidays, and they helped me do it. Until that day, it was all touch and go for me, but once I did it, I realized I needed to move on."

Willow paused for a minute before continuing. "You're the first person I've told all this."

Alan realized he didn't know what to say. It was a painful confession on her part, and he knew his actions had triggered those bad memories, things she had been trying to forget. He was having difficulty expressing the sudden emotions that had crept into him. He found it hard to acknowledge what she had said, realizing that she couldn't face him and was looking out somewhere in the distance.

"Willow… I'm sorry. I didn't know."

"How could you? Don't be sorry." Willow looked down at her hands. "Sometimes, I think that love is overrated. I have yet to see it in my life. I thought I had it, but it was just a fleeting moment of hope, and I saw it crumble. It became a fact of life that you can't expect someone to love you. There's no guarantee. There might be a semblance of it, and you think, *Yes, I am in love, and he loves me, that's it, I got it.* But no, that was just a tease until you get hooked. And then comes the destruction. Now, I can't go back and remember when I was happy. Truly happy. You see, I lost trust in my instincts. Lost trust in myself. How could I not have seen this coming? I'd always trusted my gut feelings, especially about people, but I got things so wrong that it's taken me quite a time to readjust my compass. I don't even know if I have."

"Why on earth did you marry him?" Alan asked.

"I guess I just didn't want to be alone anymore. My father was a career diplomat, and they had a busy social life, so my parents started to leave me alone at nights at the age of eight. I grew up pretty much by myself."

At one point, Alan couldn't help noticing that her eyes were shimmering again with tears. It was then that he saw a tear falling down her cheek. She carelessly brushed it away. He had been silent throughout her long speech, not wanting to disturb her rhythm once he had her going. However, he now felt he needed to say something.

"Willow, one thing I learnt in life is that you need to find the courage to forgive yourself. I know it's difficult, believe me. This is from someone who went through the thought process you're going through, but in the end, I did forgive myself, because otherwise, you constantly live in the past, constantly in anger at the world, at yourself, and that doesn't bring any kind of comfort." He paused. "I'm sorry. I didn't mean to hurt you when…"

"No, no, I'm fine. You're right, it is a relief to talk about it all. It was bottled up inside me for so long that I'm glad to have shared my story with you. I'm just too sensitive for my own good. Too romantic as well. It's just that…" Willow stopped. "You know what?" she finally said, getting up. "I'm very tired. I think I'll go to bed now."

"Of course," he said as he started to get up.

"Don't get up." Willow walked to his side and, without looking at him, placed her hand on his shoulder. Alan dared not move, but he could feel her touch burning into his skin through his shirt. Her arm was near his face, and he could smell her skin, her faint perfume that she liked to wear. Willow stayed there for a minute or two and then walked inside. Alan found her gesture strangely intimate, wanting to feel her touch again. It was a precious moment, so he sat there, savouring it. A rush of emotions filled his heart and for one minute he thought *how can any man, not love this woman? How could they have hurt her so much?*

He sat outside for quite a while, deeply troubled by Willow's story. He worried now that what relationship they had would be damaged with the information she had come forth with. He knew that she would feel awkward with him in the morning, anxiously looking for signs of judgement on his part. He himself had gone through a rough patch with his marriage, albeit in a different manner than hers. He remembered how he had struggled with Caroline, balancing work and home and not succeeding too greatly at both. Caroline's illness had come as a surprise, developing in a slow manner that threw himself and everyone in the family on the wrong course. He understood full well why Willow would have chosen to repent for her misjudgements, because he had as well by abandoning his beloved architecture and returning home to the family business after his father's and Caroline's deaths.

Alan looked at his watch to see that it was past two o'clock in the morning. *It'll be difficult to sleep after this,* he thought as he got up and picked up the empty wine bottles and glasses. As he walked inside, he noticed that there was no light in Willow's room. He closed the doors and put everything on the counter. He slowly walked toward her bedroom door and leaned in to listen. There was no noise. *Hope she's sleeping,* he thought as he walked into his bedroom and closed the door.

CHAPTER NINE

Confession

That night, Willow looked through her bedroom window and saw Alan still sitting in the same position that she had left him. She wondered what he was thinking. She didn't know why she had touched him like that, but it had felt right at that moment. Was he shocked by what she had shared? Would he now act differently now, knowing her story? Had she ruined what relationship they had? These thoughts ran through her head. *He was the one who insisted on me talking,* she thought, *but I must admit that it did do me good to unburden myself.* She had been holding it all up inside, not disclosing everything, not even to Jasmine. She lay down on the bed and curled up on her side. *Let me rest now for a bit,* she thought and, without realizing, she fell asleep.

The next day, Willow woke up later than usual, realizing that she had fallen asleep on top of the bed with her clothes on. The sun was just rising. She felt different. Maybe it was because she had unloaded a lot of emotions last night. Call it relief or just knowing that Alan knew more about her past life. She hadn't told him everything, but she saw in his eyes that he understood her.

She didn't know when he'd gone to bed last night after she left him. She walked toward the windows and saw him sitting outside on one of the lounge chairs close to the edge of the terrace. She then went into the bathroom, splashed water on her face, and looked up at the mirror. Her hair was all tangled up and dishevelled, and she looked... old. *Well, you are old,* she told herself. *You're sixty-five going on a hundred.* She smiled then, knowing what Alan would have said to that. She quickly changed into a pair of jeans and a tank top, on top of which she wore a long colourful shirt, rolling up her sleeves. She brushed her hair quickly into a ponytail and, putting on her loafers, walked out of the bedroom.

"Good morning. You're up early," Willow said as she approached him.

Alan glanced up and smiled. "I thought I might make the coffee this morning. Here, I'll bring you a cup," he said, getting up.

"I can get it."

"I've been sitting too long. Take my seat, I'll be back." Alan walked into the house. Willow sat down on his chair and felt the warmth his body had left there. It was somewhat comforting. Alan came back with a steaming cup of coffee.

"Here you are. I'll just grab the other chair." Willow took a sip. They sat in silence as the sun rose higher, changing the colours around them.

"Did you get any sleep?" Alan asked.

"Yes, I fell asleep on the bed," Willow answered. "And you?"

"A few hours." Alan replied. There was an awkward silence then. They continued to sit and sipped their coffees, listening to the day coming alive.

"Oh, look, there's a beautiful sailboat in the distance," Willow said, pointing out to the horizon.

"So there is," Alan replied.

"Someone else is up and sailing, how nice. I've never been on a sailboat, you know."

"I know," Alan replied. "You told me before."

"Did I? Hmm, I don't remember. I guess I might have. Look, it's turning toward us."

"Is it, now?" Alan said, and it was then that Willow suddenly knew. "Are you telling me that it's coming here?"

"Well, it sure looks like the captain is sailing our way."

"Alan?" she said.

"What?"

"Is that sailboat coming here?"

"Why don't we go down to the dock and see?" Alan replied, getting up from his chair. "Come on." Willow left her mug on the ground and got up to follow him. They took the elevator down. By the time they reached the end of the dock, the sailboat had anchored, and a man waved at them from behind the helm while a young boy walked toward the bow to check the anchor. Alan waved back.

"Who are they?" Willow asked, shielding her face from the sun.

"That's John—remember, from the airport? —with his son."

"Why are they here?"

"They brought my boat."

"Your boat?" Willow turned around to look at him.

"Yes, my boat."

"Why? I mean, why are they bringing it?" By now, Willow was really confused. She watched as the man and the boy lowered the dinghy in the back and got in. After a few pulls, the small motor kicked in, and they slowly approached the dock.

"Hello, good morning," John shouted as he professionally manoeuvred the dinghy to line up against the dock. The young boy jumped onto it with a tie as Alan reached for the second one that John threw at him.

"Good to see you, John, thank you for bringing her in."

"Not at all," John replied, turning off the engine and deftly climbing onto the deck. "Ma'am," he said, looking at her. "Alan, when do you want me to pick it up?"

"Six o'clock should be fine," Alan replied.

"All right, then. Come along, Roy," John said as the young boy smiled at them, and they started walking toward the steps. Willow stood there, looking into the dinghy, then at the sailboat, at a loss for words.

"What is this all about?"

"I thought a day out on the sea would be a nice change."

"But... I mean, why did they bring it here?"

"The boat stays at the marina near town. John and his boy take care of it for me while I'm not here."

"Well, then we could have easily gone—" Willow stopped suddenly. "You didn't want me to go to town because of what happened yesterday."

"I thought it best not knowing how long they would be around, and I saw how upset you became."

"I don't know what to say."

"How about we go and get ready and make the most of the day? How are your sea legs?" Alan asked as they walked back to the house.

"I'm OK. I don't get seasick, if that's what you're asking. I'll let you know that I had a small rowboat when I was young."

"Really?" Alan asked, turning around to look at her.

"Yes, I was a teenager then, and in summer, I would often stay with my grandmother who had a house by the sea. She bought me the rowboat. I became quite a good rower."

"Did it have a name?" Alan asked.

"You know, I don't quite remember, but I'm sure I would have named it. I scraped and painted the whole thing. Prussian blue with an orange stripe." Willow smiled at the thought as they took the elevator and reached the living room.

"How are John and Roy going back? Are they staying here?" Willow asked.

"No, he'll take the jeep and come back in the evening."

"You've thought of everything."

"I had time to last night." Alan smiled wryly.

"Anything special I need to take with me?" Willow asked as she walked toward her bedroom.

"Your bathing suit if you want to swim and a sweater if it gets windy. Something for your head, maybe? Your loafers are fine for the boat. I'll grab some things for the cooler." Willow watched him walk toward the fridge. She was pleasantly surprised with what he had organized, and for the first time, she felt... special. However, she knew because of her previous experiences that this was a dangerous path to walk on, and she promised herself to be cautious. She knew she had talked too much last night, and maybe that was the wrong thing to do, because it meant now that she was vulnerable. At the time, it had felt right, but now, she had hesitations.

Willow shook her head and scolded herself. *Come on, just enjoy the day.* At the end, she did take her bathing suit, even though she found the idea of changing and climbing in and out on the boat too uncomfortable. She brought along a headscarf and a sweater along with a towel, which she all pushed into her bag, and then she walked out to the terrace where Alan was waiting for her.

"So, you will try to swim?" he asked, looking at her bag.

"We'll see, how about you?"

He pointed to the small bag behind him. "Come on, let's go."

Willow saw he was also carrying a cooler bag and had changed into a white shirt with small blue flowers and a sweater around his shoulders. She looked at the hat on his head, and it looked like it belonged there. *He looks... He looks just adorable,* Willow thought.

It had been some time since she got into a dinghy, but she managed without falling overboard. As they puttered up to the sailboat, she noticed the name *Wind Dancer*.

"Nice name," she remarked. Alan helped her climb aboard while he held on. "Here, give me the bags," she said, turning around.

Alan got out after her and neatly tied the dinghy to the boat. "Let's hope we get some wind this afternoon," he said as he got behind the helm and pushed the button to pull in the anchor.

"Where are we going?" Willow asked as Alan steered the boat to open waters.

"I want to take you to a favourite spot of mine. Hopefully there'll be no one there. We can swim if we want and have lunch. It'll take about two hours to get there, so just sit and enjoy."

Willow sat down behind him and watched the house get smaller in the distance. "Where did you learn how to sail?" she asked.

"My father. He was an avid sailor, and we had a terrific sailboat. We would go out together, sometimes for several days. I was eight when he started to take me out for the day, then he moved to the farm." Alan turned back without saying anything. Willow gazed at the sea, lost in her thoughts.

"All I want is for you to have a good day today," Alan said later without turning his head.

"I will. Look—it's a beautiful day, and you're taking me to your favourite spot, which, by the way, I'm very curious about. Where is it?" Willow looked around as they were approaching a couple of small islands scattered close to the coast.

"It's the small one right behind the others," Alan replied as he slowed down. Willow could see several other boats out and about.

"It looks busy."

"Not where we're going," Alan replied. "Not a lot of people know of it."

"I'm curious now. Very curious." Willow laughed and walked toward the bow of the boat to see better. They approached the small island, which looked uninhabited but was covered with beautiful mature trees. Alan started to go around to the other side when Willow spotted a little entrance between the trees.

"Don't tell me we're going in there!" she shouted. Alan just smiled. Willow got up and walked back to his side. "Are you sure we can go in there? What about the keel, isn't it too shallow? What if…"

"We're not going in there with the boat. We'll take the dinghy. I'm just going to anchor here."

"And leave the boat by itself?"

"Yes, why?"

"I mean, what if someone…"

"No pirates around here, if that's what you mean," Alan said as he manoeuvred the boat and dropped anchor. Willow was still standing, glaring at him. He turned around to look at her.

"You might want to change into your swimsuit if you want to swim."

"And where might I be swimming?"

"It's the surprise, come on. You can always not swim, but just in case you like the place…"

Willow went down, grabbing her bag. "The bedroom is right ahead," Alan shouted from above. *As if I didn't know that,* she thought and walked into a nice, cosy bedroom. She closed the door and pulled out her bathing suit. *Well, here goes,* she thought. Jasmine had put in her black one-piece suit, knowing she would feel comfortable in that.

Willow looked in the mirror behind the door. Not too much sagging overall, a little cellulite on the thighs, bit of a stomach, breasts held up by the suit. *Why am I bothering with how I look, anyway? Better that he knows.* She pulled her shirt on and grabbed her bag to go out. Alan had prepared the dinghy and the cooler bag.

"Wait until I change too," Alan said, running inside. Willow sat on the side and waited. It was very peaceful, and all she could hear were the trees whispering with the breeze. The sea shimmered under the sun. Alan came out wearing colourful board shorts, and Willow realized that it was the first time that she had seen him this undressed. It was obvious that he worked out, because his body was muscled, even for a man his age. Suddenly, she felt very conscious of her own body.

"I'll go in first, then. I can help you get down. Hand me the bags," Alan said.

Willow got in again successfully without falling overboard and sat down. Alan pushed away and started the little outboard motor. Willow sat with her back to him as they slowly approached the secret entrance. The trees on both sides had intertwined above and created a ceiling of green with the sunlight barely making it through. It was cool and the water very clear, and she could see the pebbles and sand underneath. In a couple of minutes, they were out in the open again, and she saw that they were in a little cove with a sandy beach.

"What is this place?" Willow asked, turning around.

"People say that it was used by smugglers a long time ago. Only the locals know about it." Alan cut the engine as the dinghy slowly approached the beach. He jumped out and pulled it onto the sand.

"Give me your hand."

Willow got out and looked around. "This place is magical. I'm surprised there's no one here."

"Like I said, you've got to know the area. We try to keep it a secret," Alan said as he took the bags out and placed them on the sand.

"Hidden treasures and all?"

"Definitely. I keep the map in a secret place."

Willow laughed as she walked barefoot on the warm sand. The water was calm, and the occasional small wave rolled in and tickled her toes. The sand continued into the water with small pebbles scattered here and there, and she was once again amazed at how Mother Nature had created these beautiful spots.

"Do you like it?" Willow turned around to see that Alan had walked up behind her.

"It's amazing. When did you discover this place?" she asked as they turned to walk back to where their bags were.

"John showed it to me when I was building the house." Alan sat down on the sand by the bags. "Want to swim?" he asked, looking up at her.

"It's very inviting, and the water isn't that cold. I think I'll give it a try. What about you?" she asked.

"I'll keep guard," Alan replied.

"What do you mean? Any animals I should know about?" Willow asked, looking around.

"Only the ones with two legs," he said, smiling.

"Oh, very funny," she jokingly said. She walked to the edge of the water and felt her feet sink slowly in the sand. She personally didn't like the idea of taking off her shirt and standing in her bathing suit in front of him, but she realized she had no choice, so slowly she pulled off her shirt. Alan fiddled around with the bags, not looking at her, and Willow realized he was doing that on purpose so she would feel comfortable. She briskly walked in and, with one dive, immersed herself in the water. She came up for air and shook her head, her ponytail flinging about, and started to swim freestyle. She swam horizontally to the beach a couple of times before she stopped and turned to look at him, finding him already looking at her.

"Come on, it feels fantastic."

Alan got up and ran into the water, creating great splashes and noise, and then promptly dived in, ending up beside her.

"It's like your own private pool," Willow remarked, floating on her back. They swam together, with Alan pointing out certain corners of the cove and talking about the time when John had brought him here so many years ago.

"My fingers have shrivelled," Willow joked and swam toward the beach. Together, they came out and towelled themselves before sitting down.

"How about a nice, cold beer?" Alan asked, opening the cooler.

"I think that would be great." She smiled as he handed her a can and a perfectly wrapped sandwich. Willow looked at him then. "When did you prepare these?" she asked, remembering their exchange twelve years ago.

"Like I said, I didn't get much sleep last night, so I got up early," Alan replied, popping open his beer and drinking a large gulp. "Ahh, life is good." He unwrapped his sandwich and took a bite. Willow followed suit.

⁓ℯ๑

They stayed there another hour before going back. As Alan manoeuvred the boat out of its mooring and moved toward the open sea, he said, "Hold the helm as I unfurl the sails. The wind is picking up."

"What, me? I don't know…"

"You drive, don't you?" he said as he walked toward the bow.

"I can't…" she said, grabbing the helm.

"Just hold it steady without changing direction."

Willow froze in her spot, holding tightly as he unfolded the sails with a snap. Before they could fill in with the wind, Alan came back and took over. Willow sat down in the stern, watching with amazement as the sails filled up and Alan cut the engine. The boat gracefully rode the waves, and the only sound was of the wind and the rushing of the boat over the water. It was the most sensational feeling Willow had ever felt, with the wind against her face and whipping up her hair. A sudden rush of emotions overwhelmed her as she sat there watching Alan and the sea.

"Look, there's a pod of dolphins ahead."

She got up and held on, gazing ahead. "They're beautiful," she shouted as she slowly walked toward the bow to see them better. She sat down sideways as the dolphins raced the boat, and some jumped high in the air before plunging into the depths of the sea. The sailboat gained speed, and at one point, they were parallel to the dolphins as they went ahead of each other. The sun was in her face, the wind was all around her with the occasional spraying from the sea, and she felt alive and grateful for the wonders of nature. Willow pulled out the band from her hair and let it fly loose, feeling the wind in each strand.

She turned around to see Alan looking and was startled at how aroused she became by the look. She felt the wind in her hair and started laughing and clapping her hands in delight. It was as if she was transformed into this little girl, a girl who became alive and was literally jumping up and down in delight. *Where did I hide this little girl?* she wondered, looking on. They continued for a while, each in their own thoughts, seated apart yet knowing they were together. Finally, Willow got up and came back next to Alan as she pulled up her hair again.

"That was amazing."

"I'm glad you enjoyed it," Alan replied without turning around, "I've never seen you like this before." Not giving it a thought, Willow leaned her face against his back and put her hand on his shoulder. He didn't move at the sudden intimacy.

"Thank you," she mumbled into his sweater. "Thank you for this." Alan too did not move, and they stood there for a few minutes without saying anything. Willow finally pulled away, not wanting to but knowing she had to. She was surprised at herself for what she'd done but didn't regret it.

"We should be going back," Alan said finally, his voice a little hoarse. Willow settled down as he gracefully turned the sailboat around, and they made it back in silence, enjoying the magical moment they had just experienced, trying to analyse what had happened.

By the time they approached the house, Willow saw John and Roy on the dock waiting for them. Alan dropped anchor, and they gathered up their things in the dinghy and motored back to the dock.

"How was it?" John asked as they tied up the dinghy.

"Just wonderful," Willow replied, jumping out. "Thank you for waiting."

"Thanks, John," Alan said, "we'll talk later. Safe journey."

Willow waved at John and started walking toward the house.

"You caught the sun in your face today," Alan remarked.

"Did I? I can feel it, what, with the wind."

"It looks good," he said, walking up the steps to the elevator.

"I think I'll shower before dinner," Willow replied.

"Me too. I'll meet you here for drinks," Alan said, dropping off the cooler bag in the kitchen.

Willow walked to her bedroom and closed the door, wondering how she looked. She walked into the bathroom to look in the mirror. Her face was flushed with the sun, her hair a glorious mess, but she looked happy. *Hmm, this sailboat thing is something I should do more often,* she thought as she undressed and got in the shower.

Fifteen minutes later, wrapped in her bathrobe, she rubbed the steam from the mirror and looked again. Now her hair was wet, but the flush was still there, and she still managed to look happy. *Strange that I should feel happy,* Willow thought. *Why? Because of the sailboat? Because of Alan? Because I hugged him?*

But now, what to wear? Jasmine had packed some of her favourite things, but suddenly, she felt the need to be different tonight. Willow looked at the dress that Alan had bought her from the market. She had refused to buy it for obvious reasons, but she loved the vibrant, colourful design, and what better place than here to wear it? She blow-dried her hair before finally putting it up and placing her shiny combs to hold it in place. She put the dress on and anxiously looked in the mirror.

The woman she saw there wasn't her. It couldn't be. This woman had a glow about her face from the sun, and the new crystal earrings matched the colours of her dress that fell gracefully about her body. *Not bad.* Willow looked surprised at this woman that somehow managed to look beautiful, regardless of her age. Even the lines on her face seemed to have disappeared. "Haven't seen you around lately," she mumbled at the image. She pulled on her sandals and walked out of the room. Alan was behind the counter in the kitchen, and he turned around when he heard her.

He stood still.

"Well?" Willow asked, twirling around. "Too much?"

"It's perfect," Alan finally replied. She saw the rush of emotions come over his face as he looked her up and down. She felt beautiful and she could see him struggling with the urge to kiss her? Maybe. Instead, he just said, "I thought we might have some champagne to celebrate your first sailboat experience, which, by the way, you passed with flying colours."

Willow sat on one of the stools behind the counter as he took out the bottle from the fridge along with two chilled flutes. She saw the label immediately. "Dom Perignon? Oh my…"

"I remember this being your favourite, no?" Alan replied jokingly, referring to the bottle they had on her birthday some three months ago. *Was it only three months?* Willow thought. *It seemed longer.* Alan deftly popped the cork and poured.

"Here's to sailing, and of course, to you," he said, looking into her eyes.

"Here's to you, sir, for taking me out today." They both sipped.

"Are you hungry?" Alan asked.

"Famished. All day out in the wind and sun always makes me hungry. Even though we had your fantastic sandwiches."

"Good, so am I. John brought us a fresh sea bass and tiger prawns from the fish market, so I thought I might grill them on the barbecue. We can have the fish and save the prawns, or have the prawns and save the fish, or—"

"Let's have the tiger prawns tonight," Willow intervened.

"Good. If you'll make a salad, then? We also have fresh bread, courtesy of John's wife."

"Yum," Willow replied and smiled, sipping her champagne. When he remained silent, Willow was puzzled. "What is it?"

He didn't answer but instead continued to look at her.

"What is it, Alan?"

"It's just that…" Alan started, then stopped. "Never mind. Let's go outside and sit." He picked up the bottle and walked out onto the patio.

Willow sat down on the couch, and Alan sat next to her and stretched out his legs. She looked at him sideways, noticing that he had changed into a navy-blue shirt with the sleeves rolled up. His tanned arms had a soft blonde fuzz, and Willow had a sudden urge to touch it. Instead, she gulped down her champagne.

"Are you all right?" Alan asked while he poured her a second glass.

"It's been a beautiful day, the sun, the wind, and the ocean. I'm just… just relaxed." Willow replied, trying to hide the sudden flow of emotions that she hadn't felt for a very long time.

Willow sat, trying to analyse why all she wanted at that moment was to fall into Alan's arms and let go, but then she remembered her past mistakes and suddenly sat up.

"Maybe we should get dinner going," Willow said finally. She didn't want to sit next to him anymore and got up.

Alan looked up at her. "What's going on?" he asked.

"Nothing, I'm just hungry, aren't you?" she said jokingly, trying to disguise her feelings.

"All right, I'll get the barbecue going, then," Alan said, walking toward it while Willow went inside into the kitchen to do anything so she could suppress her emotions. She took out the salad ingredients and turned on the tap. She looked up to see Alan fiddling with the barbecue, and a sudden warmth filled her heart. She took in his tousled hair, his tall frame, his suntanned face, and she daydreamed as the tap continued to flow. *Get a grip, woman,* she thought to herself and started washing the lettuce leaves.

"How's it going?" Alan asked as he came in and walked to the fridge. He opened the door and took out the prawns. "Oh, sorry," he said as he brushed up against her back while passing. Willow had a sense that he had done that on purpose, so she turned around. She saw him going outside, and he was smiling. She shook her head and smiled to herself. *This is going to be a difficult night,* she thought. *Very difficult.*

Dinner was ready in no time, and they sat outside, enjoying the cool air now that the sun had set. It was a clear sky, and one could see the faint lights in the distance from the other islands. Their mood changed over time, and they returned to their casual conversation to the point where it started to feel like they were flirting. Willow overcame her previous trepidations about the evening, and Alan had seemed to seize upon it.

After they finished their dinner and the bottle of wine, Willow got up to clear the table while Alan put away the barbecue. He came in, glancing over at her as she was filling the dishwasher. He went to where his records were and searched through until he picked one up and placed it on the record player. Willow stood still when she heard the song "The Nearness of You" playing. Alan came over to her, holding her hand and pulling her close to him. He said, "Come dance with me."

Willow didn't know if Alan had specifically asked her to dance because of the lyrics of the song. They danced slowly around the room. Willow pulled her head back that was resting on his shoulder and looked at him. For a few seconds, they stood, their faces inches away. Alan then took his hands and put them on both sides of her face. Willow closed her eyes as he softly kissed her on the lips.

"You smell of the sun."

Willow's whole body tingled with the sensation. Alan pulled away a little, waiting for her to say something. It was then that Willow put her arms around his neck and returned the kiss. Suddenly, it grew passionate, and after a while, they were left breathless.

"I'm thinking we're too old for this," Willow mumbled.

"I'm not too old to want to make love to the woman I love," Alan huskily replied. Willow looked up at his face questioningly. "I might not be the man I was forty years ago, but I still feel. I still love." Willow hesitated, and Alan seemed to sense it. "Don't run away from me, Willow. I'll never hurt you."

"Why me?" Willow slowly asked. "I'm not beautiful, I don't have a body you would desire, I'm old, and I carry bumps and bruises all over. Why would you want me?" She looked into his eyes.

"I'm not looking for a quick release or a mad frenzy session of sex. You're a beautiful woman with an incredible heart and mind. I see you. I see the real you, and I want that real woman hiding behind the image you present to the world. I saw a glimpse of her today on the boat. I know it's in self-defence, so I'm asking you to lower your barriers and let me in. Let me touch the real you. Let me make love to the real you. Let me take you in my arms and hold you tight and show you that yes, there is still love out there. There is still hope for us."

"I remember what happened when I precisely did just that, and look where I am now," Willow responded.

"Do you not trust me?"

She didn't answer immediately, and she pulled back a few steps. "I don't want to get hurt. I promised myself I would never allow myself to get hurt again."

"I know, I understand. But there's still hope for you. I'm offering you a chance to believe in yourself again. Don't hide behind the past, and don't let it affect the decisions you want to make. Give yourself a chance at happiness again. Love isn't like the ones we see in the movies. It just doesn't happen like that. People make mistakes, but they deserve a second chance. I saw how happy you were today—on the boat, at the beach, you transformed into this totally different person. The real you came out, a woman still young at heart, wanting to be loved and cared for. And I'm saying I'm up for the job, if you'll let me. We still have many years ahead of us, and I believe that if we share that together, we'll be happy. Both of us have been through the different stages of a relationship. We don't need to go through that again. But we can enjoy each other."

"I have to think about this. I'm sorry."

"Tell me. Why are you here?"

"You have no right to ask me that," Willow said angrily, looking straight into his eyes.

"Tell me what's right, then. Tell me what to do. I don't know how to reach out to you."

"I never said I wanted anything from you. You don't have the right to say that to me." Willow turned and leaned against the kitchen sink, her shoulders sagging.

"I wish you did. For once, I wish you'd say what you want. I'm not a fool. Your husbands were fools to let you go, but I won't be."

Alan paused and slowly walked to stand right behind her. Willow didn't move. He slowly placed his hands beside hers and leaned in.

"Say what you want," Alan whispered softly into her ear.

"I just…" Her voice was trembling. Willow could feel his body warm against hers and remembered that time back at her house when they were in a similar position. She remembered him pulling away.

"Say it, Willow. Just say it, please. Don't run away this time," Alan continued, not moving, just standing close to her body. Willow was breathless. Her body trembled as he slowly placed his hands around her waist and pulled her slowly toward him. He kissed her on the side of her neck. She leaned back, letting go.

"I… Alan, I…"

There were tears in her eyes as he slowly turned her around in his arms and lifted her face up. "Say you want me like I want you." His eyes had turned dark with emotion.

"Please, please let me go" was all Willow could say.

"I will not let you go. I cannot let you go." Alan leaned to kiss her.

"Please, please," Willow murmured against his cheek.

"No, say it... say it, please. I know you want to say it."

"I can't. You have to understand." Willow pushed him away.

Alan was taken aback and looked puzzled. "What is it that I have to understand?"

Willow moved past him to go outside on the terrace. It was a warm night with a slight breeze coming in from the ocean. She sat down and pulled up her feet under her. Alan moved to join her, stopping halfway to return to pick up his wineglass. He stared at the glass in his hand and hesitated, but he turned around and came out on the terrace. He sat back in his chair across Willow and stretched out his long legs. He sighed. Willow looked up at him. He returned the look.

"You know what I think?" Alan finally said. "I think you're afraid that you've forgotten how to love. I know what I want. But do you?"

"That's a cruel thing to say."

"Maybe. But you know I'm right." Willow didn't respond, and Alan said, "Look, I'm sorry, I'm listening. I feel pretty foolish with what went on inside," he added.

"I know, I'm sorry. It's just that..." Willow stopped and drew a long breath. "I haven't had s... It's been nearly fifteen years since I've been in a relationship with a man," she continued.

Alan suddenly looked up at her in astonishment, frowning and hesitating. "Do you mean to tell me that you and James... that your husband... that you... the bastard," he mumbled. Willow was having difficulty expressing the sudden emotions that had crept into her. She saw the anguish on Alan's face. Suddenly she couldn't face him anymore and looked away.

"But why?" Alan finally asked.

"One day, in our first month of marriage, James turned to me while we were in bed and said, 'You know what? You don't know men. You have little experience on how to please a man, and I'm too old to teach you.' From that time on, he never kissed or touched me again. The humiliation I felt is… difficult to explain. You don't forget something like that. It leaves a mark on you." Willow stopped talking for a minute, remembering that moment. "Maybe he was right," she continued. Willow turned to look at Alan. "Maybe it's my fault. I led you to believe that things could be normal between us. I'm amazed at how far our relationship has come. I just felt so unwanted… It hurt so much… It…" She stopped and very slowly got off the chair and walked inside the house. She noticed that Alan didn't follow her. She stood beside the sink struggling not to cry, unsuccessfully. She looked up and saw Alan standing outside looking at her. Suddenly, the wineglass in her hand snapped in two from her grip.

"Ow, shit!" Willow exclaimed loudly. Alan ran inside beside her and saw the broken wineglass in her hand. Blood was flowing freely into the sink, swirling around the drain.

"What have you done?" Alan looked around for something to wrap around her hand and grabbed the tea towel hanging beside the sink. Willow was still crying, oblivious of the injury.

"Give me your hand, Willow, give me your hand." She silently gave it. Alan turned on the tap to wash off the blood and then gently wrapped the towel. Willow sniffled.

"Does it hurt?" Alan asked quietly. Willow shook her head in silence. "We should have some antiseptic around here to put on it." He opened one of the kitchen cabinet doors to several bottles of spices, matches, ammonium, and antiseptic. Holding Willow's hand, he grabbed the bottle and twisted the cap open. He unwrapped the towel and poured some of the liquid on her hand. Willow winced but silently looked on. By this time, she had stopped crying. Alan rewound the towel and held her hand in both of his but couldn't look at her face. They stood for a few minutes without speaking.

"That was silly of me," Willow finally said in a small voice.

Alan took a while to reply, seemingly overcome by emotion. "I should have some Band-Aids in the bathroom," he finally said and walked to his bedroom. Willow stood there hesitant, not knowing whether to follow him or stay. He came back with a box by the time she had made up her mind.

"There, that should do it."

Willow looked down at her hand, now nicely cleaned and sanitized. "Thank you."

"Just one thing missing," Alan said. He picked up her hand and gently kissed her palm. "Medicinal kiss." He held on to it. "Willow, I don't want to be alone tonight," he finally whispered without looking at her face.

"Neither do I," Willow replied after a while, and she gave him a soft smile. She slowly turned around, walked to her bedroom, and closed the door without looking back at him.

◦℮◦

Alan stood there for a few minutes to digest all that had happened. *I would have run over and banged open the door, thrown her on the bed, and taken her there and then if I was the young man I once was,* he thought. *How should I go about it now? Do I wait? Do I go in, just like that?* He knew how sensitive Willow was about all things intimate, and her past experiences with men were not much to compare to.

On the other hand, it had been a while since he'd been with a woman, and suddenly, he had performance anxiety. Once the intimate moment had passed, he was having second thoughts, and he realized he'd put himself into a bind. Was Willow expecting him to knock on the door and go in? Or had she just toyed with the idea but had decided to not go further and instead went to bed?

Alan turned around to look outside. *Might as well blow out the candles,* he thought. He stood a while, listening to the ocean waves. As Alan turned to go inside, he noticed that the windows were open in Willow's bedroom, and the slight breeze was billowing the curtains. Was she awake waiting for him? It was then that he saw her shadow standing behind the curtains. Was she looking at him? Alan stared at the image, wondering.

He went inside and walked to Willow's bedroom door. He softly knocked, then opened it slightly. The room was dark with no lights, but he could see that yes, Willow was standing in front of the windows with her back turned. She didn't move. Alan closed the door behind him and slowly walked to stand right behind her. He didn't say anything, and they stood there for a while, both lost in their thoughts. He could feel the heat from her body as she stood still.

Finally, Alan looked at her piled-up hair and gently pulled out the two combs that held it. Her white hair tumbled down. He could smell the faint lavender scent. "I've been wanting to do that for a long time," Alan said, his voice deep and husky. Willow was trembling. "Are you cold?" he asked, embracing her. She had changed into a silk button-down long shirt, and the fabric slithered under his hands.

"No," Willow mumbled.

With one hand, Alan moved aside her hair and ever so gently placed a kiss on her neck. As Willow moved back closer to his body, she responded by laying her head on his shoulder and, with her soulful brown eyes, looked into his eyes. Alan realized that he could feel her breasts through her shirt, and the sensation overwhelmed him.

He pulled her flush against him as Willow turned around to face him. His kiss was passionate as he caressed her. *How can any man not want to kiss her?* Alan thought as he lost himself to the moment. There was no urgency, no rush as they kissed. This was a strange feeling for Alan; as a young man, he would have acted differently, but now, he wanted to savour the moment, like sipping good wine. He could sense that Willow felt the same way, but it was her who finally pulled away from the kiss. Alan waited for her to make the first move.

"Why are you with me when you can have all the young and beautiful women in the world? Why me?"

He looked into Willow's troubled eyes. "It's you I want. It's you I want to make love to. You. It's not the body I want, but the woman. You make me want you, don't you see? I've never felt like this."

He looked down and saw that the tiny top button of her silk shirt had slipped open. He slowly undid another one, then another. The collar flapped open, and Alan gently slid his hand inside. Willow shuddered at the touch. Alan stopped to see whether she would say something, but she seemed to enjoy the moment, closing her eyes. As Alan caressed her, he felt her nipples tense under his touch. He was surprised to see how very much aroused he was by now, but he knew that he had to control himself for the time being. He pulled his hand away. Willow's face was in the shadow, but he saw that her eyes were open.

"Are you sure?" she whispered.

Alan's answer was sure from the start. Ever so slowly, Willow disentangled herself from Alan's embrace and walked behind him. He didn't move, waiting. Willow slipped her hands around him to unbutton his shirt, then moved them up until they reached his nipples. Gently, she caressed them until they were stiff, and for a moment, Alan stopped breathing. He hadn't felt something so erotic for a long time. Willow then slipped down his shirt from his shoulders and let it fall to the ground. She stepped back, and Alan didn't know whether he should turn around and just throw her on the bed, but then she placed her face against his naked back and gradually moved her body against his. Alan realized Willow had opened her night shirt, and he could now feel her naked body against his.

Suddenly, Alan couldn't wait any longer, so he turned around to face her. Willow's face was half in shadow when he leaned down to kiss her. He deepened the kiss as she opened her mouth and put her arms around his neck. Alan could feel her heart beating fast as he pulled her closer, and he knew she could feel his arousal. For a while they stood there, kissing as time stood still. All that mattered was the kiss.

When eventually they ended up on the bed, Willow lay on her back and Alan lay down next to her on his side. He propped himself up on his arm and looked into her eyes. He gently caressed her face. "Let me love you," he whispered in her ear. His hand touched her breast and slid down. Willow trembled then. "Let me love you," he repeated, his hand gliding down. Alan touched her delicately, wanting to see, wanting to understand the woman he was making love to, and Willow closed her eyes. He bent down to kiss the side of her neck and moved his lips down to her breast, licking her nipple.

Willow seemed to lose control of her body then, giving herself up to the moment when she reached her orgasm. Alan held her tightly as she wound down, breathless, and he noticed the tears in her eyes. The soft light that shone through the curtains played shadows in the room. Willow opened her eyes and saw Alan looking down at her, his breathing heavy. Neither of them spoke, both knowing the next step.

"I don't want to hurt you," Alan whispered in Willow's ear.

"You won't," she whispered back.

Alan kissed her, then as he entered her, Willow tensed for a second. He waited, but they had gone too far to stop and reflect as their bodies moved in unison. He felt lost in an unknown world, his feelings for Willow overwhelming his thoughts and body. Willow welcomed him. Alan arched his back as he gave out a long groan, deep from his throat, and then he let himself down by her side, breathing heavily. Willow drew the sheets up.

"You do know that I've seen it all," Alan said, looking up at the ceiling, still breathing heavily and smiling.

"You're terrible."

"I know." Alan looked at her now.

"Your eyes change colour, do you know that?" Willow asked, also turning on her side.

"They do? How?"

"Your eyes are green, but when you're deeply emotional, they turn dark blue. That was one of the first things I noticed about you."

"Funny, no one's said anything about that before," Alan mused. He leaned down to kiss her gently, then gathered her in his arms.

CHAPTER TEN

Passion

*I*t *must be morning,* Willow thought when she woke up. A slight breeze billowed the white curtains in front of the sliding doors, which were wide open. She felt it caressing her face. For a moment, she thought she heard the ocean, but in fact, it was the sound of rain. She was lying facing the windows with her left arm tucked under her pillow. This was usually the way she slept. It was a soft rain, a welcome sound, and she could hear the birds singing through it. It was very peaceful, and she closed her eyes and listened to the sounds of nature as thoughts of the previous night ran through her mind. She had never felt like that before with any of her husbands. *Why is that?* Willow thought. She had forgotten all her worries about her body, age, and inhibitions. Alan had known exactly what he was doing, where to touch her and when to slow down. There was this overpowering sensuality between herself and Alan that she had difficulty understanding. There had been only two men in her life, both she had married, and she had never been in the game of dating. *Is this what it's supposed to feel like? Is this what I've been missing? What do I do? What if he's not feeling the same?*

She slowly turned on her back to look at Alan, who was sleeping on his stomach with his face turned toward her. His right arm was possessively resting on her waist. Willow stared at him for a few minutes as she stretched her legs. She wanted to move but didn't want to wake him. As she tried to turn around, the arm around her waist restrained her.

"Where are you going?" Alan mumbled sleepily.

"I thought I might get up."

He opened his eyes and looked at her. "What time is it?" he asked, closing his eyes again.

"Five thirty. It's too early for you to get up. We had a long day yesterday," Willow added.

He still held her by the waist. "And a long night," he finally answered without opening his eyes. Willow smiled, and she saw him peek at her.

"It's been a while since I woke up with someone next to me." Slowly, Alan pulled her toward him by the waist. She glided over. Their faces were inches away. He got up on his elbow and leaned over so she was forced to lie on her back. She fidgeted under the scrutiny.

"Don't move, woman," Alan whispered gently, kissing her on the lips. After a long and deep kiss, he continued, "You are extraordinary."

Words refused to come. Willow saw that he was sincere as she caressed his face with her hand. The stubble on his face was soft to the touch. He slowly turned his face to kiss her palm.

"Am I too heavy for you?" Alan was lying full on top of her, although he was supporting himself on his elbows.

"No." They gazed into each other's eyes while their bodies reacted. Willow smiled seductively. "Is that a wake-up call?"

"At this age, frankly, I don't know." Alan leaned forward to whisper in her ear. "Why don't we give it a try?"

Willow closed her eyes, and slowly, they made love again.

A couple of hours later, they were still in bed. The rain had stopped by then, and the sun was starting to peek from behind the clouds. Alan had his arm about her as her head lay on his chest. Willow sighed.

"What is it?" Alan asked.

Willow looked up at his face. "I've never done this before. Lie in bed, cuddled up in bed without doing anything."

"It's not as if we haven't been doing nothing."

"You know what I mean." Willow laughed, slapping him on the chest.

"Ow!"

"Oh, I'm sorry, did I hurt you?" she suddenly asked, getting up.

"Lie down, I'm joking. It'll take more than that slap to hurt me."

She lay back down again. "I like the way you hold me," she said in a soft voice. Alan didn't answer, touched by the way she had said it. He knew she was sincere, and as a matter of fact, no woman had ever said that to him. He had had his share of women in his life, even after becoming a widower. However, no one had affected him as much as Willow did. She had the same effect on him now as she had twelve years ago.

"I like touching you," Alan finally responded. They lay there, each in their own thoughts, not wanting to be the first to get up.

"Do you like scrambled eggs?"

Alan was practically dozing off when he heard her. "Scrambled eggs? What's that?"

"It's when you…" Willow stopped when she noticed him laughing. "Tease," she said, rolling around. She stretched up her arms, her long white hair flowing down her back. Willow grabbed her silk night shirt from the end of the bed and pulled it on. She got up as she buttoned it down. Alan propped up on the pillows to look at her.

"I must look a mess." Willow said as she gathered up her hair.

"They're on the side table."

"What? Oh, thank you." Willow said, noticing the combs Alan had pulled out last night. She stuck them in her bun, trying to control the strands of hair about her face. She sat in front of the vanity table and looked in the mirror.

"You're beautiful," Alan said, noticing how she looked at herself. Willow looked at him without turning around. There was a softness in her eyes, and suddenly, he noticed tears, and that she became short of breath.

"What is it, Willow?" Alan asked, worried.

She slowly turned around to face him. "Something's happening to me that I can't describe. I haven't felt like this ever in my life, and I'm having difficulty controlling my emotions."

"Come here," Alan said, patting the side of the bed. Willow slowly walked to his side and sat down. "You can tell me," Alan said softly, holding her hands. "What's bothering you?"

"It's just that…" Willow suddenly burst into tears. "All my life I've been there for my family, parents, grandmother, first husband then second, always putting their needs and desires before mine. Always sacrificing myself for them. Not that I complained," she continued between sniffles, "but not once did anyone ask me what I wanted, what my desires were. Funny, isn't it? All I wanted was for someone to hold me, care for me." Willow continued crying. "I'm sorry. I'm just damaged goods."

"You are not damaged goods. Look at me." She glanced at him sideways. "You are not damaged goods, you understand? You're not. Somebody must have clipped your wings when you were young. You're just afraid to be happy." Alan pulled her down beside him, where she lay like a foetus. He wrapped his arms around her, holding both her hands and curled up right behind her body. He could feel her trembling and shaking as she continued to cry, and all he could do was hold her tightly while she let go of the pressure that must have built inside her all those years. Alan didn't know for how long they lay there as one body, but he didn't want to move before she did.

Eventually, Willow stopped crying, but still, he waited. "You can let go now," she whispered. He slowly released his hold but still held her lightly. She slowly turned around to face him, her hands tucked under her cheek. Alan watched her closely.

"Silly me," Willow said, wiping away her tears and looking at him with wet eyes and a wiry smile on her face. "I've been looking for you all my life. Life is so easy and comfortable now, and I guess this is how love feels. You've filled the hole in my heart," Willow continued. "I love you, Alan." She spoke softly and leaned forward to kiss him.

"You have no idea how long I have waited for you to say that," Alan said, kissing her back. Willow sighed and snuggled up against his shoulder.

He opened his eyes again when he heard the water running. He must have dozed off, because he hadn't felt Willow leave his side. *How could any of her past husbands not have seen the woman that she is?* he thought. He knew he was lucky to be the one with her now, and there was a selfishness in his thoughts, for he knew she had suffered emotional abuse. Given the chance last night, she had shown the woman hidden behind the mask, and he was fascinated to learn more about her feelings this morning.

"You still in bed?" Willow asked, opening the bathroom door. Alan had been so lost in his thoughts that he didn't realize that she had showered and gotten dressed.

"Still up for scrambled eggs?" she asked, smiling.

"Give me fifteen minutes," Alan replied, getting out of bed.

That afternoon, they spent time around the shady pool. Willow swam as Alan watched her, then they both sat on the side, enjoying each other's company. Alan gathered her in his arms, leaning to kiss her on the neck.

"Hmm." He nuzzled her while she slowly put her arms around his neck.

"What?" she asked, laughing.

"You smell of the pool."

Willow laughed. "Your hair is dripping." Alan answered her by kissing her fully on the lips. Willow was surprised by the force of it.

"You surprise me sometimes, you know."

"Sometimes?" Alan laughed with his face buried between her shoulder and neck. He slowly licked her earlobe and bit tenderly.

"Are you planning, by any chance, on having me for dinner?" Willow said softly.

"Not a bad idea. You look good enough to eat."

Willow pulled away from him playfully, embarrassed by his frankness, and looked frantically around to find something else to talk about. "Shouldn't we get out and prepare dinner? You said you would barbecue tonight."

"You're changing the subject." Willow glanced up at him. "OK, OK, don't glare at me." Alan laughed. "You let yourself be teased so easily."

They both got up and, after a quick shower, dressed and went into the kitchen. Alan walked out to the barbecue and turned it on. He was still laughing. Willow glanced outside to look at him. To admire him. She felt an ache in her heart just looking at him, wondering if she would be able to hold onto him.

"Got some wine to go along with this fire?" Alan shouted.

"Sure. I'll grab a bottle. Red, white, or rosé?"

He turned around with the tongs in his hand. "You choose whatever you want."

For a minute, Willow stood there, understanding what he was trying to do. She appreciated the gesture. "All right, I'll choose."

She grabbed up two wineglasses and a bottle of white wine from the wine fridge and went out on to the terrace to join him. Alan grabbed the corkscrew and the bottle. Willow stopped to gaze at the sky.

"Oh, look, a new moon," she exclaimed suddenly. Alan looked up as well. "Look at gold. Something gold." Willow glanced at her fingers, noticing she had no rings.

"Why?" Alan asked.

"It brings good luck to look at something gold when you first see the new moon. Quick." Willow looked around frantically. Alan calmly placed the wine bottle on the table, grabbed her, and pulled her into his arms.

"Hey—what are you doing?" Willow struggled in his arms, but he was strong. Alan held her tightly. Willow couldn't move; nevertheless, she looked up into his eyes. They had again turned darker.

"I need just to look at you when I see the new moon. You're going to bring me luck."

Willow was at a loss for words. She rested her head on Alan's chest, and it was so comforting that she didn't want to move away. *Is this new for him too?* she thought.

"I think the barbecue is ready, don't you?" Alan looked back over his shoulder.

"Five more minutes." Willow was reluctant to be let go, and they stood there for a while, not saying anything, just enjoying the moment.

Finally, it was Alan who moved away. "Let's get this fish going, then."

"I'll get the rest of the food," Willow said, walking into the kitchen to grab the salad bowl. She noticed Alan looking at her fondly. She poured a little bit of olive oil in a deep dish and some balsamic vinegar on top. She placed some olives in another dish and picked up the basket of fresh bread. She walked back out, balancing everything in both of her hands.

"There's something called a tray that you can use," Alan remarked.

Willow glared back. Alan just smiled. He poured out the wine into the two wineglasses and offered her one. She came to join him. They silently sipped. The sun had set, and there was a soft breeze coming in from the sea.

Suddenly, Willow trembled.

"Are you cold?"

"No, just... too happy," she replied. She returned to the table to light the candles. Alan joined her and picked up an olive.

"Hey, these are good. Did you buy these the other day?" Alan asked as he broke a piece of bread and dipped it into the olive oil. Willow watched him as he ate the dripping bread. She had a sudden urge to kiss him, so she got up and leaned down to kiss him fully on the lips. He tasted of olive oil.

"What was that for?" Alan asked. Willow coyly smiled. Alan shook his shoulders and returned to the barbecue. He flipped the fish and took another sip from his wine. Willow went into the house and came back out with a shawl in her hand. Looking around the garden, she came up behind Alan and softly leaned in. She felt the muscles in his back tense.

"You know, I could just feed this fish to the cats and have you for dinner," Alan growled.

Willow smiled into his back. "That fish looks cooked."

"Just give me a moment to settle down."

Willow chuckled and turned around to sit down. Alan lifted the fish and placed it on the plate next to the barbecue. He closed the cover, picked up his wineglass, and walked back. Willow was tossing the salad. He placed the fish between their plates and settled down, leaning back.

"Ahh." Willow served the salad. "Shall we pick from the plate?" She demonstrated by plucking a small piece of white flesh from the fish and swallowed it. Alan looked on, mesmerized.

"You know, this is a side of you that I would never have imagined you possessed."

"Meaning?" Willow wiped her fingers on her napkin and took a sip from her wine.

"It's so good." Alan shook his head and made for the fish. "You seemed so proper and dignified and reserved that I find it hard to believe, yet here you are, eating with your fingers." Alan dipped another piece of bread in the olive oil and licked his fingers.

"You don't know me," Willow responded.

"It's a work in progress, but I have you pretty much figured out. I don't think you know the person you really are. No, let me rephrase that—you're at last showing who you really are."

"And?"

"I'm loving every moment of it," Alan replied, smiling up at her. Willow was lost for words.

The next evening, Alan checked himself in the mirror before he left his bedroom. He had left his wet hair to dry naturally, and he had finally shaved, so he looked much tidier than the previous days. There was a relaxation in his face lines, and he looked… happy. Just as he opened his door to go out, he saw Willow in the living room. She had put on a colourful tunic over capri pants, and he noticed that she was barefoot. She was bent over the record player, placing the needle, when suddenly, he heard Earth Wind and Fire's "The Way You Move." She stood up and started to move with the rhythm, and Alan realized he had never seen her like this. He stood there, hidden by the door frame, watching her. Willow seemed entranced by the music and was moving and dancing when she twirled around and saw Alan. She stopped immediately.

"Don't stop, you look like you were enjoying yourself there." Alan smiled as he walked closer to her. "Earth Wind and Fire, hmm?" he asked, taking the cover in his hand.

"I grew up with their music," Willow said.

"You must have been quite the disco girl," Alan remarked.

"I've never been to a disco," she said softly.

He looked up. "What? No disco?" he asked, not believing what he had heard.

"Yes, no disco. No bar, for that matter."

Alan shook his head. "Where have you lived all your life? On a secluded island?"

"I told you I was an introvert. Besides, no one asked me." Willow reflected. "I don't want to talk about it. It's in the past now." She walked toward the kitchen counter. Alan followed her.

"I didn't mean to hurt you. I was just caught off guard, that's all." Alan took her in his arms and gave her a hug.

"I know," Willow said. "I have a long list of things I haven't done in my life."

"I'd like to see that list," Alan replied. "Maybe I can help you cross off some of them."

"Well, with the sailboat, you did. I've also never driven a convertible." Willow smiled.

"Why didn't you say so? I mean, I have a convertible, you saw me in it, we drove in it, how come..."

"I couldn't just say 'Let me drive your car.' Besides, I'm sure you'll let me now," Willow jokingly said. "Come on, what are we having for dinner tonight?" She changed the subject and sat on one of the stools.

"I thought I might cook for you," Alan replied.

"What did you have in mind? Let me guess—pasta." He gave her a look. "Told you I have a sixth sense."

"Yes, it'll be pasta with my own secret recipe, so don't ask. Just sit there and pour us some wine."

"You want red, white, or rosé?" Willow asked as she opened the wine fridge.

"Red this time. I think I have some Merlot in there somewhere." He pointed at the wine rack in the corner. Willow found the bottle, and after pouring two glasses, she handed one to Alan, who was getting several things out of the fridge. She settled down to watch him work.

'Do you think we drink too much wine?" Willow asked, looking at the glass in her hand.

He looked up from what he was doing. "There's no such thing as too much wine."

"If you say so." Willow laughed. He crushed some fresh garlic as Willow watched. "I can get used to this."

"I don't mind. I can get used to having you beside me," Alan said, looking up. Willow blushed. "Are you blushing? Really? After all we've done these past days?"

"You're embarrassing me."

"You should be embarrassed. Here you are, taking advantage of a handsome guy like me. And at your age." For a minute, Willow looked at him, wondering if he was serious. "Willow. You should know by now that I love to tease you. You act like you're a young girl—which, by the way, you are."

"Sure, a woman of sixty-five is a young girl, of course. What was I thinking?" Willow laughed.

"You worry too much. Just relax."

⌀⌀⌀

The next day, Alan took Willow for a hike to the other side of the cove. There was a trodden path leading from the house, and when they reached the other end, Willow could see the whole house and the landscape around it.

"This is where I designed the house," Alan said, pointing. "It gives you a vantage point to the whole area."

"I can see why. From here, the whole place takes a different meaning."

It was near sunset when they walked back. Willow went outside to wait for Alan.

"Come on, let's go," Alan said from the terrace door. Willow turned around to see him with a basket and blankets in hand.

"Where are we going?" she asked, getting up.

"Down to the beach." Alan waited for her to enter the house.

They walked to the elevator and went down. "It's a beautiful evening, and I thought we might have a picnic on the beach. I'll build a campfire."

"Another strike on my list," Willow said as she watched him lay out the blankets.

"What list?" Alan asked, turning around.

"Of things I have never done."

Alan stood up, looking at her. "Never been near a campfire?"

"Never went camping either."

He shook his head in amazement. "Help me gather some wood."

Together, they walked toward the trees lining the end of the beach. While he built the fire, Willow took off her sandals and walked along the water. The sand was warm under her toes, and she lifted her arms toward the sky, as if to embrace the world surrounding her. She returned to see that the fire was going, and Alan had opened the basket and was pouring wine into two glasses. He got up, walked toward her, and handed her a glass.

"This is beautiful. You've thought of everything," Willow said, smiling. They drank in silence, watching the small waves slowly roll onto the sandy beach. "What else do you have in that basket of yours?" Willow asked mischievously.

"Food, what else?"

They walked back and sat down on the blanket to eat. The fire burnt merrily and glowed as nightfall came. Alan added some more branches and came to sit next to her.

"I love the sound of the sea," Willow said. "Always have."

"Yet you told me you've never surfed or dived in it."

"I bet you have," she replied.

"Oh, yes, I love surfing. Or at least, I used to. I don't anymore since the accident, and because I've gotten older as well."

"What accident?" Willow asked.

"I spent my teenage years surfing whenever I could. Riding a wave is a breathless experience, you know—the adrenaline, sun, salt, and sand. It's one of the best ways to forget your daily problems since it's just you and the wave and the sea. You don't think of anything else but perfecting the ride. The accident was after Caroline died. I tried riding a big wave that I shouldn't have, because I wasn't that focused. I couldn't overcome it, and I crashed. Somehow, my surfboard hit me, and I broke my collarbone, among other things. That's when the family, with Daisy in the lead, forbade me from going surfing again."

Willow noticed how animated his face became when he started talking about surfing. "That must have hurt. I've never really watched surfers live, only from movies or TV. What a rush of adrenaline it must be, with the roar of the waves and the sound of the wind, the water spraying all around you while you use the forces of nature to your benefit." Alan looked at her with surprise. "What?" she asked casually.

"You continue to surprise me. You described it so perfectly, as if you yourself were there."

Willow smiled. "I read a lot, and I have a good imagination. But it must have hurt when you crashed."

"It did, but like I said, at the time, I was reckless. My family worried."

"I'm not the adventurous type, so no surfing for me. Or diving, for that matter."

"Why?"

"I'm a Taurus, an earth sign, so I like to be grounded."

Alan laughed and said, "So it's because of your astrological sign that you're not adventurous."

"Of course. You're a Leo, right? With a touch of Virgo."

"How do you know?"

"I checked your birthday. Besides, it's so obvious."

"Tell me, how so?" Alan asked, looking at her.

"First, you're a fire sign. You're generous and kind-hearted. You're confident. You're determined. You're ambitious. Me, I like stability and consistency. I'm a creature of habit. We're worlds apart in the way we deal with things, so really, we're not compatible."

"Yet fire burns the earth with its flames."

Willow looked at him, surprised. "Hey, you do know about the signs. Yet here you let me go on rambling." Alan smiled. "What's your spirit animal?" she then asked.

"I haven't thought about it. What about you?"

"Polar bear."

"Really?" Alan said. "I wouldn't have thought so."

"Polar bears are big and white and fluffy but, when threatened, can become fierce and wild. Very protective of their cubs and family." Alan looked on quizzically. "I can be fierce, you know."

"So it seems," he said. "You were saying you like to be grounded, right?" he asked, moving closer to her. He looked on, and Willow suddenly felt shivers down her spine.

"Yes, grounded," she responded softly.

Alan leaned forward and took out the combs in her hair, letting it tumble down. "I can do that, ground you." He pushed her down onto the blanket. He leaned in close to her ear. "Have you ever made love on the beach?" he asked.

"No, what do you mean? What if someone sees?" she said, fidgeting under him.

"And who might that be? There's no one around except the stars." Alan said, nuzzling her neck. She giggled. "Did you just giggle?"

"Your stubble tickled me."

"Oh, so we are ticklish?"

"No—yes, I mean—no, Alan, stop, please," Willow squealed as Alan tickled her.

"You're just like a little girl."

"Stop, please stop," Willow said as Alan continued to tickle her.

"Would you rather I ground you?"

Willow looked up into his eyes.

"I take that as a yes." Alan said, kissing her on the lips as Willow wound her arms around him. The fire cast soft shadows as they made love.

The night became cooler as the fire slowly burnt down. Alan leaned over to grab the last of the branches and threw them on the fire. They blazed up into the sky. Willow touched his naked back. "Come back under the blankets. It's cold."

He snuggled down next to her while Willow put her head on his chest and watched the fire. "You're beautiful," Alan said as he stroked her hair.

Willow turned to look at him and smiled. Only he could make her smile like that. "I must look like a well-fed cat," she murmured, teasingly caressing him. Alan closed his eyes, and Willow savoured the moment with him, the peaceful quiet except for the crackling of the fire.

After a while, they got up, and Alan pulled on his shorts while Willow wrapped herself up in the blanket. Alan poured sand over the fire and made sure it was out as she gathered up the rest of the blankets and basket. They walked barefoot to the elevator, hand in hand. While going up, Alan looked fondly at her.

"Sorry about the sand in your hair," he said mischievously.

"Yes, about that—I think I have sand in all the wrong places," Willow replied, hitting his arm. Alan hit back, and they both laughed. She felt like a teenager.

"Are you sleepy?" Alan asked.

"No, are you?"

"No," he said as the elevator door opened. Willow walked to her bedroom as Alan headed towards the kitchen.

"Oh my, look at my hair," Willow exclaimed from her bathroom. He stopped midway and turned to follow her.

"I think you look beautiful, the messy hair and sand and all," he said, grabbing her from behind. They looked at their reflections. "Mine looks even worse," he added, brushing his hair with his hand, making sand particles fly off.

"I need a shower," Willow said, turning around.

"Want company?" Alan asked, still holding her tight.

Willow turned around to face him. "I think I've been adventurous enough for the day, don't you think?" she said coyly.

"I'll accept your word for it. Besides, I need to save up on energy. See you in a bit," Alan said, winking and walking toward his room. Willow looked after him when he waved without turning. She smiled and closed the door.

Once in the bathroom, she quickly dropped the blanket and turned on the shower. The warm water felt good, and she washed off all the sand and shampooed her hair. Her body felt relaxed, even soft, and she realized that she had never felt like this before. *Was I always like this but didn't show it, or was it because I had never found the right man until now?* she thought. She grabbed a bath towel and wrapped herself up. She towel-dried her hair, too lazy to blow-dry it, and looked around for something easy to put on. She remembered

Jasmine had packed her sleeveless white cotton nightgown with laces in front, so she pulled that on and walked out.

Alan was in the kitchen with only a colourful turquoise pareo tied around his waist, water still dripping from his wet hair.

"Look at you," Willow said. "I likes."

Alan turned to look at her, taking in the white nightgown. "Better not stand in the light with that," he remarked as he brewed tea. Willow looked down at herself.

"Really?" she asked.

"Really," Alan answered as he poured the tea into two cups. Willow ran to sit on one of the couches. "I don't mind," Alan said. Willow blushed, and he seemed amused by it. "You're one of a kind."

She noticed that he was laughing silently. "You're terrible, you know that? Terrible," she said as she sipped at her cup.

"That's why you love me," Alan said nonchalantly.

"Do you ever think about what would have happened if we had met each other when we were in our twenties? Before we were married to someone else?" Willow asked.

Alan didn't answer immediately, and she noticed he was thinking over what she had asked. "It would have been fantastic, but I wonder if we would have appreciated each other then as we do now. Yes, there would have been benefits of being together when we were young, but would we have survived the years? I don't really know. I think our life experience has made us better in a way—minus the troubles and anguish, of course."

"You may be right," Willow said, becoming silent.

"What made you ask that now?"

"I don't know. I feel so different, and I like it. I was wondering if I would have been different back then if I was with you."

"Different in a good way?" Alan asked.

"Now you're fishing for compliments."

"I'm just a guy. Guys need to be complimented." Alan laughed, finishing his tea.

257

"Well, you look downright adorable in that pareo, with your wet hair and... and..." Before Willow could finish her sentence, Alan was beside her on the couch.

"You were saying?" he said as he pulled on the laces of her nightgown.

"You're distracting me."

"That's the whole point. You talk too much." By that time, he had unlaced the front of her nightgown. "Where do you find all these exotic scents? They're driving me mad."

Willow placed her cup on the table and turned to face him. She put both her hands around his face, caressing the soft stubble and noticing that his eyes were changing colour again. She found it very sensual. She caressed his wet hair, softly holding his gaze all the time.

"Your place or mine?" she asked in his ear.

"Mine," Alan said, getting up. Holding her hand, he walked her into his bedroom.

⌒℮◜

It was past one o'clock in the morning by the time they had finished. Alan leaned back on his pillow and stared up at the ceiling. The soft breeze from the open windows caressed his hot body, cooling him down slowly. Willow closed her eyes and sighed. He dragged himself up on his elbow and looked down at her.

"What?" Willow asked, her eyes closed.

"My throat is dry. I feel like I've been in the desert for a week. I know we have some ice cream in the fridge. What do you think?"

"Hmm... I'm so lazy," Willow replied, squirming around under the sheets and coyly looking at him from under her lashes. Alan swung his feet over the side of the bed and sat up. He picked up his pareo from the floor and tied it around his waist.

Barefoot, he walked out of the room and into the kitchen. He opened the fridge and clattered around for bowls and spoons. Alan placed two bowls of heaping ice cream on the kitchen counter, as well as two wineglasses, and Willow walked into the kitchen, her nightgown on. He had the bottle of wine tucked under his arm.

"You should've been a waiter," Willow said, laughing.

"I was one." They sat facing each other over the counter. "I worked as a waiter during my university years. I was quite good at it."

"I bet the ladies tipped you well," Willow remarked.

Alan looked back at her with a sardonic grin. "And it wasn't always money, my dear."

"Oh, I'm so shocked," Willow said, laughing, and picked up a bowl. She scooped up some ice cream, then slowly licked the spoon while Alan looked on.

"You know, if you keep doing that, you're not going to end up having any ice cream," Alan said.

"And?" Willow continued to lick the spoon.

"Don't tempt me."

"And if I do? Will you pick me up and drag me back to bed? Again?" Willow coyly remarked. Alan lifted an eyebrow. Willow dropped the spoon in the bowl. "You couldn't if you tried. I'm way too heavy to be carried like some romance novel heroine." Alan moved toward her, and she quickly put up her hands. "OK, OK, I'll eat properly."

Alan had uncorked the bottle of wine and was pouring two glasses. "You know, I haven't felt like this since I was a young man. I never would have thought that I... you know, we..."

"Could be sexually active?" Willow finished his sentence.

Alan looked up from his glass of wine. "Yes, did you? I mean, you keep reading about people at our age. You know how things change, libido and all that? I'm rather enjoying what I have with you, and I feel guilty that others don't," he concluded.

Willow placed her bowl on the table. "I feel sexy with you, and it was never like this when I was a young woman. You know what I think? I believe mature couples have better love lives. We have fewer distractions in the form of pregnancy concerns, busy work life, kids, and so forth, so we have more time for a deeper intimacy. Besides, we have more know-how." She winked at him.

"How did you become so smart?" Alan asked jokingly.

"I was always smart," Willow replied, finishing off her ice cream.

"I want to keep you as you are now," Alan said while eating his.

"As I am now? Why?" Willow asked.

"I see you change. You've changed since you got here. I got to see the real you."

"Oh, please, I am who you see."

"No, you're not. Generally, you only show people what you think they want to see."

"What?" Willow asked.

"Let me rephrase that. These past few days, I got to see the real you. You weren't like this when we first met. You're totally different now."

"Are you out of your mind? I haven't changed."

"I'm not asking you to. I just want to see the real woman behind this mask you put on. You gave me a glimpse, but I want more. I want to see the woman who surrounds herself with wonderful colours, creating a painting out of everything that surrounds her. The woman who loves to smell the clean linens, the flowers, the fresh air, surrounding herself in this cocoon of aromas. I never noticed the smell of freshly washed sheets until I met you."

"I don't know what to say. I... I didn't think you noticed."

"I notice everything about you." Alan stopped when he saw the effect his words had on her.

"I didn't think I could be loved as you love me. You're my hero."

Alan couldn't find the words to respond and suddenly felt a knot in his throat. He looked up at her then with tears in his eyes and saw

Willow's soft smile.

"It's our last day here, isn't it?" she asked him.

"Yes, I promised Jasmine I would bring you back tomorrow. She has to go back home."

"I'll miss this place."

"We can always come back again. You can leave your dogs at the farm with Robyn. Lots of children and people to take care of them. Then we can stay longer."

"I would like that. Not that I don't love my home, but this place will always hold a special place in my heart."

"Come on, let's go to bed. I think we should sleep this time, no?" Alan teased, putting away the bowls and glasses.

❦

The next morning, Alan packed the jeep with their bags. Willow stood outside on the terrace, breathing in the sea air and remembering the precious moments she had spent here.

"Ready to go?" Alan asked from the door.

"Yes," Willow said, entering the house while Alan locked everything up.

They drove down to the airport in silence. John was already there, and so was the chopper.

"Thanks, John. You'll take a look to see everything is all right at the house?" Alan asked as Willow got out.

"Of course." John nodded at Willow as she got into the chopper, and Alan was close behind her as he placed the bags inside.

"Have a nice flight, and see you soon," John said as the blades started to rotate. He pulled away, waving at them. Willow looked out of the window, trying to catch a last glimpse of the house. She could sense Alan watching her, and she looked back at him as they left the island. They arrived at the airport without trouble. Willow noticed that the convertible was waiting for them.

"Want to drive?" Alan asked. "But it's stick shift, I don't know if you're used to it."

"Oh, no," Willow replied. "Stick shift? Damn!"

"Come on, it's not that hard, I'll show you. Get in." Alan opened the door on the driver's side. Willow got in reluctantly and fastened her seat belt as Alan got in the other side.

"Now, as you can see, there are three pedals. The one on the left is the clutch, and you need that to change gears. The others you know."

Willow looked at all three, then at Alan.

"Now," said Alan, "you—" Before he could finish his sentence, Willow had turned on the engine and, with great expertise, shifted gears and drove out of the airport at great speed. Alan watched with astonishment as she deftly handled the sports car and got on the highway.

"You tricked me," Alan said over the wind.

"I said I'd never driven a convertible, not that I couldn't handle a stick." Willow laughed, throwing her head back as they sped along. In a short time, they arrived at her house.

"Welcome back, Mom, Alan," Jasmine said, coming out of the house.

"Alan let me drive."

"I can see that. Must have been quite the experience," Jasmine said jokingly while he got Willow's baggage out of the car.

"That was one fast drive. Wow. She can still amaze me," Alan answered.

"She was the most popular mom for the carpool among us kids because she was so fast." Jasmine laughed.

"Blame Grandma, I learnt how to drive from her. The grand old lady was a very fast driver, wearing driving gloves and all. I just try to follow the tradition. You should know that Jasmine is a mean driver as well."

"I'm glad I know. Next time, I'll be more careful with what I say," Alan said, looking at the two women. "May I hug you, Jasmine? I want to thank you for organizing this trip with me."

"Of course," Jasmine said shyly as Alan gave her a big hug.

He turned to look at Willow. "Your mother is an exceptional woman," he said tenderly, looking on. There was an awkward silence then—Alan not wanting to leave, Willow not wanting him to go.

"See you, Alan. I'll take your suitcase inside, Mom," Jasmine said, apparently catching on that they needed a private moment.

Alan came close to Willow and took both her hands in his. "I don't want to go, but I need to," he said softly, not looking at her.

"I know. I understand. We'll see each other again soon, I hope."

"You can be sure of that," he said, releasing Willow's hands and walking back to his car.

"Goodbye, Alan, drive safely." Willow winked.

"Ha ha." Alan waved and drove off.

Willow watched after him for a while before going in. The dogs rushed forward and jumped up, licking her hands and face. "Enough, enough already, calm down." She laughed, sitting down in the living room. Jasmine came and sat opposite her.

"You're glowing. It looks like you had a nice time."

"It was magical. Just magical. Alan and I… we…" Willow didn't know how to continue.

"I think I understand. I'm just happy for you."

Willow noticed Jasmine's bags by the door. "You're leaving already?" she asked.

"I must. Sam is flying in this evening, and I promised I'd be home."

"You've done more than possible. Come, I'll see you off." Willow embraced her daughter fondly and watched her leave as well.

Once she was back inside, the house suddenly felt very empty. Willow opened the patio doors, walked outside with her dogs, and sat on the bench to watch the pond. The garden looked well, it being the end of summer. The flowers and trees were in full bloom, and the grass a plush green. She stretched out her legs as she thought of Alan and wondered what he was doing.

After leaving Willow, Alan had stopped by the farmhouse, needing to talk with Robyn before going home. He found her in the stables.

"You're back," Robyn remarked as she continued to brush her horse. She stopped brushing as Alan came closer.

"You look different." She paused. "You look happy."

"I am. Robyn, I…" Alan stopped, trying to find the right words to describe his emotions.

"Don't say a word. Your face and body language says it all. I'm happy for you."

"Why?" Alan asked.

"Why what?"

"Why am I like this?"

"Because you've been in love with her for the past twelve years and now you've had a chance to be with her. Was it worth the wait?"

"You have no idea. I feel like a young man when I'm with her. She has this effect on me, I can't describe it. I just want to be with her always." Alan leaned against the stable door.

Robyn turned to look at him. "Then be with her always." Her answer caught him off guard. "You might be my big brother, and I love you, but sometimes, you act like a boy." She kissed him on the cheek. "Do what your heart desires. Come on. I'll make some tea."

CHAPTER ELEVEN

Avalon

The following week was extra busy for Alan, as he was catching up with paperwork and answering letters and calls that had come in during his absence. He toured around the vineyards with Robyn and Daisy and oversaw preparations for the upcoming harvest season. He stayed in touch with Willow, sometimes calling, but more often writing her emails or sending her messages. He missed her presence, ever more so after their stay at the island. He missed touching her, missed the way Willow's hands felt over his body, missed her scent. As he was revisiting his memories with her, Daisy walked into his office.

"Dad, you look miles away. Daydreaming, are we?"

Alan scowled at his daughter. "I don't daydream. Not at this age, anyway."

Daisy sat down in one of the armchairs facing his desk. "You're not fooling anyone. You've been mooning around the office since you got back. Anyway, I just wanted to ask if you still don't want any birthday celebrations this year, as you usually say every year?"

"Yes, definitely no celebrations, no gifts."

"What about with Willow?"

"She hasn't said anything since we last talked. I was just thinking of going to see her, it's been more than a week now."

"She surprised you with her birthday, so pay her a visit on yours and see if she remembers," Daisy offered.

"Could do that, I guess," Alan said, already excited at the prospect of seeing Willow again. She had been supportive of him as he stayed away for business reasons, but Alan knew that she missed him, something she would never venture to say in order not to disrupt his work. Willow was like that.

"I'll give her a call," Alan offered.

"Do it now. I want to be sure."

"You're not the boss of me," Alan remarked half-scoldingly.

Daisy handed over his phone. "Call her."

Alan dialled Willow's number and waited. She picked up on the third ring. "Hello, Alan, how are you?" Willow said, out of breath.

"Where were you?" Alan asked.

"I was outside, but my phone was inside, so I sort of ran," Willow explained. "I'm happy to hear your voice."

"I wanted to ask you if I can come over this Thursday evening? I've had enough of wine business, and I miss you and your cooking," Alan added.

Willow joyfully replied, "Anything special you want? Besides the chocolate mousse, of course?"

Alan smiled. "Surprise me. I should be able to get away by six."

"Sounds good, see you then. Say hi to Daisy."

Alan put down his phone. "Willow says hi to you. Wait a minute, how did she know you were here?" he asked suspiciously.

"She must have guessed," Daisy quickly replied. "I have to go. We have guests over for dinner, and Ivy will kill me if I'm late." She left the room, leaving Alan pondering what had just happened.

༶

That Thursday, Willow busied herself preparing dinner. She had made the chocolate mousse the day before, and they were nicely setting in the fridge. She decided to cook a roast chicken with scalloped potatoes and green beans fresh from the garden, which she planned to toss in olive oil and garlic. She paid special attention in setting the table outside, this time going with an elaborate lace tablecloth—a relic from her grandmother—and set out the green-coloured crystal wine and water glasses. She placed crystal rings around the matching napkins and arranged the silverware. She had hesitated between the tableware she normally used and the elaborate flowery set she had inherited from her mother. It was one of her mother's favourites, so she decided to use it. She looked at the elegant table, then went and cut some orange and yellow roses from the garden and placed them in a shallow crystal bowl in the centre of the table. *Now it's perfect,* she thought.

Willow had sent the dogs to the dog hotel, wanting no distractions for the evening. After surveying the whole arrangements and the food, she quickly went upstairs to take a shower. She had chosen to wear her black, wide-legged silk pants with a kimono-style wraparound top that tied to the side. She let her hair down this time, blow-drying the ends into curls and put on a black velvet headband. She put on her grandmother's drop emerald earrings but not the matching necklace, thinking it would be too overbearing. Some makeup, a touch here and there, and then she slipped on her comfortable black flats. She paused to look at herself in the mirror, trying to see herself through Alan's eyes. *He's in for a surprise,* Willow thought as she went downstairs and put on some music.

As she walked back into the kitchen, she noticed that Alan had arrived. *Right on time,* she thought as she buzzed him in. Alan had the top up on his convertible, so Willow waited for him to get out before greeting him. She noticed that he had, as always, dressed elegantly in shades of blue. Willow opened the door to see him with a bouquet of tall stemmed red roses. *Two dozen, from the look of it,* she thought.

Alan was looking at the willow tree and the garden beyond before he turned to her. "You're a vision," he said as he handed over the roses.

"These are beautiful, thank you," Willow said, admiring the flowers. He gave her a soft kiss on the lips. They walked into the house.

"What is that smell? It's... it's... killing me."

"Chicken?" Willow added, laughing as she placed the bouquet on the kitchen counter. Alan came close and pulled her around to face him, and he looked at her hair, the headband, the earrings—the whole outfit. He leaned down to kiss her again, his hand brushing her long hair.

"I've missed you," Alan mumbled after a long, lingering kiss.

"Me too," Willow answered.

"Where are the dogs?" he asked, looking around.

"At their hotel," she said as she walked into the living room to get a vase for the roses.

"Why?" he asked, sitting on the kitchen stool as she poured water and opened the bouquet.

"I wanted no distractions tonight." Willow cut the ends of the roses and placed them one by one in the vase. "These are lovely," she said as she continued not looking at him.

Alan leaned forward. "Tell me. Why?" he asked again.

Willow stopped what she was doing and leaned to kiss him gently. "You didn't think I would forget, did you?"

"How did you know I would be coming, and—" Alan stopped midway. "Daisy?" he asked.

"Don't blame Daisy, I asked for her help to get you to come here." By that time, Willow had finished placing the roses and took the vase back into the living room. Alan was still sitting when she got back.

"And the chicken?"

"That was a wild guess. All men like roast chicken," Willow replied, laughing. "Let's have some wine and celebrate."

"I don't like birthdays," Alan grumbled.

"What's there not to like? You get to celebrate the you that you are. Wait a minute, that's too many yous." Willow laughed. "We get to celebrate the man that you are."

"If you put it that way." Alan watched as she took out a bottle of chilled white wine and placed it in the wine cooler.

"Come on, let's go outside," Willow said, taking his arm.

Once out on the patio, Alan stopped to look at the elegantly set table. "You didn't have to go to all this trouble."

"I didn't have to, but I wanted to. Besides, I know you appreciate it," Willow said as she poured out the wine. "Let's go and sit on our bench."

They walked down by the pond and sat down. "How's work?" Willow asked.

"Good. Buying the winery was a good decision, and now, we have foreign investors interested. I might have to travel next week. We'll see. How about you? What have you been doing since we got back?"

"I've started painting."

"What? That's great news!" Alan exclaimed, turning to look at her.

"I know, it's been ages since I held a brush. I had no motivation, no insight into what I wanted to paint. You know, I'm visual, and I used to see the painting before I even started, but not since... well, a long time ago. I need to be in the mood, in the moment to be able to create. Anyway, long story short, I started again. I might have to convert one of the outbuildings into a workshop."

"I can do that for you," Alan offered.

"I know you can," Willow replied, holding his hand. "But let's see the results of my endeavours first, then we can decide."

"Will I get to see?"

"Maybe," Willow replied coyly. She glanced at her watch. "We should go in, the chicken should be ready." Once they were inside, Willow opened the oven door, took out the pot, and placed it on a trivet. She took out the scalloped potatoes as well.

"This looks incredible. I'm literally drooling."

Willow threw back her head and laughed. "I just need to toss these beans, then we can eat. Will you carve the chicken? You can find the necessary utensils in the top left drawer."

When everything was ready, Willow brought in the plates to serve themselves before sitting outside.

"Where did you learn to cook like this?" Alan asked as he ate.

"My grandmother. She was the cook of the family, and my great-grandmother before her. The talent skipped over my mother and came to me. Unfortunately, it skipped Jasmine as well. Luckily, she has Sam to cook for her."

"I cook too, you know," Alan replied.

"I know you do. I still remember that pasta dish."

Alan leaned back and looked at her. "I can't imagine how your two husbands missed out on a person like you."

"They both enjoyed my cooking but rarely complimented on it. Would you like some more?" Willow asked, noticing that Alan had nearly finished his plate.

"Do we have something else after this?"

Willow gave him a sly smile. "Maybe."

"Then definitely not. Let me help you with the plates."

"Is the wine finished?"

Alan looked at the wine bottle. "Practically."

"Then bring in the wineglasses. I have the flutes chilling."

Once Alan brought everything in, Willow said, "Now go and sit outside and wait."

"Why?" Alan asked.

"Please, just go." Willow shooed him out. She took out two bowls of chocolate mousse and, from a drawer, took out a birthday candle and stuck it into one of them. She took out the chilled flutes and the bottle of Dom Perignon, walked outside, and gave them to Alan. He smiled at the label. She walked back in, lit the candle, and came back outside again.

"Happy birthday, Alan," she said, bending to give him a kiss.

"You're spoiling me," Alan said as she sat down.

"Make a wish."

Alan did it silently and blew the candle out. Willow clapped her hands softly.

"You're like a kid," he remarked, pouring the champagne.

"Here's to you," Willow said. They both took a sip as he put the candle aside and started eating the mousse.

"Do I remember this taste or what?" Alan said, eyes closed, savouring the dessert. As Willow got up, he asked, spoon in hand, "Where are you going?"

"I have a surprise. I'll be back."

Willow came back holding a big package with a blue ribbon on top. Alan looked on questioningly. "Is that what I think it is?"

"Yes, let's see if you like it. I'm rusty, but it turned out better than I thought."

Alan slowly ripped open the package to uncover an oil painting. It was the ocean, in all shades of blue and green, with huge waves crashing toward a beach. The tips of the waves were white with foam, and the spray rose into the cloudy sky. Alan leaned to look carefully at a dark figure under one of the waves on a barely visible surfboard, silver in colour with a cobalt blue streak. The figure looked like a shadow of the waves from a distance, yet it was distinctive when one looked closely. The figure and the ocean and waves were like one entity.

"I'm speechless. I don't know what to say, this is... this is... magical."

271

"Really? Do you like it?" she asked excitedly.

"Like it? I love it. Do you know that I used to own a surfboard just… just…" Alan turned around. "How did you… I mean…"

"I'd never painted something like this but wanted to try, so I asked Daisy if she had any photos I could look at."

Alan looked lost for words. His eyes watered. He placed the painting on one of the chairs and came over to Willow. She got up, and he grabbed her. He gave her a hug, holding her tight. Willow could feel him trembling, so she didn't say a word, silently happy about the effect her painting had on him.

After a few minutes, Alan pulled away without letting her go, his eyes glistening with tears. "You have no idea how much I love you, Willow." He kissed her. "I need a drink." Alan went back to sit down, gulping down his glass. "I need a few moments to gather myself here."

"Do you want another mousse?" Willow asked. "Maybe next time, I should make it in a big bowl just for you." She got up to go inside.

There, she watched him, giving him the space he needed to compose himself. When she had decided to paint again, she had looked inside the trunk she had placed in storage. The brushes were still good, but the oil paints had dried out from old age. She had to go out to buy new ones; it reinvigorated her, and she looked ahead to the challenge. The last time she had painted was just before her divorce a long time ago. She bought the large canvas, and setting up her easel and paints had excited her. When she saw Alan's reaction, she realized that she hadn't lost her talent after all, and that was gratifying.

She decided to go out again. "Here you are, birthday boy," Willow said nonchalantly. The sun had set, and the garden lights had come on. "Are you OK?" she asked when he remained silent. She came behind his seat and put her arms around him.

"I'm overwhelmed but OK," Alan replied, finishing off his second bowl. "Are there any more surprises? Because I don't think I can take any more."

"Will you hang it?" Willow asked.

"Of course. I just need to find the perfect place," Alan said, touching her arm. Willow placed her head on top of his, and they looked out onto the garden, now lit under the starry sky.

Willow moved away, and Alan asked, "Where are you going?" She didn't answer and just walked into the house. She headed towards the CD player and placed the CD she had previously set aside. She returned to the patio as a solitary trumpet and the sultry voice of a woman started singing "The Very Thought of You."

"Is that Chris Botti?" Alan asked as Willow returned to his side.

"Yes, with Paula Cole. Come dance with me," Willow said, holding out her hand.

"Hey, that's my line," Alan replied, getting up and taking her into his arms.

They danced on the patio, Alan holding Willow close as she lay her head on his shoulder. They said nothing, just listening quietly to the music.

◦⁀◦

Something changed that night. Time seemed irrelevant now. Later in bed, the lovemaking was slow, their bodies knowing by now exactly how to touch and respond. "I wish I could stay here like this forever," Alan mumbled into her ear as he lost himself in his release.

The next morning, he left after breakfast, promising to let her know when he would travel, which turned out to be in three days. "I'll be gone for ten days, but I'll stay in touch," Alan said over the phone.

Willow realized that she needed to keep herself busy while Alan was away, or she would go crazy. She decided to go through the storage room next to the garage and clear it out. There was a lot of stuff that belonged to James, so she spent her days salvaging what she needed, filling out boxes for donation and cleaning. The dogs stayed close by, keeping her company. At night, she would be by her computer, waiting for emails from Alan, who kept her up to date with developments.

Already a week had passed by, and Willow couldn't wait for him to get back, when he sent an email saying that he was returning the day after tomorrow.

The following day, Willow cleaned out the now-empty storage room and looked around to see if she could turn this into a workshop like she wanted. *Alan could do it,* she thought, smiling, and went out for some grocery shopping now that Alan would soon be back home.

That evening, Willow was just about to turn off the lights to go upstairs when she noticed Honey's ears perk up. "What is it, sweetheart?" she asked, kneeling. Could it be the rain that had started a minute ago? Sophie and Lucy stood up, and all three dogs looked tense. "What is it, girls?"

Willow walked toward the security monitor in the kitchen. That was when she noticed a car by the gates. She turned on the lights to see Alan standing by the car in the rain. *What the...* She pressed the buzzer for the gates to open and walked outside. Alan had parked his car, and he turned around when he heard her.

"Alan? What are you doing here? When did you get—" Willow couldn't finish her words, for Alan had briskly walked toward her in the pouring rain and kissed her passionately, literally sweeping her off her feet. They somehow managed to get inside, still kissing and turning, managing to miss much of the furniture. The dogs were running around them, and Lucy was barking.

"Alan." Willow managed to get in a word. "What is it? What are you doing here? You were supposed to be coming tomorrow, and you're soaking wet."

"You've ruined it for me," Alan said, holding her by the shoulders.

"Ruined what?" Willow asked anxiously.

"My life as it is. I just couldn't stop thinking about you. During the meetings and work, I just kept thinking about you, where you were, what you were doing, and I realized that all I wanted was to be with you, beside you, to see your face, to hear your voice, to be. . ." He kissed her again, holding her close to his body. This time, Willow stayed in the moment, trying hard not to think about what he had just said.

Suddenly, Alan pulled away and stared at her. His eyes burnt through her skin while he held both her arms. "I realized that I too have been waiting for you all my life," Alan finally said. Willow looked at his face, his hair dripping from the rain, his wet clothes, and his passionate look. "You have no idea what you mean to me," he said, taking her hand.

Together, they quickly walked up the stairs to her bedroom. He walked in first and turned around as Willow closed the door and, facing him, leaned against it.

Alan quickly closed the gap between them and held her against the door. Their faces were inches apart, and both were breathing heavily. He kissed her then, first slowly, and once she responded, he kissed her in a frenzy, leaning against her. The blue night lamp cast a soft shadow on his face, and when they both stopped to breathe for a moment, Alan buried his head on her neck, and she could feel his heart beating fast. Willow had her arms around his back, listening to her own heart, her own body responding to his, wondering if she was in a dream.

"What is it with you?" Alan whispered. "I want to watch you smile, I want to touch you, I want to feel you, I want to be there beside you, I want to share my life with you. You're under my skin. Why do you have this pull on me?"

"You bring it out," Willow replied softly. "You bring out the woman in me that I never knew I was." They continued to stand there against the door, waiting for a change in their mood that would never come.

"I could have you right here, right now," Alan said.

"I'm not going anywhere," Willow whispered.

◦↶℮↷

The next morning, Willow woke up, feeling something was different. She turned around and saw that the bed was empty where Alan had been sleeping. She rose and opened the bedroom door, but the dogs also were nowhere to be seen. *Strange,* she thought. *Where is everyone?* She glanced at her bedside clock and saw that it was just past six in the morning and that the sky had already started to lighten up.

She walked to the window facing the garden. There was Alan, sitting on the bench with the three dogs lying by his side. There was a soft mist in the air as the ground warmed up with the first sign of the sun peeking through the trees.

Willow got up and dressed, putting on a warm cardigan, and went downstairs to make some coffee. When she approached, the dogs perked up their ears and started wagging their tails, and Alan turned around.

"Ahh, coffee." Alan said, taking a cup from her hand. Willow settled down next to him.

"It's beautiful, you know," Alan said. "Sitting here watching the sun rise and the garden come alive. The birds are already here."

"I should put out some more feed," Willow said. "The ducks will be flying in anytime now." They sat in silence.

"Does your house have a name?"

Willow turned to look at him. "A name?"

"Yes. Some houses have names, you know. I just wondered if you'd named yours."

"No, actually, I haven't," Willow replied.

"Avalon."

"What?"

"Avalon. You should call this place Avalon."

"You mean the place King Arthur was carried to after his death? Don't you think it's a bit morbid?"

"Legend says it's an earthly paradise where heroes are brought to be buried. It also means 'island of apples,' so a very appropriate name, since you have many apple trees here."

"How come you know so much about this?" Willow asked.

"I had a thing for the legend of King Arthur and the Knights of the Round Table when I was a kid." Alan turned to look at her. "You should call it Avalon."

"Maybe you're right. I always wonder what'll happen to the place once I'm gone."

"Where are you going?"

"Don't joke with me, I'm serious. I wonder sometimes about death, don't you? I don't want to die, but I'm curious. Is this it? What was this all about? You die, and they put you in a hole, or they scatter your ashes, and then what? You're gone and forgotten."

"No one can forget you. Why this sudden onrush of morbid thoughts?"

"I don't know. Living alone, you think of things like this. Anyway, I've decided that I want to become a tree. Of course, Murphy might see to it that my roots never hold in the garden, and I die again, but I think it's worth a try."

"What in earth are you talking about?" Alan turned and asked. "What's going on?"

"I want my ashes to be put in a biological urn so that I might grow as a tree. I can be planted right here in this garden."

"I didn't know you could do that."

"Well, now you do. Of course, no guarantee that I will succeed."

"Listen. You and this place are one. The house and gardens are you, and you are them, each corner a reflection of you. Just walking around is a discovery into your character, a reflection of your soul. You've poured out your heart into this place, and I'm so lucky to be able to share it with you—" Alan stopped. "Why are you crying?"

"No one's ever said anything so beautiful to me in my life. No one's understood what this place means to me other than you. How is it possible that you see this?" Willow wiped her eyes with her sleeve. "There. Now you've made me cry."

Alan leaned down to place his cup on the grass and took the one in her hand. "Come here," he said, opening his arms. Willow snuggled up to him while he cradled her on his lap.

"You know, all I wanted out of life was someone to love me, be with me, understand me, and I would have dedicated my life to him. Someone who would sit with me in the morning with a freshly brewed coffee and watch the sunrise. Someone who you didn't need to even talk at that moment because you would feel the same thing, the same emotions waking up to a new day. Someone with whom you could watch the birds come in and feed, listen to the sound of nature. And then afterward, go and pick the day's vegetables from the garden and walk around to observe which flower had died or which rosebud had decided to open that day. Someone to take notice of the grass, and the silent swaying of the leaves. To make note of things that needed to be done and come back.

"In the evening, sit outside with a drink or maybe a glass of chilled wine and watch again as the sun sets and twilight creeps in. By this time, you would've done your day's work, and you put on some smooth jazz music and lean back. Maybe close your eyes and breathe in the fragrant scent of the honeysuckle or jasmine creeping up your terrace. Enjoy the way the wine goes down your throat, a sensual sensation. You look at your partner, and you see that he's looking at you, knowing how you feel at that moment, but doesn't say a word—not that he doesn't care, but he already knows how much you enjoy sitting out there on your bench under your tree with a glow on your face from the sunset.

"As it gets darker, your solar lights blink on like fireflies. You know you have to get up to prepare dinner, but maybe just a little bit longer, what's the rush? you think." Since Alan hadn't said anything, Willow continued, "Never rush dinner. Always set the table with candles, go the extra mile. Now, you can converse about many subjects while dining, taking care to listen to each other, hopefully laugh at some silly event or joke. At night, you cuddle in bed, sometimes making love, sometimes just lying together with the smell and touch of your bodies, knowing you aren't alone in this world."

"I'd like to be that person, Willow," Alan said, leaning down to softly kiss her on the lips. Willow rose from his lap and looked into his eyes. "I was going to ask you last night, but then things got complicated," he said with a half-smile.

"Ask me what?"

"I was thinking, if it's all right with you, that I might bring over a few things and stay with you from time to time. If that's all right, of course."

"You mean live with me here?"

"You might put it that way, yes, if it's—"

Willow put up her finger against his lips to silence him. "You know my answer."

"I guessed as much but wanted to hear it from you. I won't be in your way, but I just love watching you do things. I'll just sit out here while you work with your flowers and vegetables—me and the dogs, that is. I'll even help around the house, maybe go back to designing again."

"What about the winery? Your family?"

"I'm going to hand management over to Daisy. She does it already, anyway, and if she needs help, I'm always around. As for my family? They just want me to be happy."

"You won't regret it?"

"The only thing I regret is the past twelve years away from you. So, I'll be the one to pour you a glass of wine, and we can come out here and watch the sunset together."

"Is that a promise?"

"It's a promise."

CHAPTER TWELVE

Oblivion

Alan kept his promise. But all good things must end, and this story ended with a phone call.

"Hello?" Willow answered the phone.

"Willow?"

"Yes?"

"It's me, Daisy."

Willow hesitated before answering, "What is it?"

"I don't know how to say this…"

That feeling of premonition…

"Dad had a stroke last night," Daisy concluded.

"Oh my goodness!" Willow said, sitting down. "Is he all right? Where is he?" She hated to hear what her answer would be.

"Dad passed away last night. We're all devastated. I'm so sorry to bring such news."

"But we spoke yesterday, he was fine, he sounded fine…" Willow stopped talking.

"I know. He was excited about going back to the island with you. It was just so sudden. He had stopped by to see me and Ivy. I poured him a glass of wine with me, and while I was in the kitchen preparing dinner, I jumped at the sound of glass breaking. By the time I came to his side, he was gone. The doctor said that it was a massive brain aneurysm that could've been caused by a blood clot due to the accident he had several years ago while surfing."

What to do? What to say? Willow's emotions were all over the place.

"I... I... Is there anything I can do?" Willow finally asked.

"We've called all family members and informed his lawyer. He's coming over. I'll let you know the arrangements as soon as possible."

"Daisy, how are you? How are you dealing with this?" Willow managed to ask.

Daisy sighed and said, "You can never prepare yourself for a moment like this. My only consolation is that he didn't suffer. He would've hated that. He was so happy since he met you, Willow. I'm grateful for your friendship. Er, I... I need to go I have another call waiting. I'll stay in touch."

"My condolences to the family, Daisy."

"Thank you, Willow." She hung up.

Willow sat there at her desk, too numb to react. She looked at her hands, then glanced outside. She got up to walk around, feeling a painful sensation in her whole body. It felt like a fist had gripped her stomach, and she doubled over, rushing to the bathroom. She hardly had time to pull up the toilet lid when she vomited up a storm. Her whole body was being pulled inside out, and she could hardly breathe. As she sat down on the bathroom floor, the tears came pouring. She cried out loud with the pain, not only from her body, but from her heart as she reeled with the thought of not being with Alan again, not to hear his voice, not to feel his touch. It was unbearable, it was unjust. She cried out, wanting to hear her voice echo on the bathroom walls. How would she survive this? How would she continue to live now and be a strong woman again? Why? Why? she kept shouting. *Why me? Why now? I don't want to be strong anymore,*

I don't want to be brave. Willow laid down her face on the cool bathroom floor. The pain in her stomach was somewhat relieved when she'd vomited, but her body ached. She just lay there, closed her eyes, and tried to find the energy to get up. But not yet. Not just yet.

The dogs came rushing in, and Honey started to lick her face, but Willow didn't have the energy to move or say anything, so she lay down, liking the cool tiles on her cheek. She didn't know for how long she stayed there, but she finally managed to lift her head up when she heard her phone ringing. She let it go to voice mail.

Willow stood up and looked at herself in the mirror. She hated the woman she saw, old and ugly. She walked back to her desk, picked up her phone, and listened to the voice mail. It was from Robyn. *I'll call her later,* she thought, not having the courage to talk to her yet. She dialled Jasmine instead.

"Mom, hi! How are you?" Jasmine said. "Mom, what's the matter?" she continued when Willow didn't reply.

"Alan… Alan…" Willow couldn't continue as the tears came back.

"Mom, what happened? Mom?" Jasmine insisted.

"He's dead," Willow finally managed to say.

"What! How, when… Oh, Mom."

"He went home to pick up a few things and see the family before we went to the island. Apparently, he had a stroke and was gone in minutes."

"Oh, Mom, oh no" was all Jasmine was able to say. "We'll try to come over as soon as possible."

"You don't have to. Not yet, anyway. I don't know when the funeral will be. I'll let you know."

"You shouldn't be alone."

"I want to be. This time, I want to be. Don't worry about me. I just have to think and be alone."

"OK. I love you, Mom."

Willow turned off her phone without replying. Just for tonight, she didn't want to hear anyone, do anything. She went upstairs to her bedroom and looked around. She saw Alan's sweater on the chair and picked it up. His scent filled her nostrils, and she hugged it as if it was Alan himself. She put it on and went back downstairs, walking aimlessly around the house. The dogs watched her lying down, knowing and feeling that something wasn't right.

⌒⌒⌒

Three days later, Willow received another call from Daisy.

"Willow, how are you managing?" Daisy asked.

"I feel dead. Life has no meaning. I feel empty. Useless," Willow replied. "But taking each day as a new day. How about you? How's the family holding up? I talked with Robyn the other day."

"It's been hard. I walk and turn around the corner as if I'll see him."

"Tell me about it," Willow said. "I know. When's the funeral?"

"That's why I called you. We'll be having a celebration of life for Dad on Thursday next week, and I wanted to know if you wanted to take part in it. Knowing how close you and Dad were, I thought…"

Willow hesitated. "What's your family saying about this? Do you think it would be appropriate? I don't know, Daisy."

"Of course it would. That's also why I'm calling. We had a meeting with Dad's lawyer about his will and wishes. We want to talk to you about it."

"Me? Why?" Willow asked.

"I'd rather not say over the phone. Can you come?" Daisy asked.

"When?"

"How about tomorrow?"

"I don't know. This is news to me. Why do you want me there?" Willow asked.

"It's important that you hear it from all of us."

"Us?"

"Mr. Harris—the lawyer, me, Robyn, and William. Grace is flying in tonight."

"What time?"

"Let's say two p.m.?" Daisy said.

"At the farmhouse?"

"Yes, see you tomorrow."

"Thank you, Daisy. I'll be there." Strange. Willow didn't know what to make of it.

The next day, Willow drove down the now-familiar road to the farmhouse. Before she could knock, Robyn opened the door.

"Willow," Robyn said, then hugged her, tears welled up in her eyes.

"Hello, Robyn." Willow pulled back. She too had tears in her eyes. They understood each other.

"Come on in, everyone is here." Robyn closed the door after them.

"Mr. Harris, this is Willow."

Willow shook the elderly man's hand. His shoulders sagged. "Willow, Alan was a close friend. We've known each other for over thirty years."

"I'm sorry for your loss," Willow mumbled. "Hello, William"— Willow nodded— "Daisy, Grace."

They all stood there, staring at the floor, no words to say. "Let's sit down, shall we?" Mr. Harris said. As everyone settled down, Willow thought, *Why am I here?*

Mr. Harris cleared his throat. "I'll start the discussion. As you all know, Alan was a meticulous organizer and liked to have all details set out in preparation for any event. His death was no different. His wealth and estates, the vineyards, and personal items he left to the family."

"As is fit," Willow said, still not knowing why she was there. "I have no expectations and never did ask for anything from Alan, if that's what this is all about," she said, looking around questioningly.

"No, no, Willow," Robyn intervened, "we're saying no such thing. No one here is even thinking of it. It's just that—"

"I think I should continue, Robyn," Mr. Harris said.

"Of course." Robyn leaned back in her seat.

"Last month, Alan came to me to add something to his will. He also left me an envelope to be delivered to you, Willow, in the case of his death." The lawyer leaned back and pulled out a blue envelope from his briefcase. From a distance, she recognized Alan's handwriting, the beautiful cursive lettering of her name. She touched the envelope, caressing the handwriting. As she choked up, she could barely say the words "thank you."

"That's not all, Willow." She looked up. "He did leave you something. I've discussed this with the family," the lawyer continued, glancing at their faces, "and we just want to know if you'll agree. It's a difficult decision."

"What is it?" Willow asked, now curious. "What is it that he left me?"

"Himself."

Willow must have stared a long time, because the lawyer suddenly got up and came by her side. She looked up at him.

"Are you all right? Would you like a glass of water?" he asked, worried.

"Please," Willow croaked. Grace got up to fetch the water. "What do you mean himself?" she asked after taking a few sips.

"Alan came to my office two months ago. He talked passionately about you and how he enjoyed being with you. I hadn't seen him this happy since… well, for a long time. He knew that you had no need for anything, that you loved living in your house with your garden and all the wild animals that visit you. Alan was happy there with you. Then, he told me he wanted to change his last will."

She looked on, not understanding. Daisy intervened. "Willow, Dad loved you so much. He wants to be cremated and his ashes to be put in a biological urn so he can return to life as a tree in your garden."

Willow's heart skipped a beat. "But that was my wish for myself," she mumbled.

"I know," said Mr. Harris. "He told me, and he wants to be in your garden if you'll allow it. But maybe you should read what he wrote for you before you decide." He glanced at the envelope lying on Willow's lap.

"No, no. I mean, yes, of course yes, he can be planted in my garden—but no, I'll open the envelope later at home, if you don't mind. This is just too much to absorb in one day. But yes, by all means, arrange anything, everything for his wish to come true," Willow managed to say.

⁓

That night, Willow sat down in the living room and opened the envelope.

My love,

If you are reading this, then I know I am gone.

I wish we had more time. I regret the years we lost for the obvious reasons we both know. I will always cherish the short time we had together—not dreams, but memories that I will keep with me always.

I know you wanted to continue your existence after life as a tree, and I want to be there along with you. I want to set my roots in your beautiful garden so that I can watch over you and wait for you to come beside me.

Don't be sad for me, my darling Willow. I know you'll mourn, but don't let life slip past your fingers because I'm not there with you anymore. You're a strong woman—always have been—and I know you'll overcome your feelings and live once again as you've done many times in the past. For me, you were my swan song.

When the time comes, I will be here for you.
Goodbye, my love.
Alan

Willow thought, *No, Alan, you were my swan song. How will I go on living without you?*

EPILOGUE

"Is this the tree?" Jane asked. She turned around to look at the old woman, who remained silent.

"I think I'll stop here," the woman finally answered. "I'm tired."

"Of course, of course. I'm sorry to have taken up so much of your time, but it was fascinating to hear the story. Thank you so much for sharing it with me," Jane said as she got up.

"Good luck with your show. Tell Simon I approve."

"I will. But I don't know your name," Jane said.

"It's Jasmine," the old woman replied. For a moment, Jane stood still and looked questioningly. Jasmine smiled.

Jane walked back toward the house, surprised and confused at the same time. She was thanking Lilian, and just as she was walking out, she heard someone come in. She glanced sideways to see a tall old man with a beard.

"Where is she?" the man asked Lilian.

"Usual place, Sam," Lilian replied softly.

"She's going to catch a cold out there one day," he replied gruffly and walked out. Jane saw him walking toward Jasmine.

"Is that—" Jane started, turning to Lilian.

"Yes, he is," Lilian replied before Jane could finish her question.

"Thank you again," Jane said. As she walked out, she saw the name *Empryeus* printed on some forms laid out on the counter. Lilian noticed Jane looking at them.

"*Empryeus* belongs to the foundation. I thought Simon would've told you," Lilian said.

"So that's how you know Simon," Jane remarked. She suddenly remembered the story Jasmine had told her, and reality hit her.

"Are you all right?" Lilian asked walking, toward her. "You look very white. Would you like to sit down?"

"No, I'm fine, thank you." Jane walked out toward her car. Once inside, she texted Anne.

Anne, I got the centrepiece. We'll talk when I get back

She then texted Simon.

You have some explaining to do, but thank you so much, I got my centrepiece

Simon texted back several minutes later.

So, you met Jasmine. Have dinner with me tonight

I can't wait to get back, Jane replied.

☙

Jasmine slowly got up from the bench and walked toward the tree trunk. There was a soft wind, the one that usually came before sunset, and the leaves of the tree rustled and shimmered under the golden pink rays. Jasmine leaned against the tree and put her head against the trunk. It was very quiet, and the only sound was that of the waterfall from the pond and a few songbirds chirping in the distance.

Sam reached her, still standing against the tree. "Jasmine," Sam said softly, reaching out to her. Jane turned and walked into his embrace.

"I miss her so much," Jane whispered.

"I know," Sam replied. "You must be careful, though. It's getting chilly these days," he continued, taking off his jacket and putting it around her shoulders. "Come on. Let's go in. You can tell me about your day over a glass of wine."

"Only if you'll tell me yours." Jasmine smiled up at him, and they slowly walked back toward the house.

By the time they went inside, the wind had died down to a soft breeze, caressing the tree's leaves. The sun was setting as the garden readied itself for the night. The waterfall of the pond had quietened down, yet the occasional bird chirped on. The tree stood still, watching the house come alive inside and hearing laughter. It was a peaceful moment until a little squirrel came running among the grass and clambered up the tree trunk. It had a little nest somewhere between the branches, and it too settled down for the night.

It was a beautiful evening, and if you looked from far away, you could see the house with lit windows and hear sounds of voices and music. The garden sparkled with its lights, and the faint scent of honeysuckle and jasmine streamed through the air, reaching the tree. The leaves shuddered for a moment, then settled.

All was quiet now.

THE END

Printed in Canada